About the Author

Jennifer S Read was born in Yorkshire and moved to Scotland in 2002. She lives in the beautiful county of Fife. As well as writing, she is an artist and teacher. This is her first book.

The Masked Threat

Jennifer S Read

The Masked Threat

Vanguard Press

VANGUARD PAPERBACK

© Copyright 2025
Jennifer S Read

A CIP catalogue record for this title is available from the British Library.

ISBN 978-1-83671-007-3

Vanguard Press is an imprint of
Pegasus Elliot Mackenzie Publishers Ltd.
www.pegasuspublishers.com

First Published in 2025

Vanguard Press
Sheraton House Castle Park
Cambridge England

Printed & Bound in Great Britain

Dedication

For Carrie Rae Gallant, who was with me every step of the way. I am so grateful.

Acknowledgements

I must acknowledge the importance of my wonderful neighbours, who encouraged me to write. My dad, Ian Martin Read, who is sadly no longer with us. He taught me to love thrillers and murder mysteries, and he was a talented wordsmith. My wonderful family, and my mum and Nick, who always believed in me and support me every day. My Venetian family, Gina, Franco, Pietro and Abi, (who inspired Clara.) You gave me so much. Thank you, my wonderful proof-reading friends, Caro Freeman and Pam Bridge, they helped me greatly. And finally, Kirsty, who came with me to Venice at Carnevale, and let me watch life and get inspired. I salute you.

Day 1 of Carnevale

The mist rose from the canal and enveloped the little bridge.

It painted yellow halos around the lanterns hanging from the Trattoria, and changed the colours of the streets to muted versions of their usually vibrant hues.

The mournful foghorn sounded across the city, and Clara pulled her jacket more tightly around herself.

The dampness was worse than any cold; it seeped into your bones.

She had planned to stop at her favourite local bar for a spritz on the way home, but now that the fog was rolling in, she just wanted to get back to the warm apartment on Calle de Cercheri.

It was unlikely that Luca would be back before nine, so she could indulge herself for a long soak before getting dinner started.

At this time of night, her route was quiet. It was too early for the nighttime revellers to have emerged in their fine costumes, and it was too late for the day-trippers and holidaymakers who would be back on their cruise ships or in their Airbnb after a full day of sightseeing.

She knew this pattern well, being a self-employed tour guide. It had taught her the ways of tourists. Most days, she enjoyed passing the secrets of her wonderful city to people, showing them just how magical this unique place was.

The visibility was considerably lower when she got to the street door to the apartments. She let herself in and breathed deeply as she made her way down the long corridor to the lift.

Every time she took the lift to floor five, she was thankful to be fortunate enough to rent such a great flat.

The heating was humming away, and the salon was warm, dry, and cosy.

She worked her way around the room, pulling the shutters closed and lighting the low lights, closing out the fogbound night.

She took off her coat, and hung it neatly in the cupboard, and put her slippers on.

She made her way to her bedroom and switched on the bedside lamp. She got her night things ready, ran a bath, and turned the water flow down to give herself time to begin the dinner.

This was the best bit about February: the cosy evenings in before the heat of spring and summer. She supposed that her love of cosying in on a dark night came from her English half; her mother always made the winter seems special.

Her Venetian father preferred to be outside in the air, no matter what the weather. She chopped an onion and garlic as she thought about her parents.

She must go over and see them for a few days once Carnevale was over.

The savoury smells caught her attention as she fried

anchovies in olive oil with garlic. A simple baked pasta dish would be best if Luca was to come home late.

In the three years that the friends had lived together, Luca had become accustomed to Clara's eclectic style of cooking. She ignored so many of the Italian rules of cuisine, but what she made was always delicious.

They had intended to share the food preparation equally, but his job as an investigator for the Carabinieri frequently meant that he was back too late to cook.

With the dinner on a low heat in the oven, Clara took a glass of wine to the bathroom and indulged in a hot bath. She put a Puccini aria on the sound system in her bedroom and let the liquid notes carry her away.

Betsy Noakes just loved Venice! It was so neat, with all its canals and cute buildings. It was just like Disneyland, but real, right? She'd been here a week, and already her Instagram feed was through the roof with 'likes' for the reels and posts she had put up of Venice.

Her best one so far was the picture that she had taken of her Aperol spritz glass against that cathedral thing at the edge of the lagoon.

She was excited that Carnevale started today. She was going to go to as many of the celebrations as possible.

'The procession of the Marie's' was a definite. Before that, though, she wanted to attach a padlock, specially brought from home in New York, to the quaint side of the bridge near her hotel.

There were already quite a few padlocks attached and she was excited to add hers.

There was a sign in Italian with a cross through an

image of a padlock, but as others had done it, she didn't need to pay that notice any mind!

The mist was rising up from the canal. The Ponte degli Scalzi was so elegant, and it was close to the station, just across from Burger King.

She liked these evenings best, when the lights were lit in the bars and restaurants; it looked even more like the Venice from Disneyland.

She was disappointed that the gondoliers didn't seem to sing as she had thought, but that was a minor detail.

She climbed to the top of the white stone bridge and saw some padlocks already in place, hanging from the metal handrails. She knelt down and took the engraved padlock from her backpack.

She had the engraver put 'Betsy ♥'s, Venice' and the year on it. On the reverse, she had chosen "New York's finest!" She clicked the lock to the rail and took some photos for Insta. She turned the camera to face her and grinned broadly for the video, as she flung the keys to the padlock over the bridge side and into the water.

She then adeptly switched the screen to face the padlock, zooming in on her engraving, so it was clear to see. Flipping the screen again, she panned the view and then said, "Venice, baby," and laughed, showing the world what a swell time she was having.

She leaned against the bridge side and watched her video back twice. Satisfied with her work, she picked up her backpack and put it on.

She began her descent from the bridge in the direction of Burger King. All this Italian food was well and good, but she needed a burger and fries! Fixed on her goal, she didn't notice the swish of dark velvet skirts.

She didn't notice the masked face, impassive and ornate in gold. The detailed costume with the gondola headdress gleamed in the lights from the eateries.

It was quite crowded with people. Betsy felt the crush of tourists surround her and tried to step into the side for a moment and let them go by. She yelped, aware of a sharp pain in her back, just below her backpack. The pain intensified, and she found that she couldn't get her breath. She couldn't breathe.

There was a hot, wet feeling. She felt around the place, confused. Her hand was covered in blood, her own blood.

Her last thought, before she collapsed was one of puzzlement. "What just happened?" As she slumped to the ground, the masked figure swished past and into the crowd.

Their cape swelled as they rapidly turned the corner down Calle Zocco, over a bridge into Castello.

It was only moments before someone noticed that the woman wasn't okay. She was making a gurgling sound. A small group gathered, and a man stepped forward and said he was a doctor. He asked for space, and the group of bystanders formed a ring around the woman and the doctor.

The throng of people moved around the ring of protection like water around a fixed object.

The doctor checked her and then stood up. With a shocked expression on his face, he said, "She's been stabbed! She's dead!"

A woman screamed.

Somebody had the presence of mind to go into the

Tabac and get the owner to phone the police and ambulance.

The doctor waited by the lifeless form of Betsy Noakes until the Carabinieri arrived. Some of the bystanders drifted away, but others joined, wanting to gawk and revel in the drama.

Luca was powering down his computer and tidying his desk when the call came in. Nino looked at him quizzically.

When he answered the phone, he raised his eyes to heaven and shook his head. Luca was wedded too much to the job.

Where was the balance in his life? What was the point of it all if you didn't have fun? He waited, swigging the last of his now-cold Americano. He pulled a face. "Needs grappa!" he muttered to himself

When Luca had finished speaking in rapid Italian, he pushed back his chair and ran his hand over his face. He felt very, very tired.

"What do we have?" Luca opened his eyes and looked at Nino. "We have a dead American tourist on the first day of Carnevale."

Nino groaned. "Why did you answer the phone? Stupido!"

Luca and Nino stood looking down at the body of Betsy Jane Noakes. Fellow uniformed officers were working hard at crowd control. At least the volume of people had lessened as dinner service began, and the various celebrations for Carnevale were starting in Saint Mark's Square. Carabinieri from the technical roles,

16

worked quietly and systematically, photographing and bagging evidence.

Soon, an ambulance boat would take her away to the mortuary at the hospital in Castello. Luca was looking through the notes made by the first officers on the scene. They had thought that robbery was the motive, but the woman's backpack was intact. Her phone, wallet and passport were all still within.

Nobody had reported an argument or fight prior to the woman collapsing. She had made no fuss, just a short yelp, which must've been when she felt the knife going in just below her ribs. The post-mortem would tell them more.

Mulling this over, Luca half-heard the chime of the church bells and realised that he really needed to let his flatmate, Clara, know that he was okay. He tapped out a text, and she responded immediately. She would wait up. She had a day off tomorrow and knew he would need to talk about whatever he was dealing with.

Leaving the technical team to complete their investigations at the scene, Luca and Nino made their way to the hotel where Betsy Noakes was staying. Thankfully, she had kept her key on her, and the monogram of the hotel, along with the room number, was embossed in burgundy plastic. If there were family members or companions with her on this trip, it was going to be a difficult and emotional set of interviews.

They introduced themselves to the inscrutable hotel receptionist. She raised one quizzical eyebrow at their question and then tapped furiously at her keyboard. "A twin room. She travels with a female friend, Chloe

Mathewson."

Establishing that Miss Mathewson was in the room, Luca and Nino took the lift to the fourth floor. Then they heard a female American voice shout, "Betsy? You forget your key again!" before the door was pulled open.

Music was thumping from a Bluetooth speaker inside, and the smile on the girl's face turned appraising at the sight of the two young men. "Well, hellooo to you!" she drawled. Her smile left her face as they introduced themselves and asked to speak with her.

She killed music and sat on the left-hand bed, picking up a cushion to hold for comfort. Nino and Luca remained standing; they hated this bit.

Luca had better English, so it was his task to break the news. All colour drained from the girl's face.

She looked ashen beneath her tan. For a moment, there was no sound, just the distant chiming of the quarter hour from a nearby church.

Then there was a scream. A raw, long, ragged scream. Luca and Nino looked away from Chloe's face.

She looked surprised at the noise that she herself was producing. There was a shouting from the corridor, and a pounding on the bedroom door. Nino answered it to find a worried-looking Australian tourist.

He heard the scream and was concerned that something bad was happening to the girls. Reassuring him that something bad had already happened but was not happening now was tricky for Nino, but he managed to convey the message, and the tourist went back to his own room.

Luca put his hand on Chloe's arm. "We will get you consular assistance," he said. "There is an honorary US consul in Venice, whom we will call to be with you tomorrow. We will need you to come to identify your friend." Chloe sobbed and gulped back the tears. Nino filled a tooth mug with water and gave it to her.

This was going to be a long night for all concerned.

It was 10:45 when Clara heard Luca's key in the door. He looked exhausted. The fog plastered down his unruly dark curls, and he looked bedraggled.

She fussed around him, removing his wet coat and scarf. She plumped up the cushion on his favourite armchair and went to the kitchen for a beer and a bowl of pasta.

He said nothing as he worked his way steadily through both. He gave her a grateful look as he took on the delicious flavours.

When his meal was finished, he spoke, "Grazie, Cara!" Her kindness was one of her greatest qualities, he thought.

She took his plate, and empty bottle and brought him another, and then sat on the sofa opposite him waiting for him to begin.

He took a long swig and sighed. "This isn't good, a death at the beginning of Carnevale. It's a tourist."

"Robbery?" asked Clara.

"Noooo," Luca drew out the word and looked baffled.

"Her stuff wasn't taken. Her backpack was still on her back. She was stabbed just below it. We know it didn't leave her back; there was her blood soaked into the fabric.

19

She had no previous connection with Venice. This is her first trip. She and a girlfriend are doing Venice, Rome, Florence, and then moving onto London and up to Scotland, or they were…" Once again, he rubbed his face, Clara knew this to be a gesture of stress.

Luca was a quiet, thoughtful man, but he felt things deeply. He hated unfairness and wrongdoing. This was shaking his moral code.

"What did her companion say?" she ventured. Again, he winced as he remembered Chloe Mathewson's raw emotion.

"She had gone out to get some shots for Instagram. She had a padlock to add to the Ponte degli Scalzi."

"Oh no, not another of those! Don't tourists understand that it's forbidden?" said Clara, exasperated. "The weight of the padlocks causes the sides of our beautiful and ancient bridges to break and fall into the canal. It's such an ignorant thing to do!"

"We need to go through her mobile phone to see what she's been posting and photographing. It's with technical at the moment. Tomorrow, I must go with her friend and Graham Finch, the consul, to the mortuary to formally identify her."

He closed his eyes. He looked so tired and defeated.

Clara wondered if this was entirely the right profession for him. It was almost one in the morning, and Clara stifled a yawn. Time for bed.

She began to turn off lights and Luca went towards his room. He was deep in thought and walking, as if on auto pilot.

In the grand Palazzo Dolfin Manin, the lights in the exquisite Murano glass chandeliers glittered. They didn't usually light the Grand Salon during the hours that the palazzo was closed to the public because of cost, but tonight, with the fog so thick, Isabella and Rocco Manin felt that they needed cheering up. It was the first day of Carnevale.

They remembered being excited children and watching the waterborne flotilla of decorated crafts sailing by their windows on the Grand Canal.

It was always a special time, a time of family and tradition.

Isabella still tried to mark the traditions, but it wasn't the same now that there were just the two of them left. The last of the Manins. Nobility from Venice's glory days, when the shimmering city was an important centre of the world: rich and influential, with so many artists, craftsmen, and musicians. They were almost glad that they were the only ones left to witness this pastiche. The tawdry kitschiness that laid itself like a heavy wet blanket over their Venice, cheapening it, mocking at its historic grandeur.

If their ancestor, Ludovico Manin, could see this diminishment, he would spin in his grave. Ludovico had been the last Doge of Venice in 1797.

The twins, Rocco and Isabella, were extremely proud of their pure Venetian lineage. One of the reasons neither of them had married was that it was so difficult to find pure Venetian's with the right noble pedigree to marry in the first place.

Rocco handed his sister a glass of Prosecco. It was presented in an ancient Venetian glass, one of a pair usually on display for tourists. This glass symbolized their heritage, and it felt fitting to use on such an auspicious evening.

Earlier, Isabella had been to the bakery and collected the 'Frittelle,' a traditional type of doughnut, that were only eaten during Venice Carnevale. They were filled with raisins, cream, chocolate, or pistachio.

She took her glass and her sugary doughnut and went through the salon door out onto the balcony. The lights of the palazzo, opposite glittered delicately, through the fog, and vaporetti full of people – some in elaborate costumes – buzzed left and right.

The Grand Canal was busy and the voices of the revellers from the Rialto bridge carried to her on the night air.

Rocco joined her. He raised his twin glass to her and took a long pull at the fizzy, blonde liquid.

"We mustn't be late tonight," he said. "It's a four-tour group day tomorrow, and we don't have Lilia to help."

Isabella tossed her dark hair and looked at him. "I know you're annoyed that I gave her a day off, but her mama is sick, and she has to get to Burano to see her. It was the right thing to do! We can manage. We have managed before. They're only tourists, Caro!"

"I hate it, you know, this life? I hate that we have to open our ancestral home, that it is now owned by the city. I hate that it's not even Manin property anymore. We are merely caretakers now!" Rocco's handsome face flashed with anger and bitterness.

"You know that was all Uncle Leonardo's fault though? He sold the palazzo and then proceeded to drink and womanise through the proceeds. We can't change it. At least we can still live here." Isabella put a conciliatory hand on his arm.

"To live in the servant's apartment! Not really the same, is it?" He grumbled.

"Easier to heat, Brother dear! And look at the positives. They pay us to be here to care for what we would always have cared for. It could be very, very much worse!"

"Just yesterday I found chewing gum pressed into the moulding of the grand table in the hall," Rocco said.

"It's the casual disrespect that hurts me, actually physically hurts me. All this wealth sails into our city, and we, the original Venetians, have to be grateful for the small crumbs from their table. It's not us who benefits. There are less than 50,000 people living full-time in the city now. Fewer of that number are Venetian."

"But you can't solve it, Rocco! Eat your Frittelle and forget about it. You are spoiling the evening." With that, she went inside, leaving him to moodily eat and watch the revellers cavort, oblivious to his torment.

Day 2 of Carnevale

Luca and Nino got off the police boat close to the hotel. Standing, wearing a camel coat, and a homburg hat, was Graham Finch, the US consul for Venice. It was a grand title for an honorary role that didn't pay well. Graham ran his surgeries from his office, where he exported Italian pasta and produce to the US, He was a kindly bear of a man and his late 50s. Luca felt sure that Graham would help Chloe through the nightmare, of her friend's sudden and baffling murder.

Together the three men made their way into the foyer. Luca was surprised to see the same woman in reception, he greeted her and commented on her long shifts.

"What can you do?" was the response, accompanied by a shrug. "It's hard enough for a Venetian to make a living in this city. I work double shifts and still live with Mama!" He'd heard this refrain before from many of his friends in their mid-30s.

It was difficult to live independently in Venice. He was grateful once again for Clara and their flat share. He thought of his friend fondly.

He had been very much in love with Clara when they first met. Her grey eyes and blonde good looks had captivated him. She was sporty when he was bookish. She played basketball and could've turned pro if she'd wanted to move to the United States.

Luckily for him, she had stayed in Venice, and incredibly lucky for him, they were now best friends. While he was musing on all of this, the receptionist had rung up to Chloe's room. The lift doors opened to reveal a very subdued girl. She was dressed in dark clothing, and her eyes were swollen from crying. Her face was blotchy too. She put a pair of oversized sunglasses on to hide her eyes.

Graham immediately stepped forward. "Oh, honey!" he said, and gathered her up into a bear hug. She sobbed noisily on his shoulder, but the Italians could see that it was a comfort to have a fellow countryman with her at this impossible time.

Graham was speaking softly to her, and he handed her an enormous white monogram handkerchief. She blew her nose, squared her shoulders, and went over to where Nino and Luca awaited. "We have a boat to take you to the mortuary," Nino said.

The little party left the lobby and made their way to the Polizia Locale boat. A few people watched with interest as the woman, sombrely dressed, with large dark glasses, was helped into the motor launch. The men stepped in behind her, and the local police gunned the engine and sped off.

It was flashier than it needed to be, and a hapless gondolier nearly lost his footing from the sudden wash that the launch kicked up.

It was a pleasant morning with a watery sun trying to burn through the fog from yesterday. The sky was streaked with greys, blue grey and lemon. The buildings looked magical rising up from the dark, turquoise water of the canal.

The Polizia Locale were enjoying this rare important journey and had put the blue lights on for good measure, although Nino shook his head when one of the young officers reached to add the siren.

Normally, these police boats monitored the waterways, looking for infringement of state laws and water protocol.

Taking a tourist to the mortuary after a murder was much more glamorous and interesting. They left the canals and skirted into the lagoon. Here, there was open water, with markers of ancient tree trunks lashed together to form bollards. A cormorant was drying his wings in the morning light. Strange, straggly trees rose up from the lagoon as if growing there.

They were markers, an indication of various fishing grounds that boat traffic needed to avoid.

The effect was eerie, and Luca noticed Chloe sit further back, hugging her bag to herself – the way she had held the cushion the previous night for comfort.

Isabella Manin opened the shutters of the Palazzo.

She put in place the red silk ropes and posts which kept visitors away from the more delicate paintings and artefacts.

She made her way room to room, straightening objects and checking that all was in order. When she got to the Grand Salon, she tutted in an annoyance at the glass and plate with sugary crumbs resting on a side table. She gathered them up and went to the small side kitchen, which they usually used to cater receptions, to wash up the glass. She carefully dried it, and replaced it in the display case by its twin.

She straightened the information card: "Venetian drinking glasses, 1680," and locked the glass door.

Where was Rocco? She pressed the intercom buzzer to the upstairs caretaker's flat that they shared – no answer.

She checked the time on the exquisite gold filigree clock on the Grand Salon side table. Two hours. There were only two hours until the first of the hoard arrived!

Sunlight and shimmers from the Grand Canal were playing their reflections on the walls of the room, picking out the colours in the tapestries and frescoes decorating the walls. The whole room was bathed in a delicate peach light. She sighed and took a moment to enjoy her surroundings. This was one of the most beautiful houses on the planet. She was proud to call it home, even with all the modern challenges.

Still no sign of Rocco.

This was too much. She started to feel anxious. The first group would have a tour guide with them. Nevertheless, they would still need to be split into two groups to be shown the Palazzo efficiently. What was he thinking?

Was he being petty and making a point about her decision to give Lilia the day off? She waited in the hall. She could see the pavement in front of the Palazzo from here. She glimpsed a figure, in full Carnevale costume: cape, heavily adorned wig, and mask, as they swished

27

passed. The turquoise colour of their silk skirts matched the sunlit shade of the canal green perfectly.

Still concerned for her brother's whereabouts, worry soon took over, and she began pacing the cool marble of the entrance hall.

"Isabella?" it was Rocco.

Finally, he was coming down the main staircase, buttoning his blue shirt cuffs. His hair was slightly damp from the shower. "Where were you?" she hissed.

"I slept in, Cara! I'm sorry." There was no time for more recriminations as the first party of chattering tourists arrived with their careworn tour guide.

This group was mostly Chinese and followed a stuffed toy lion attached to a pole that the tour guide held aloft.

The twins began their well-practiced routine. Rocco stepped forward, smiling. "Welcome to our home, Palazzo Dolfin Manin."

Their working day had begun.

The cruise ship was docked at Stazione Maritima, near the Piazzale Roma transport hub by the entrance to the lagoon.

It would be leaving at noon, but several of its passengers had disembarked last night in the fog to spend the night enjoying Carnevale, as well as spending an evening and sumptuous dinner in Venice.

Gunter and Adele Walner had done just that. They had been tendered into the city to the beautiful hotel, Danieli and had walked through Saint Mark's Square before dinner.

Gunter had taken lots of photographs of the people, costumed and mysterious, as they thronged and paraded. Seeing people in antique dress, made him recall the research he had done into Venice's past and the purpose of Carnevale: to do forbidden things and give into hedonism before the strict religious yoke of lent landed on their shoulders.

It was a chance to give in to excess, and it was very exciting. Adele had been disappointed that Gunter hadn't wanted to dress up too. He was too much of a rules person. Though he enjoyed the spectacle, he would not participate.

He spent a lot of his leisure time behind his camera.

He recorded life rather than truly experiencing it firsthand. The dinner had been delicious and candlelit. The mist rising from the canals greatly added to the atmosphere.

The couple sat in the breakfast room after a pleasant sleep, overlooking the paved Riva Degli Schiavoni. They were almost exactly opposite Zaccaria, the pontoon that they would need to meet the tender boat to take them back to the ship.

The soft light played on the water of the lagoon, and misty silhouettes of the tower, and domes from the other bank, shimmered. Gunter was snapping away again, while Adele urged him to drink his coffee.

They checked out of the hotel and took their small pieces of luggage across to the entrance to the pontoon.

There were ancient stone steps into the green-blue water of the lagoon, green with seaweed and crusted, with growing mussels, fed by the mineral-rich waters.

Gondolas bobbed rhythmically as the water lapped. The sun began to warm, and even though it was February, it felt almost springlike. The gulls called and swooped across the plaza.

A lone rubbish collector, dressed in fluorescent yellow overalls, pushed his wheeled barrow from bin to bin, systematically cleaning up after a night of revels.

Adele paused at one of the stalls to look longingly at the Carnevale masks on display. They were encrusted with gems and lace, completely plastic and mass-produced, but in that setting, they evoked the magic of this annual event.

Gunter was over by the steps, photographing a gondolier navigating his craft in between the other boats already docked.

He moved forward to get a better view onto the one of the low pontoons between the Zaccaria stop and the gondolas.

He was looking down his lens changing the amount of light that the camera was using. He was in his own little world.

He was oblivious to all his surroundings except for the view through the camera.

Behind him, a costumed woman seemed to glide. She wore the blank, white porcelain mask of Carnevale, and below her high golden wig, a turquoise scarf hid her hair.

Gloves, made of the same turquoise material, were on her hands, and her dress was the same green turquoise of the water of the lagoon when the sun caught it. She was adorned with a gold velvet cloak, and her dress was encrusted with embroidery – stitched images of sea

30

creatures and mermaids. She carried a gold trident in her right hand.

Early though it was, tourists stopped to photograph her, and she turned, automaton-like, to strike a pose. Satisfied, the tourists moved onto photograph the next spectacle.

It was just Gunter and the masked lady on the pontoon now. The air was full of the chiming of church bells and the raucous calls of herring gulls.

Suddenly, she pounced at the German. With great force, she pushed him sharply forward.

He was unaware of her presence and was holding his camera in both hands. He had no way to save himself and fell forward straight into the water.

As he fell, he hit his head on the stone steps. He splashed violently once, then sank. A few seconds passed, and he reappeared, bobbing up at the side of the pontoon. The masked lady had been scattered with water from his fall and from the splash.

She took her trident and pushed it down onto Gunter's head, holding him under the water. She stood calmly and decoratively, looking out across the lagoon, as if nothing was happening. When she felt all struggle end, she raised her trident from the water and delicately removed a piece of bright green seaweed.

She turned on her golden stacked heel and glided back to the main plaza, stopping from time to time to be photographed.

Gunter Walner's lifeless body floated on its back, his dead eyes looking to the heavens. Soon, Adele would come looking for him. He was first noticed by gondolier getting ready to take his boat out.

"*Mia dio*!" he said, crossing himself.

He began to shout at his fellow gondoliers, and they came running. "*Abbiamo un uomo morto*!" We have a dead man!

Luca and Nino were speeding back to the city from the mortuary.

Chloe was white-faced and sitting close to Graham. She would go with him to his office so that they could call the US Embassy in Rome. They would work together to inform Betsy Noakes's parents and sister.

Graham would take care of Chloe's flight home and the cancellation of the rest of the trip. For obvious reasons, she just wanted to get home now.

Luca's radio began a burst of urgent-sounding Italian.

He was only half listening, still processing in his mind, the sorrow he witnessed when Chloe identified her friend,

Nino caught the full message, though. "Tourist drowned in the lagoon, practically outside the Danieli! Not an accident, the normal force says!"

"Not another tourist!" Luca said despairingly. He rubbed his hand over his face. "It's the second day of Carnevale! This is terrible!"

"Are we being called to attend?" Nino wanted to know.

"We have a meeting with Bianca Avedo, the prosecutor we can't go. We have to finish this first, then I think we speak to the commander."

Umberto Grazie was preparing for the post-mortem on

Gunter Walner.

Grazie was a grumpy, studious man in his early sixties, and had heard all the jokes about being saddled with the surname "Thank you."

Throughout school, he wished to change his name to anything different, but maturity had knocked the corners off his embarrassment. What wasn't up for debate was how thorough and talented he was at his job.

He was the best pathologist in Venice, and that wasn't his own opinion, but that of the prosecutors who valued his clear, decisive, evidence-based testimony, which had seen so many criminals punished and justice done.

He began methodically, and went through all the facts in front of him. The cause of death was drowning. There was a blow to the head, which was likely to have been sustained by hitting his head on the stone steps as he fell.

There were no defence wounds, or any indication that the man had tried to save himself when falling. His heart was strong. There was no sign, either, that he had suffered a stroke or sudden collapse. What particularly interested Umberto were the marks left on the shoulders and forehead; they appeared to be made by a pronged implement, like a pitch fork or garden fork, and the bruising they had left suggested that considerable force was exerted to hold the deceased man down, under the water, to ensure drowning. He recorded his findings into his dictaphone, ready to type up an email to the prosecutor later. This was most definitely murder.

Clara was trying to concentrate. She had bagged her favourite table at Adagio café in San Polo. It was a small

33

establishment that grew to double its size when the outside tables and chairs were in place.

They did excellent coffee and gondolier snacks: small pieces of delicious bread with toppings, a bit like open sandwiches.

Today, she was working on her tour admin and working out her diary for the rest of Carnevale and into Easter.

As she answered an email on her phone from a tour company. The phone rang. It was Sofia, her friend and fellow tour guide.

"Have you heard there is a serial killer in Venice killing tourists!" she said excitedly. Sofia loved drama; the gossip had clearly begun, as both victims had allegedly, been tourists.

Conclusions were being jumped to! Sofia wanted to know if Clara knew anything, living with a Carabinieri.

Clara wasn't about to break Luca's confidence, and so said that she hadn't seen him properly in days.

She omitted the long chat they had shared the previous night and his fears. She ended the call early. She gathered up her things and finished her coffee.

She needed to find out about the second murder. If the rumour mill was already talking about a risk to tourists, that would spread! And a risk to tourists would be a risk to her business too.

Isabella and Rocco were one tour through the four-tour day. The first group had been reasonably attentive.

The sunlight on the water had caused the majority to flock to the windows of the Grand Salon to take selfies of

34

themselves against the view.

"Why do they always make the two-fingered peace sign?" Rocco asked Isabella in an irritated growl.

"I don't know! They just do!" she whispered back.

As the group filed out of the Palazzo, the twins sighed and began the task of going room to room tidying, ready for the next group, who were coming in one hour. Isabella watched her brother's slumped shoulders.

She understood how he felt. He was diminished by what he regarded as a life of servitude. It depressed him when he considered what he had been born to and what life was giving him. The Palazzo was owned by the city, so it wasn't even possible to see each tour as a revenue stream that they could add value to. They were paid a fixed salary for their work, which included the requirement to host evening receptions too. A portion of their salaries were deducted to take into account the caretakers flat, that they lived in. It rankled that they were given leave to remain in what they considered their own home.

The fact that their uncle Leonardo was the culprit for this state of affairs wasn't something that they like to dwell on. It was far easier to moan about the city and how they were in this situation, because of the terms of the agreement with the authorities. Isabella replaced the ropes and took a glass cloth and cleaning spray to the display cabinet in the hall.

It was sticky with finger marks.

Sometimes she reflected that she really hated the tourists. It was so much worse in the summer, of course. She loathed the way that litter floated down the canal from

35

casually tossed coffee cups and hamburger wrappers. It congregated by the private boat dock under the Palazzo.

Rocco had a large fisherman's keep net with which to fish the rubbish out. In the summer, he was forced to do this twice a day to keep on top of it.

One of the things she hated and found incomprehensible was the tendency to put rubbish by the side of the municipal bins, not in them. Why not? Why go as far as the bin and then lay the trash on the pavement by the side?

Irritation fizzed through her. Something should be done! There needed to be a stand, a protest, something to change the tide of casual disrespect that visitors showed to their unique city. She pushed her hair behind her ear and went to get the vacuum cleaner. Someone had thrown coriaridoli in one of the bedrooms. The colourful confetti that was thrown by revellers all over the city during Carnevale had found its way in volume to the cool marble floor and rugs of the state bedroom. "*Ratti*!"

"*Ratti sporchi*!" she shouted, and began to clear it up.

Bianca Avedo kept her ear to the ground, and she had heard the chatter from the city. Two murders in so many days, of tourists, was highly unusual for Venice.

Which, considering the high volume of people visiting annually, had a relatively low crime rate.

There were more incidents of theft than murder. More bribery and corruption too, but a very low homicide rate.

This was the same for the whole of Italy, which had the lowest rate for murder in Europe, aside from

36

Luxembourg and Slovenia.

She was worried too, by the fact that the victims seemed entirely blameless. They had come to Venice to see the wonderful buildings, and absorb the unique experience of a 'floating city'.

They weren't connected in any way. There hadn't been an altercation in either case. It was baffling.

Her reverie was broken by her assistant, Dario, who knocked briefly on the office door and entered to announce the arrival of Luca Conti and Nino Greco from the Carabinieri. The two young men were rather scared of Prosecutor Avedo. She was fiercely intelligent, and known for calling out woolly thinking and laziness. She gave 110% daily, and she expected the same from everyone on the cases that she brought to court.

Luca, the more scholarly of the two, led the meeting. He had prepared a comprehensive report with help from Technical's findings and Umberto's post-mortem on Betsy Noakes. She put on her reading glasses and, in silence, began to read. Halfway through the document, she raised her eyes to them and indicated that they take a seat.

Generally, this was a good sign, but it could also mean a lot more work to do, which it usually did Nino inwardly sighed. He liked to be out and about in the field.

He didn't much care for due diligence or procedure.

"Va bene!" she said, finally. "All right! What are your thoughts? You will have heard that there has been a second murder of a tourist this morning?"

Luca rubbed his hand over his face, and Nino raised his eyes heavenward. *He's got a theory!* he thought.

37

Luca's theories always generated more work and often ate up weekends – and once, a holiday! As his partner, Nino appreciated Luca, but sometimes it was difficult to take his constant, studious appetite for work.

"I've been concerned by the lack of an obvious motive in the murder of Miss Noakes. She hadn't been in Venice long enough to have made enemies. Her friend is obviously and genuinely distraught at her death and was in her hotel room at the time of the murder, which is a considerable distance from the bridge, where the murder took place. We now have a second murder. I'm not fully aware of every fact in regard to this crime, but there is one common thread between both deaths. Tourism!"

Bianca nodded once. "Yes! I was afraid of that." She removed her glasses and shook her head.

"It's Carnevale! The city has a huge number of visitors, all excited to participate in ten days of revelry. If we have a maniac killing tourists, it's going to be a very bad for our image, for the perception of the safety of Venice."

All three sat in silence, processing what could be the thin end of a very sizeable wedge of a problem.

"Conti, I would like you to review any CCTV from the area around the Hotel Danieli and see if there's anything similar to what you find on Miss Noake's mobile phone's photographs and videos. Some common thread in each death. We are lucky that we have technology to inspect – it might throw up a link. Meanwhile, I will speak to your commander. I f you are right, and tourists are being targeted, there will be another victim sooner, or later. I want him to keep both of you informed of any development. We will have cases to build to bring the perpetrator or perpetrators to justice. Go! begin your investigations!"

Luca and Nino stood up. They shook Prosecutor Avedo's hand and made for the door. They had a lot to do and a lot to think about. The implications of the two murders were chilling. As they opened the door, they were met by a breathless Umberto Grazie.

"Good! You are all together. I need to speak to you all!" He was red in the face and sank into the chair that Bianca offered him.

He took a moment to breathe deeply.

"I've just had the toxicology report from the murder of Betsy Noakes. The blade that was used to stab her had also been poisoned. There is a degree of cruelty in that fact. The intention was absolutely to kill not to wound."

Luca rubbed his face. Bianca shook her head, and Nino muttered, "*Mio Dio*!" The serious situation was getting worse by the second.

On returning to their headquarters, they realised that word had carried fast, and they were immediately ushered in to see their division commander.

He was a serious-minded man with a keen eye for detail.

He knew what chaos multiple murders would cause during Carnevale and how politically sensitive these two deaths were.

Luca offered up his theory, and was impressed that his

39

superior didn't dismiss it out of hand. The commander ordered Luca and Nino to work both cases with help from the ordinary force. Nino looked a little bit sick at the prospect of many hours of work ahead.

He was somewhat mollified by the fact that overtime would absolutely be paid. There had to be some compensation for this disaster that was about to be his social life.

Day 3 of Carnevale

Massimo Lungi was in his office. In front of him, he had the details of a traditional grocery store that had been in the same family for six generations.

It was a well-known, thoroughly Venetian institution. Currently, it was being run by Antonio, who had recently lost his wife.

She had been the culinary brains behind the shop and had sourced the best prosciutto and aged Parmesan to complement the breads, oils, and ingredients that they also sold.

The shop wasn't on the market, but Massimo knew of Antonio's grief and how lost he felt since the death of Francesca.

He would be easy to manipulate into selling up. The location was good, nestled in the labyrinthine streets at the back of Strada Nova in the Cannaregio. It was an area that thronged with tourists.

Despite its popularity, Massimo didn't plan to keep it as a grocery.

Oh no, he was going to use the business model that he had applied to the fourteen shops he already owned.

It would be souvenirs, made in huge numbers in the Chinese factory that his business partner had a share in.

It would sell all the usual things, masks obviously,

plastic models of gondolas, complete with striped jumper wearing gondoliers. They sang 'Oh Solo Mio' when you pressed the button!

He had recently received a consignment of Murano glass copies too.

They would go well in the shop. A fraction of the price of the genuine glass made on the island cost and looked genuine enough for a tourist.

He was pleased with them.

It had been his idea to send a couple of willing students, who worked in his Murano shop, to photograph some of the local glass artists' work and send the photos to China for copying and mass production.

He felt very satisfied that he could obtain Antonio's grocery store for a fraction of its value.

He picked up his phone and dialled the number. Glancing at his reflection in the mirror opposite his desk, he cut a dashing figure.

The electric light caught the diamond and gold of his watch and pinky ring.

It reflected off his blue-grey silk suit and the depth of his walnut-brown tan.

The tan was from a bottle, professionally applied at this time of year. He smiled at himself. "Pronto!" The phone was answered by tired-sounding Antonio.

Massimo gave himself a wolfish grin and began to speak.

He went in for the kill with honeyed words and hollow promises.

Poor shattered Antonio didn't stand a chance, it was

agreed, verbally in ten minutes. Massimo then instructed his lawyer to draw up the sales contract.

Antonio replaced the receiver of his old manual telephone.

He looked bleakly at the neat shelves and drawers of inviting produce. He began to weep quietly. What good was it all without her? Without his Franca by his side, it was all as dry as dust.

He suspected that he had just been swindled, but in his current frame of mind, he didn't much care.

Sadly, he and Francesca hadn't been blessed with children, so there was no one waiting in the wings to take over and keep the business running.

It would happen sooner or later. He hated being in the shop without her. Every second there reminded him of his loss.

He was dabbing his eyes when Isabella Manin entered the shop; the little bell chimed in the way that she remembered since childhood.

This shop always smelt of delicious things. She liked to shop here; it was part of the genuine, original Venice.

Today, she needed coffee, Parmesan, and some ready-made dried pasta. She didn't have time to make her own, but Antonio supplied a wonderful handmade range that saved her time – time that she didn't have.

She noticed Antonio's wet eyes and greeted him as 'Zio,' uncle.

She asked him how he was. Since Zia Franca died unexpectedly three months ago. She had been very worried about him.

43

As he told her of his plans and the deal that Massimo Lungi had struck with him, she felt growing dismay and fury.

She could see plainly that Antonio had been taken advantage of! This was a terrible deal, and a terrible loss to the city.

She urged him not to sign anything. She wanted to speak to Rocco, and also urgently to Antonio's niece, Lucia, who would no doubt know nothing of the situation.

Lucia was as passionate about Italian produce as Zia Franca had been.

Isabella felt sure that Lucia could support Zio Antonio through his grief, keeping the shop going in a way that would honour Francesca.

Isabella paid for her purchases and hurried home.

It was, thankfully, early in the day, and Lilia was handling a small tour at ten a.m. in the Palazzo. She and Rocco had the morning off.

She must speak to him and work out a way to stop Massimo Lungi in his tracks.

Isabella arrived back home to the Palazzo in a whirlwind. She took the staircase from the grand entrance hall two steps at a time "Rocco!" she shouted as she ran. He came out onto the small landing at the top of the servant staircase, looking worried. "Where's the fire, Cara? What has happened?" Agitated, she put away her provisions, and he took the coffee beans from her and began to fill the machine as she told him what she had learned and witnessed. His movements became very small and precise.

44

He looked at her, and she noticed a fire, fury, burning in his eyes. "This cannot happen. We must do something! I know just who to call."

They took their coffee into the sitting room of the caretaker's flat and firmly closed the door. Out on the landing, the sunlight danced on the wall of the servants' stairway, bouncing off the water of the Grand Canal below. It rippled over the ancient glass of the windows, all original, each one with a tiny acid-etched lion, the symbol of the city of Venice.

Luca had experienced one of the most exhausting, but also stimulating, days of his career to date. He was exhilarated, but he knew that, as soon as he sat down and relaxed, he would fall into a dreamless sleep.

His brain felt almost itchy, as if it had thought too many thoughts.

The motive for the murder swirled around his head repeatedly; nothing so far had offered up any common thread, except the nagging theory that tourism was at the heart of the crimes.

He let himself into the building, and, as he called the lift, was quietly relieved that today had not brought a new murder. He was obviously wrong about that part of his theory, and he was heartily relieved that he was!

Clara was setting the table and pouring wine.

The air was fragranced with the smell of herbs and roasting meat.

As they finished eating, Clara told him about her conversation with Sofia. Luca listened intently.

It was always important to know what the city was

45

thinking.

By listening to the people, he might get an inkling as to what this was all about.

He was beginning to tell her about the twists and turns of his day when his mobile began ringing.

It was Nino; he answered and then rubbed his face as he heard what his friend was telling him.

The body of Massimo Lungi, a prominent businessman known for his ruthless negotiations in the city, had been found dead.

It was definitely a murder.

Lungi wasn't a tourist; however, the way that the murder had been committed had caused the commander to contact Nino to request that he and Luca attend the scene.

Luca ended the call and put his coat on again. With apologies to Clara for leaving her with the washing up once again, he left the apartment.

Clara looked at the closed front door and wondered perhaps if Luca was right after all about his theory, three days of Carnevale and three murders.

What was happening to their city, and why?

Massimo Lungi had been found by his office cleaner when she let herself in to clean at the end of the day.

She had found him slumped over his desk, his forehead resting on his keyboard. She hadn't moved him.

She had assumed that he had suffered a heart attack and had called the Politzia.

They had attended, but immediately realised that this was no natural death.

When Luca and Nino arrived, the technical team were

photographing each item at the scene. Massimo Lungi was now propped up, against the backrest of his chair.

It was easy to see the marks of the ligature, which had been used to garrotte him.

The strangest thing, however, was that he had fabric stuffed in his mouth.

Luca and Nino watched in horrified fascination as a technician, carefully extracted the red and yellow fabric to bag it.

It was a T-shirt, gaudily printed in China, with "I ♥ Venice" and a cartoon depiction of a gondola on the front.

There were boxes of similar shirts stacked at the side of the office, along with some boxes of glassware that looked like crude imitations of Murano glass.

Nino and Luca looked at one another. "There's the tourism connection!" Nino said.

Luca nodded. He felt sick. He really, really didn't want to be right about this, but the death of Massimo, who was known to run a whole lot of souvenir shops and was known to buy out established businesses and convert them, was clearly pointing to tourism.

We have a tourist padlocking a bridge. We have a tourist returning to his cruise ship, and now we have a man who makes his money by selling imported, cheap souvenirs, putting out of business artisans, and Venetian traders.

Nino and Luca left the offices of Lungi associates. They left their colleagues to progress the investigations. They crossed the nearest bridge and found a bar.

When each had a large Negroni in front of them, they

began to discuss their fears. "I think we have the reason why these murders are happening," Luca said heavily.

"It's all about a disagreement with tourism and Venice. Whoever is carrying out these killings is making a comment, a protest perhaps, about tourism. We know that Betsy Noakes fixed a padlock to the Ponte degli Scalzi, which is forbidden, but frequently happens.

"We know that Gunter and Adele Walner were cruise ship passengers and were heading back to their huge cruise ship, docked just outside the lagoon, when Gunter was drowned. Now we have Massimo Lungi! We need to find out tomorrow, what deals he was working on, to see if there's something specific or whether it was just a general comment on the scourge of cheap souvenir shops flooding the city."

"We are no closer to the perpetrator!" Nino sighed. "Even if this is the motive, we are still having to be reactive to each death. We haven't got anything concrete to go on! No fingerprints. No CCTV! We are completely in the dark!"

Isabella had phoned Lucia, Antonio's niece, and she had gone to see him straight away at the shop. The old man had wept as his niece explained that she would love to help him with the store. She felt it was important to Zia Franca's memory that they continue.

"She is in every inch of this place!" Lucia soothed. "That isn't a sad thing; it's how we make her live on. We could put her portrait up behind the counter. We could add a special range of products that carry her name. Really honour her!"

48

"That's a wonderful idea, Cara," said Antonio sadly. "I have already agreed to the sale, though. I can't go back on my word; bad things happen to people who cross Massimo Lungi."

"Let's sleep on it," Lucia said, and they locked up and went back to his apartment on Campo St Felice.

Day 4 of Carnevale

The next morning, they opened the shop. They had both spent a troubled night. They were still pondering the impossible conundrum when two Carabinieri officers entered.

Antonio was stunned when they asked him about Massimo Lungi.

He confirmed that he had regretfully agreed to sell the grocery store to Lungi the previous day.

"What is this about?" asked Lucia.

They listened in amazement, as the officers explained that they were investigating the murder of Massimo Lungi.

"On his computer was an email to his lawyer asking for a contract to be drawn up, making the sale of this shop. Who else knew about these plans?" the officer in charge, wanted to know.

Antonio in his shattered state, couldn't remember who he had told. As the day progressed, he had told every one of his regular customers who had called in that day.

It had been a busy day.

There had been many, many customers. All had been upset by his decision to sell up. The officer inwardly sighed in frustration.

He knew that the rumour mill would have been buzzing with this news, and the information could have reached a wide variety of people, second or third-hand.

The murderer could have been anyone.

"My friend, Isabella Manin, told me by phone, yesterday morning about the sale. She was concerned for Zio Antonio. I came straight away and I was with him all day. We worked together. He only told the regulars. He felt he owed it to them. I have been trying to convince him to cancel the sale. We can run this together to the memory of Zia Franca," said Lucia

The second officer knew of the Manins, a well-respected noble Venetian family.

He made a note to contact Isabella to see if she could shed any light on the developments.

In the Palazzo, Isabella took a call from Lucia. She sat down heavily on one of the decorative chairs in the Grand Salon. She had been dusting, and she put down the polish and cloths to take the call.

Rocco heard her say, "Dead? I don't believe it!" before she closed the door. He continued to mop the marble floor of the entrance hall, deep in thought. He waited impatiently for her to come off the phone.

Eventually, she opened the door and looked at him, her eyes glittering. "You'll never guess! Massimo Lungi has been murdered!"

Lilia let out of sharp intake of breath and crossed herself. "What happened?" Rocco asked quietly.

Isabella recounted everything that Lucia had told her. She ended with the good news that Lucia and Antonio weren't going to sell up.

They had decided to carry on for Zia Franca, and they

would have told Lungi that the sale was off, if they hadn't been visited by the police and informed of his death.

"The Carabinieri don't suspect Antonio, surely?" Rocco asked.

"I don't think so," Isabella answered. "It's a mystery!"

"No mystery that Massimo Lungi was almost a crook!" said Lilia indignantly. "Good riddance to bad rubbish!"

With that, she went back into the catering kitchen to refill her water bucket. The Manin twins watched her departing back and then turned to each other. Isabella smiled at Rocco, and Rocco made a small, discrete bow towards her.

The moment was gone in an instant, and they resumed their tasks, this time with renewed vigour.

Luca was reviewing the CCTV from outside Massimo Lungi's office.

The camera caught the view from the small canal, passing the office entrance, and about four doors down on the right.

It was a digital system and automatically downloaded to the hard drive every hour. He had the time of death from Umberto between four p.m. and six p.m. The cleaner had discovered the body at seven thirty p.m. He selected the hour of three p.m. and settled in to watch the comings and goings of the street.

The small stretch of Venice was busy at that time of day.

There was a steady stream of visitors going back-and-forth. At one point there was gridlock as two separate parties of walking tours tried to pass along in opposite directions.

A delivery man, unloaded water cooler bottles from a boat onto the side of the canal, and then delivered them to the office premises next door.

A gaggle of school-aged boys tussled and laughed together as they went into the bakery opposite Lungi's building. They came out with a fritelle in each hand. He was watching them run off, out of the CCTV camera's range, when he spotted a couple of Carnevale-costumed revellers.

They were dressed in matching costumes.

The male wore a black tricorne hat with a white cockade, a black-and-gold decorated mask, and a waistcoat made of the Venetian flag. A strong scarlet topcoat, black breaches, white stockings and black buckled shoes finished the look.

He held the hand of his slightly taller companion in his white glove hand.

She had a dress of the same scarlet tone. The bodice was also the Venetian flag and her cloak was too. The lion rippled as the wind caught it.

She had a white extravagant wig, which contrasted starkly with her matching black and gold mask. On her wig, she had a hat, fashioned into the shape of a gondola.

They walked slowly down the street, stopping and posing to be photographed from time to time.

Luca expected them to continue along towards the canal, but they stopped and disappeared from view as they entered Lungi's building.

Immediately, Luca felt a prickle of interest. He waited and watched.

The pair were only out of shot for perhaps ten minutes or so. They emerged as impassive as before and sailed away in the direction from which they had come.

What had they been doing?

The fact that they went back the way they had come pointed towards the distinct possibility that they were purposefully visiting Lungi's building.

He downloaded the footage to a USB stick and went directly back to headquarters.

He wanted to take another look at Betsy Noakes' phone for the photos and videos.

He also wanted to review the footage they had obtained from the Danieli's cameras overlooking the wide pavements of Riva degli Schiavoni.

He was eager to see if the costumed people appeared in either footage.

He felt a bubble of excitement in his heart. "We might have something to go on!" he murmured to himself as he got to his desk.

He told Nino what he had seen and handed him the USB stick so he could watch it too. Nino looked at him and whistled softly through his teeth.

"It's something! definitely something!"

Nino collected the Danieli CCTV, and Luca retrieved Betsy's phone from the evidence locker. They began to study the footage, lost in concentration, willing the red-costumed Carnevale characters to appear once again.

There were lots of photos on Betsy's phone. It took

some time to get through them to the night of her murder. Luca watched the video where she attached the padlock to the Ponte. She panned her camera to the padlock, then to herself, and then around the bridge, taking in the view along the canal. The panning shot was done rapidly, but Luca caught sight of something. He paused the video and got up excitedly.

"I need to get technical to make this frame larger. I think I've got something!"

Nino continued to scan the Danieli's camera. It didn't show the pontoon where Gunter Walner was drowned, because of the gondola shed, which was masking the view. A herring gull kept perching on the ledge by the camera, and he had to look past the bird to see what was happening at ground level.

He noticed many costumed people, but nobody in the red of the couple that Luca had identified.

He did see a single woman, dressed in gold and turquoise walking alone towards the Zaccaria pontoon.

She disappeared from view behind the annoyingly positioned gull.

He continued to watch and saw her move back the way that she had come, only twenty minutes or so later.

What piqued Nino's interest was the gold trident that the woman carried.

He remembered Umberto's note about the marks of a pronged implement, like a fork, which had been used to hold Gunter under the water.

A trident could be just such an implement.

He jumped up and went to find Luca. It seemed that

there could be collection of killers, which was worrying, but the link seemed to be the adorned costumes of Carnevale.

Isabella was sitting down to a quick sandwich, when the two Carabinieri arrived to speak with her. She offered them coffee and took them into the Grand Salon.

The younger officer looked round in wonder. 'It's magnificent, isn't it?' Isabella smiled. "I always wanted to know what it looked like inside," he said, still looking at the splendour of the large room.

"May I?" he asked as he walked towards the tall glass doors, looking onto the canal.

The arched doors opened onto a covered logia, with matching arches. Beyond the white marble of the logia, the Grand Canal flowed. The sound of the canal, and the busy Rialto bridge, swelled up and into the calm of the salon.

The senior officer looked meaningfully at his junior colleague.

"We mustn't keep Signorina Manin for too long Gianni." Once the door was closed peace was resumed. Only the ticking of the clock broke the silence. The senior officer reviewed his notes and put the time and date, along with those present, at the top of the page of his notebook. "Alora! We are in the early stages of an investigation into the murder of Massimo Lungi. The businessman was found dead in strange circumstances yesterday. Did you know him?"

Isabella explained that while she knew of him, she had never met him. She waited patiently for this to be written down.

"What is your connection with the shop Drogheria Malvestio?"

"It's my favourite grocery," she answered, frowning slightly. "I went there yesterday and bought coffee, this coffee, in fact!" – lifting the cup to them – "the family are friends of ours. I went to school with the proprietor's niece, Lucia."

"Did you contact Lucia yesterday? And if so, why?"

Isabella made a gesture to indicate she had nothing to hide and explained what Zio Antonio had told her, and her worry that the old man was being swindled.

She naturally contacted her friend to inform her.

She had been correct in her hunch that Lucia had previously been unaware that her uncle had been persuaded to sell.

"When you were in the shop, were there any other customers?" Gianni asked.

"I was very early, we had to open the Palazzo, so I was the first customer. Zio Antonio was very upset when I arrived; he was crying. He told me about the sale, and his distress made me feel very concerned. I came straight home and phoned Lucia before the first of the tours began."

These facts were noted down.

"Finally, Signorina Manin, where were you yesterday between three p.m. and five p.m.? It's a routine question, just to eliminate you from our enquiries."

Isabella looks thoughtful. "Between three and five? We were clearing up after a tour. We had a civic reception in the evening last night, so we were here, myself and my brother Rocco. Our staff member Lilia had finished at three p.m. She had done an early tour, so we were here, together prepping for the evening event. As you can see, this place needs plenty of attention to keep it looking so beautiful. We had canapés to prepare, drinks to arrange, and glasses to polish. It was quite hectic."

Satisfied, the two officers said their goodbyes and left by the main door. Isabella stood, watching them go.

She leaned against the doorframe and put her head against the cool, polished wood. Her heart, she realised, was racing.

Luca and Nino were collating all the information that they had from the three murders. They were adding in the CCTV footage as well. Luca had a printout from Betsy Noakes' video at the Bridge.

It showed a costumed woman wearing a gold mask, dressed in black velvet with a gold ornate headdress with a gondola, A-top a dramatic wig.

The figure was stationary, watching Betsy, looking directly at the camera

In the hubbub of the busy bridge, this was the only stationary figure, clearly paying very close attention to Betsy's actions.

"We haven't got motive, but we do have a perpetrator. It's such a shame that they are so heavily disguised!" sighed Nino.

"We need to take all this to Avedo. It's progress, but not really what we would choose. In many ways, we are deeper into the unknown than before!"

Luca rubbed his face and ran his hand through his hair

for good measure. "This is weird, so very weird!"

Gianni knocked respectfully at the door to Luca and Nino's tiny office. He worshipped the pair, secretly.

They had been to university and were senior level.

He had worked his way up from the normal force, but certainly wanted to be like Greco and Conti. He had brought them the write-up of the interviews with Antonio Malvetio and Lucia, his niece, as well as Isabella Manin from the Palazzo Dolfin Manin.

They thanked him and began to read the transcripts.

Dino Tolle had run his mask stall in Saint Mark's Square for over ten years. He sold handmade artisan masks at first, made by the traditional craftsman and women who had been perfecting their trade for centuries. Lately, however, he had decided to move to an alternative source of supply. He sent some examples of the best sellers to the factory that Massimo Lungi used, to see if he could make cheaper copies. He was highly delighted with the results, which reduced his cost per mask by 80%. Of course, he still charged the full price to the customer; that was normal! Just good business.

Several fellow sellers had done the same thing.

It had been a shock when one of the makers began his campaign against the mass-produced copies.

It was embarrassing! Surely, the artisans needed to work on reducing their costs instead of putting their efforts into protesting by the side of his stall.

The protests had continued for a few years now. The hostility was steadily getting worse.

The authorities weren't interested. They saw it as a

59

business matter that needed to be settled privately.

Last week, Dino, who felt that he was the victim in all this, had arranged for a couple of thugs from Mestre, the town across the lagoon bridge from Venice, to teach Karl a lesson.

They had beaten him up, and he was currently in Castello Hospital. Dino felt satisfied that the protest would end.

However, when he arrived that very morning to open up, there were more protest banners pasted to the outside of his stall.

It had been very annoying!

Then, as if that wasn't enough, Karl's daughter, Ana had arrived with some of her school friends, and had begun noisy demonstrations with loudly shouted slogans.

The demonstrations had drawn a curious crowd, with people asking where the merchandise was made!

He told them Italy, naturally, but the backlash from the teenagers was embarrassing and unruly. The Polizia had been called, followed by the Carabinieri normal force, who had told him to close his stall and leave the area.

Ana and her friends watched Dino close up and decided to go for a coffee and a meeting to plan their next steps, somewhere away from Saint Marks.

Ana was scared. She and her dad lived alone and were struggling to make ends meet.

The rent on the flat on Guidecca was increasingly tricky to find, and food, school books, and clothes were gifted and borrowed, which left both father and daughter feeling ashamed.

Karl was an excellent craftsman, and he made beautiful plaster masks as well as the multicoloured velvet-style half masks. He had trained in his native Czech Republic as a young man making puppets, then had moved to Venice to work as an apprentice to a master mask maker.

It had been a good business well paid and varied.

When Ana's mother had left them, Karl had been able to support them both juggling childcare with work from home in his workshop.

Trouble had begun three years ago, when Dino Tolle had stopped ordering from him and the other makers and had started to sell mass produced plastic creations.

There were copyright infringements too, as they were clearly direct copies of the masks made by Karl and the other artisans.

Dino Tolle had seven stalls throughout the city; he was also very influential with the other stallholders.

Now, there were no stall traders who bought from the makers. They all imported from China. The meagre trade had reduced to just a few shops tucked away on streets where the footfall was less.

It wasn't enough to live on.

Ana was worried that her father was becoming depressed.

He wasn't suited to a desk job. He was a true craftsman, and that's what made him happy.

In the crowded coffee shop, Ana and her friends squashed into a corner. They put their banners and placards by the door to the toilets, and Claudia ordered Americanos for them all. Ana was busy telling the girls how her father was, and how long it would be, for his broken ribs to heal.

Her main concern was for his broken fingers. Without his hands, he couldn't make any new masks to sell in the small number of shops that were there to buy them.

Ana's clear, singsong voice carried to adjoining tables, where others could clearly hear. One or two traders recognized Ana and came over to ask after her father.

Someone sent across a plate of Fritelli for the girls to enjoy. She spoke with emotion and maturity beyond her years.

As she spoke, she was not aware of the person listening intently. They had their back to her and made no sign that they were listening.

Ana was speaking with the lady who had gifted the pastries. She hadn't heard the full story of Karl's troubles and the reasons for the protests in Saint Mark's Square.

Step by step, Ana took her through the years of struggle and the recent violent attack that hospitalized her father.

"It's all Dino Tolle's fault!" She finished with spirit. "He is the reason why the artisans of Venice are starving!"

A small ripple of clapping broke out from the traders drinking espresso at the bar. The unobtrusive figure left some euros on the table and swiftly left.

Nobody noticed their departure, or even that they had been present at all.

Dino had been away from his Saint Mark's stall all day, but he was itching to see what those kids were doing to it while he was away.

He knew that the Carabinieri wouldn't be standing guard, that's for sure!

He already had the feeling that they suspected he was involved with the assault on Karl, that stupid foreigner!

It was getting dark. The Sun was setting over the back of the lagoon and the sky was streaked with rose and peach. As the colours intensified, he entered St Mark's Square.

He took an outside table, at one of the cafés and ordered whisky. He could see his stall from his vantage point.

Nothing looked amiss at the moment, but he knew that if it was going to be graffiti, or posters that mischief would happen under the shadow of darkness. Before the square was properly lit.

He was going to catch them at it! He drank his whisky and brooded. His mobile phone pinged.

A text message from an unknown number:

"Meet by your stall at seven p.m. I have information to your advantage; it will end the protests." He texted back:

"Who is this?" and the reply, "A friend" came back instantly.

As he was there, anyway, he reasoned that it wouldn't be too much of an inconvenience to see what information was being offered.

To keep the cold out, he ordered another whisky and prepared to wait until it was time to investigate.

The sky had become crimson and then faded to the shade of a bruise before Dino shifted his position and approached his stall.

It was a hexagonal structure, with sides and a roof.

When trading, the shutters could be removed to show the racks of masks and trinkets within. The shutters that he could see, as he made his way across the square, looked undamaged and poster-free.

He checked his Rolex, 6:50 p.m. He would wait and see.

He heard a low whistle from the other side of the stall, the side in darkest shadows. The whisky had made him cocky and bolshy. He wasn't playing games!

He lumbered towards the direction of the sound.

There was a cloaked figure, a man, it seemed, dressed for Carnevale in a dark frock coat and breaches.

"What do you want?" he slurred, stepping forward towards the shadowy figure. It turned to look at him and was wearing a white plaster mask.

He recoiled!

He didn't have time to think before he felt the knife go into his back. A pure white heat of pain.

He felt winded, then woozy. The world spun out of control, and he fell to his knees. He saw two faces, both impassive in white masks, looking at him, and then nothing. The clock in the square began to strikes seven p.m.

But Dino Tolle didn't hear it. He had left this world for good.

At 7:30 p.m., the lights in Saint Mark's Square were lit, ready for the evening's revelry. The restaurants and bars lit their part of the square with fairy lights and lanterns.

Costumed people began to promenade, cameras flashed, and coriandoli was thrown in huge clouds of multi-coloured confetti.

In all this fun and exuberance, a lone, stationary, life-sized marionette hung from the closed stall at the side of the square.

Strings were attached to its hands and feet.

A rope held the head up, connected to an oversized wooden crosspiece, just like the controls for a traditional puppet.

The face wore a mask of the beaked, curved nose of 'La Peste,' the doctor mask that had its origins in the time of plague in the city.

On the head was a doctor's hat.

The puppet was swathed in a black cloak.

Some Japanese tourists saw the marionette hanging there and began to take photographs. People posed, beside it, assuming it to be an installation for Carnevale.

It was only when somebody got blood on themselves from putting an arm around the figure that alarm spread.

There were screams, and some people ran away.

There was enough panic and drama for the Carabinieri local, to move across from the Doge's Palace side of the square to find out what was happening.

There, they found that under the Peste mask, there was a very dead Dino Tolle. They radioed it in and called for backup.

Luca and Nino were still at the office when the call came in. It was the fourth day of Carnevale. The fourth murder.

By now, the feelings of shock had gone from the minds of both detectives.

They had been replaced by a feeling of resignation and determination to catch these masked criminals before they completed their daily atrocities.

Before they left for the scene, Luca search the police database for any information about the deceased.

Dino Tolle had quite a few pages dedicated to the trouble he was experiencing with the artisans. In addition, he was listed as a probable suspect in the assault of Karl Zeber, a Czech-born, mask maker who had been badly beaten up only that week.

There was a note from that very morning about a protest at Dino Tolle's stall in Saint Mark's Square.

Ana Zeber, the teenage daughter of Karl, had been one of the groups who had been demonstrating.

The demonstration had been against the practice of copying artisan work and selling the copied works (cheap Chinese imports).

The name of Massimo Lungi was connected.

It was the same connection: tourism and the cheapening of Venice's traditional artistry in favour of mass production.

More than ever, Luca felt that he had got to the reason for the murders. He understood what the perpetrators were saying.

This understanding didn't get him any closer to stopping the murders, however.

A protective white tent had been erected around

Tolle's stall, and the deceased had been carefully cut down.

Technical were frustrated that the crime scene had been contaminated by the people who had thought the puppet was an art piece.

They were doing their best to extract each element of the evidence carefully. Luca and Nino watched them working away in their paper suits.

"Props have been used again," observed Nino.

"In the murder of Lungi, the T-shirt was used post-mortem, and here it looks as if, after he was killed, he was turned into a puppet and displayed this way." He gestured to the stall, where the wooden cross piece of the puppet mechanism was being carefully fingerprinted and bagged.

Luca told Nino about the protests and about Ana and Karl Zeber. Karl had been a puppet maker, originally in the Czech Republic. Was this perhaps an attempt to misdirect their investigations?

They needed to pay a visit to Karl in the hospital and also to Ana. She was only seventeen and would need careful interviewing.

"I can't believe that she did this, though," Luca said. "It would've taken strength to hoist a deadweight unobtrusively onto the stall, even if it was in the half-light of the evening, before the square was illuminated."

Taking advantage of a police boat, Luca and Nino headed across the lagoon to Giudecca, the long spine Island, across from Venice.

It was an island with an entirely different feel to the main city.

Much quieter and with huge square buildings, built of warm, terracotta bricks.

They docked by the Hilton hotel, which occupied the huge old pasta factory. They walked briskly along the wide pavement, aside the old garrison headquarters, passing the Fortuny building, which still produced metres and metres of velvet fabric per year.

Karl and Ana's apartment was tucked away in one of the residential side streets. The building was plastered with dark terracotta. Its neighbour was yellow.

The shades were warm in the glow from the street lights.

Nino shook his head at the sign on the lift: "*Ascensore fuori servizio.*"

"Great! A broken lift! T hank goodness they only live on the third floor!"

They trudged up the utility staircase. From time to time, the lights went out, and Luca had to wave his hands above his head to reactivate the motion sensor.

The building had a feeling of tidy decrepitude.

The people who lived here did a lot with very little.

The Zeber apartment door carried a plaster mask, exquisitely made, above the door knocker.

At the sound of the knocker, the pop music that had been playing in the apartment abruptly stopped.

A girl's voice called "Chi e?" Luca announced them, and the door opened just a crack.

"I'm sorry," the girl said, "the cat is determined to escape!"

The door closed again, and there sounded like a

scuffle. There was an indignant yowl and the sound of swearing.

After a pause, the door opened again, and Ana stood before them, sucking a fresh bloodied scratch to her hand.

Once seated in the small, tidy sitting room, Luca began by offering his sympathy for her father's attack.

Fire sprang into Ana's eyes, and she shook her blonde hair, and almost spat. "It's Dino Tolle's doing! He ordered it. Are you here to tell me that you are bringing him to justice?" Nino took over and quietly explained what happened earlier in the evening.

As he described Dino's murder, Ana covered her mouth with her hand.

The cat scratch, a vivid red against her pale skin. She looked genuinely surprised.

As she processed this new fact, she began to look concerned.

"You can't suspect Dad?" she stammered "He's in hospital. He has broken ribs and fingers. He couldn't have done this!"

Luca reassured her that they didn't think Karl was involved in the murder.

"Please tell us all that has happened today. We know you and your friends were making a demonstration at Tolle's stall earlier. Please, just tell us what happened."

Ana was a good storyteller. She recounted step-by-step how the girls had taken homemade placards and a banner to his stall. They had also produced a leaflet, which they handed out to tourists, comparing the painstaking work of the artisan with the factory-made, mass-produced imports. They highlighted the issue of copyright infringement, showing the original masks made by the artisans and the crude copies on sale.

She spoke of Dino Tolle's fury and how he had lied to the tourists when they asked where the merchandise had been made.

She jutted her chin and defiance when she told them of the Carabinieri's attendance.

The girls had left, and then gone to a café, she told of the interest that they had received from the traders in the café.

With a certain pride, she spoke of her speech that had received applause.

Luca and Nino looked at one another. Anyone could've been listening to her, and it was entirely possible that the murderer or murderers had heard her impassioned speech and decided to act on it.

Her and her father's plight fitted entirely into the 'protest' that the string of murder seemed to be becoming.

She told of the ordered gift of Fritelli and the lady who had given it to them. She offered the lady's name for their enquiries.

"Did anyone present seem to be paying particularly close attention?" Luca asked.

Ana thought. She gazed into the middle distance, clearly replaying the memories of earlier in the day.

"Noooo, I can't think that anyone stood out. I know all the people who sympathized, and I can give you their names."

She took one of her protest flyers and began writing

the names on the back of it in purple glitter pen. Handing the list over, she looked from Nino to Luca. "I'm not sorry that Dino Tolle is dead. He was taking the bread from our mouths and he did not deserve to live! It wasn't me or my friends who did this thing, though, I almost wish it had been!" Luca admired her spirit.

"Were there any people in Carnevale costumes in the bar or at your protest?" Nino inquired. "Not in the café. There isn't space for big skirts and wigs, and they would've needed to take their masks off to eat or drink. It's too local a place, not for tourists."

"What about at the protest?" Luca prompted.

"Of course! There were costumed people – it's Carnevale, and it was Saint Mark's Square. But there weren't any taking leaflets, or standing to listen. The costumed ones only want to be photographed; they are entirely self-obsessed!"

Luca nodded and looked at Nino. They both rose from their seats and Luca handed over his contact details.

They told Ana that they would visit Karl in hospital the next day, but there was nothing to worry about.

He wasn't a suspect.

As they left the flat, they heard scratching and yowling from behind the door in the hall. Ana closed the front door.

As Luca and Nino began to descend the stairs, they heard swearing and yowling once again as the cat was released.

"No need for a guard dog when you live with a creature like that!" Nino smiled.

"It seems to attack its housemates more than intruders,

71

though!" quipped Luca, waving his hands above his head as they were once again plunged into darkness.

The lights from Venice twinkled as the police boat carried Luca and Nino back across the water after the trip to interview Ana.

They were both thinking deeply about what she had told them.

Clearly, the murderer was local – someone who knew to take coffee in a café that was for the people of the city, not something touristy.

It almost felt to Luca as if this was the spirit of old Venice, complaining about how the city had been changed. Had been diminished.

He reflected upon the costumes that they had seen the assassins wearing. Red, black and gold were Venetian colours. The fabrics were velvet, and lace. The gondola headdresses, used twice in different costumes.

The Venetian flag used as a waistcoat and as a cloak.

The turquoise blue green of the canals, referencing Venice's maritime status and a trident.

There was also the choice to dress the last victim, as La Peste, the beaked-nose plague doctor, representing the years when the threat to the city came from the Black Death. It had wiped out 50% of the population.

That was 40,000 plus deaths in Venice alone in 1348! It felt like a metaphor to Luca.

It felt as if the murderers were communicating, a clear and serious message: *Tourism is killing the city.*

It was a chilling thought, and most uncomfortable of all for Luca to acknowledge, was that it was a view that he sympathized with.

As they docked at Zaccaria, they watched the promenade of costumes, the lights glittered, and music swelled from some event in Saint Mark's Square.

The Hotel Danieli looked festive, full of revellers, taking dinner and seeing and being seen. "What are we doing to our city?" Luca muttered.

Nino looked at him thoughtfully. "We can't change it, though. It's bigger than all of us!"

Luca glanced at his partner and shook his head. "I think people have been saying that for decades, and I think that's been part of the problem. We think we can't do anything to change the rot, so we don't. If this was a person with a disease, we wouldn't just let the illness take them from us. We would get treatment for them!"

"It's not the same," said Nino.

He felt that it was very late, and they both needed to eat. It was a lack of food that was making Luca so gloomy.

He watched his friend walk off towards home until the careworn figure with the mop of dark curls was swallowed up by the crowds, and he couldn't see him anymore.

He turned in the opposite direction and made his way home.

He knew his mama would have something delicious warming in the oven for him. Tomorrow was another day, and they had so much to do.

Day 5 of Carnevale

Clara was getting worried about Luca. She had read something in La Nuova, the Venetian newspaper about a link between the three deaths.

It was speculation, but the fourth death confirmed the opinion that the journalist was expounding. The piece criticised the Carabinieri, which Clara knew to be unfair.

She had witnessed in only four days how the string of crimes had troubled her friend. All she could do was keep him fed, listen to him, and make sure that he got some sleep.

It was a time of firefighting and treading water to make sure that Luca didn't mentally go under.

She made coffee. Sunlight was flooding into the salon, and she decided that it was warm enough to serve breakfast outside on the terrace.

She knocked gently on Luca's bedroom door, and he called for her to enter. He was sitting on his bed, wearing yesterday's clothes.

"I fell asleep on the top of the bed," he said ruefully.

"You slept in your clothes!" she exclaimed and fussed him into the bathroom, turning on the shower to warm up.

She knew he would feel better when he had let the hot water revive him.

Feeling like his mama, she bustled into the kitchen and

began making him a bowl of porridge in her mother's English style.

She knew that would help sustain him for another challenging day as it unfolded. He stood at the door to the kitchen, towelling his hair dry.

"I'm so sorry, Cara! I'm not coping well with this," he said, looking embarrassed. She had so many things to say to him, so much admiration and love.

She suddenly realized that she was in love with Luca. She had probably been for years! The deep feelings surged up from her heart into her mouth, but she squashed them down again.

He didn't need an emotional declaration now, when he was so full of stress from the case.

Instead, she smiled, touched his arm, and told him that she thought he was coping brilliantly with an impossible situation,

She led him gently out onto the sunny terrace and set a bowl of porridge in front of him. He looked up, confused.

"It's medicine! Eat!" she said as he picked up the spoon, looking doubtful.

She poured him a coffee and sat down to join him in the gentle spring sunlight.

The sound of the bells from various churches chimed, and the air was full of the liquid notes and the sound of gulls calling.

This afternoon, at the Palazzo, they were holding a reception for the city, part of the Carnevale celebrations.

Isabella counted once again the number of provisions and glassware that they needed for five p.m.

This was the masked reception, scheduled for the early evening as an aperitivo before a grand dinner and party for Il Ballo Del Doge.

Some guests were going to a production of La Traviata, Verdi's masterpiece, set during Paris' carnival, at the La Fenice opera house, not far from Saint Mark's Square,

Rocco and Isabella had been chosen because of their direct lineage to the last Doge of Venice, Ludovico Manin.

It would impress the high-status guests of the city's authorities.

It was a chance to show off and the twins felt resentful that they were being forced to take part in a charade to increase the city's status.

It felt cheap and they felt used.

There was no choice but to participate, however, it was part of their contract that allowed them leave to remain in their home.

They had only eight hours to transform the Palazzo Dolfin Manin into a party venue. Luckily, they had been allowed to shut to visitors for the day.

Lilia was bringing her two nieces to help, and the city had provided four costumed and masked waiters to serve the drinks and canapés.

A string quartet was to set up on the balcony, outside the Grand Salon.

It was thankfully warm enough to have the doors open, and they had hired a patio heater to prevent the musicians from getting a chill from the dampness of the canal after sunset.

Luca and Nino were on their way to the hospital to interview Karl Zeber.

The little police motor launch skipped over the wash from the Alilaguna airport boat, taking people back to Marco Polo Airport and bringing in new tourists.

The sun was hazy and warm as they skirted the salt marshes, on their way to Ospedalle SS Giovanni e Paulo.

There were several white, elegant egrets looking for food in the shallows, and some of the marsh grasses were beginning to flower.

Luca raised his face to the sun and breathed deeply.

He loved getting out on the water. He was a true Venetian. He needed the salty air in his nostrils.

He already felt better after Clara's hearty breakfast. After all this is over, he thought, I'm going to talk seriously to Clara. I love her, and I think we make an excellent team.

I want to be more than friends, and I have to tell her how I feel.

If I don't, I will regret it for the rest of my days, even if I risk losing her.

Nino noticed his friend's thoughtful expression. I hope he isn't thinking about the case, he thought.

Nino had been waiting for Luca and Clara, to realise what everyone else saw as obvious, that they were made for each other.

It was Luca's clear devotion to Clara that had, early on, prevented Nino from asking her out on a date.

The boat slowed and got into the right lane of the hospital.

Ambulance boats, sirens blaring, zipped in and out of the channel to the left.

It was another extremely busy day and Luca snapped out of his revery, to once again, concentrate and begin his enquiries.

The nurse showed them into a sunny private room next to the nurse's station. Karl was propped up in bed, both arms and hands heavily bandaged.

He regarded them out of swollen purple eyes. He had been thoroughly beaten up, and the bruises were working their way out.

His blond hair contrasted, starkly, with the kaleidoscope of colours on his poor face. Luca told him that they had seen Ana and he looked worried.

"Is she okay?"

They reassured him that she was coping admirably, despite the fierceness of their feline companion.

Karl grinned and then winced at the pain. "Micka isn't exactly the most sociable and lovable of animals!" he said.

Nino began by telling him of the death of Dino Tolle.

Karl closed his eyes for a minute and seemed to say a prayer. He explained what the previous three years had been like, as less and less work went to him and his artisan colleagues.

Then the betrayal of seeing his designs mass-produced cheaply, so he couldn't compete. The intimidation that he had received when he began his protests.

Then finally, the terrifying attack, when he had been set upon by the hired thugs.

He had just delivered work to one of the costume

78

shops that he supplied, and as he walked back to the Vaporetto stop, two figures emerged from the shadows and began to attack him, kicking and punching him, and then hitting his hands with what looked like a handmade cosh. He had passed out as the attack continued.

When he came round, there were people standing around him, and they called the ambulance. He had been there, in the hospital ever since.

Carabinieri Normal, had interviewed him as soon as the doctors had strapped him up and reset his broken fingers.

When Karl had finished, silence hung in the air. Luca and Nino digested what Karl had said.

They knew that Karl hadn't harmed Dino Tolle. It was quite the reverse.

Luca stepped forward to the bed. He put his hand on Karl's arm.

"I'm so sorry that you and Ana have been subjected to such trouble. Everyone deserves to live life without fear. I hope that now, in time, you and your daughter can feel safe again."

Karl looked at him, and tears welled up in his bruised eyes.

He just nodded and clumsily, patted Luca's hand with his bandaged fingers. Nino looked away and cleared his throat.

They had completed their enquiries here. Karl wasn't to blame.

It was almost time! Everything was ready, the chandeliers glittered, and the glassware shone and

79

sparkled in the lights.

Everything looked inviting and glamorous.

At that moment, as Rocco and Isabella stood in the entrance to the Grand Salon, taking in the impressive spectacle, the string quartet began with some Vivaldi.

The afternoon sun broke through the light cloud, and sent a path of gold across the gleaming polished Carrera marble floor.

It was breathtaking.

Lilia and her nieces began to pour glasses of Prosecco into fluted goblets and the masked waiters filled the credenza surfaces with platters of canapés.

Isabella and Rocco went to the entrance hall, ready to join the receiving line of dignitaries, who would be welcoming the guests.

As usual, the twins were directed to the end of the line. Last at their own party.

As usual, the slight on their lineage, by lesser people, hurt their pride.

They smiled and made small talk, even though, if you looked closely, you would have noticed that the smiles and pleasantries did not meet their eyes.

The Manin's were working under great stress and unbelievable, personal pressure.

The entrance hall was full of the sound of laughter and excited chatter. The guests were mostly masked and dressed in extravagant costumes.

There were a lot of tall wigs and wide skirted dresses, made wider by hoops.

There were men and women mingling, and as they

lifted their masks to drink the Prosecco or eat the canapés, the illusion of gender was sometimes shattered.

A glamorous woman in a cream, brocade dress and pale pink curled wig, delicately lifted her white mask to reveal the bearded face of a swarthy man.

A noble-looking man in a tricorn hat and blue velvet frock coat and breaches lifted his mask to reveal a pretty woman.

All was illusion, and nothing was as it seemed.

Into this glittering throng Eunice and Ivan Bemrose sailed.

She was resplendent in maroon silk and velvet, with a half mask to match. Her iron-grey hair was topped with burgundy ostrich feathers.

Dressed in the same colours, her bespectacled husband followed in her wake, as slim as she was large and blousy.

He looked rather overwhelmed by the grandeur and the noise.

As they reached the receiving line, Eunice began to speak loudly with a strong New York accent. Everyone stopped what they were doing for a moment, as she bellowed her greeting to the welcoming dignitaries.

"We just love your darling little country! It's so small and primitive! Why, Venice is positively antique! You could use some help fixing up the paint on some of those old buildings, though. You should learn from the states. In our Venice at Disney World, they've got it just right. You need to get your tourism people on it, tidy the place right up!"

As she loudly and rudely continued with her views and

suggestions about how the Venetians could fix their city, Ivan shook his head and quietly apologised to the open-mouthed city counsellors.

Rocco made a small bow and introduced himself and Isabella to the Americans. As soon as she heard that this was their ancestral home, she began telling them all the ways that the space could be improved, if only they had her vision.

It was too plain, too old-fashioned, it needed new mirrors and proper drapes in coral and plum.

It needed fire colours, yellow and orange and cerise.

She had a particular talent for creating 'impact' she told them. During her diatribe, she barely stopped to breathe.

Isabella and Rocco had the impression of being born down upon by a large, burgundy bulldozer.

Suddenly, Eunice heard the quartet playing through the doors on the balcony and abruptly walked away from Rocco, even though she had been mid-sentence.

Ivan shook Rocco's hand, and Isabella watched the little man scuttle after his hideous wife.

In the Grand Salon, for a moment, Eunice was speechless.

The beauty and noble grandeur began to work on her soul. She shrugged off these feelings of awe and began to expound to anyone in earshot – which was everyone in the Palazzo – just how the room could be changed to modernise it.

She was a loose cannon, and the other guests began to ignore her and focus once again on having as good a time as possible at the city's expense.

Dominico Scalla, the excursion organiser for the five-star cruise ship that the Bemrose's were travelling with, came over to speak with the couple.

He was an oily, obsequious man who always considered the possibility of a sizeable tip, whenever he spent time with customers.

He was prepared to flatter the monster that was Eunice, to increase what, he had mentally anticipated, was a four-figure sum.

He had invited them to this Aperitivo before he accompanied them to La Fenice to see the opera La Traviata.

Inwardly, he fervently hoped that the music and performance would manage to stop Eunice from speaking for the duration.

Isabella heard what Mrs Bemrose was saying and felt fury.

This overblown wind bag of a woman was commenting on her heritage, her land, her home – and finding it all wanting!

Who was she to judge? To prescribe! How dare she?

To allow her rage to cool, she went to the catering kitchen to check on the stocks left of Prosecco.

They were disappearing fast, and she knew that it would be unthinkable to run out.

She was moving more bottles into the wine fridge when Rocco joined her.

"That woman is a joke! A complete monstrosity!" he spat, clearly as annoyed as his sister by the woman's rudeness.

"I hear that she's going to the opera," Isabella said, pushing her hair from her eyes. She looked weary.

"I know that she will ruin La Traviata for everyone!" said Rocco grimly.

"Perhaps she should just leave, check out early! We don't need people like her in the city."

"Rocco!" Isabella said, with mock reproof.

More could not be said, as one of the cream-coated, masked waiters came through the door to collect two more platters of canapés, impassive in his black-and-gold mask.

Somehow, the twins steered the early evening soirée to a close, and said goodbye to their guests, who were excitedly preparing for one of the biggest social occasions of Carnevale: the Ball of the Doge.

Dominico Scala gathered up his party of ten, including the Bemrose's, and took them to the gleaming motor launch that was going to convey them in style to La Fenice.

As they began to embark, Eunice could be heard loudly commenting that the boats were bigger and more comfortable in the states.

Isabella gratefully closed the doors and put the bolts across.

This evening, had been more of a trial than usual. It was that awful American that had made it particularly difficult.

The ornate, winged sign to La Fenice was lit, and casting a warm light over the steps. The audience was arriving – some dressed for the opera, others in Carnevale costume. Still others, dressed smartly, covertly photographed the finery.

There was a palpable feeling of anticipation and excitement.

Dominico shepherded his guests up the stone steps into the entrance hall.

He had reserved a large, elevated box – at great expense – at the back of the theatre, which offered a wonderful view of the stage and all the layers of intimate boxes surrounding the auditorium. Lit by faux candles, electric now, but still attached to the original sconces.

The light was warm and womb-like. As the party took their seats, Eunice began loudly to comment on how everything was so quaint, and just plain 'dated!' The other women in the party rolled their eyes and chose chairs as far away from her as possible.

All the other boxes were full. People watched one another across the theatre. Opera glasses were used to take in the scene.

Comments were made about who was there and who wasn't. The costumed people could have been anyone and may have been attending with other people's husbands or wives. The mystery, illusions, and endless possibilities created a tense and electric atmosphere.

As the overture began, the theatre fell silent. Even Eunice could tell that talking at this moment would be frowned upon.

She was dying to speak. She liked to comment on everything that she experienced. People deserved to hear what she, Eunice Bemrose thought about it!

The music swelled, and Ivan looked calm, and almost

relaxed, he was going to enjoy this. The lights dimmed, and Verdi's Opera began.

As Violetta appeared, and began to sing, all eyes were fixed on the first act. The costumes and the arias were sumptuous.

Everyone hung on every liquid note, every gesture. La Fenice worked its age-old magic, and Verdi's Opera wove the spell it had been casting since it was first sung in this very theatre in 1853.

Act one finished, and the audience disappeared to the bars or the toilets. Dominico Scalla's party went to find refreshment.

Eunice loudly told Ivan what she wanted him to bring her. The lengthy list was mostly unachievable, and he resolved to bring her an ice cream and take the consequences of her inevitable disappointment on the chin.

She turned back to the view, and he dutifully followed the other guests out of the door of the box.

Eunice settled herself, resting her arms on the upholstered edge of the box, her hard, piggy eyes, judging everything that she saw.

Engrossed in her people-watching, she didn't hear the click of the door behind her, nor did she notice the two figures dressed in matching cream frock-coats and breaches. The white curled wigs contrasted with their black and gold masks.

If Eunice had looked around at that point, she would have seen them, and assumed they were two of the waiters from the earlier Aperitivo reception at the Palazzo.

As it was, she only noticed that something was amiss when she felt strong arms grab her from both sides.

She was lifted off her seat and off her feet.

She let out a squawk of surprise and indignation, which changed to a scream as she was pitched up and over the box's edge.

She was falling.

She hurtled down past the Royal Box, four floors.

There was a loud crash, and the woman landed, her neck snapped at a sickening angle. Her ostrich feathers were still fixed into her hair.

Those who were still in the auditorium let out a collective gasp of surprise, and then shocked shouts began.

A woman sitting near the dead body fainted.

Calls were made for the theatre manager, and the police.

All was in uproar. There was only one person silent in the melee.

It was ironic to see that the silence came from Eunice Bemrose. Silent now for the rest of time.

For her, La Traviata, 'the fallen woman' had become true in a very literal sense.

As soon as Luca's phone rang, he had a sinking feeling.

It was day five of Carnevale, and the later it became during the evening, the more nervous he felt.

The frustration he experienced was growing.

Having to be entirely reactive was extremely difficult.

It was making him feel differently about his beloved city. Everywhere he looked there was a fear that the killers could be watching.

Every display of excess was presenting a risk. After the call from headquarters, he phoned Nino.

The noise in the background sounded as if he was in a bar. They agreed to meet outside La Fenice.

Clara was watching him, as he put his phone down.

She had heard his half of the conversation and she had gathered the gist of the situation. Luca rubbed his face, showing the ever-present stress once again.

"Do you need a hug, Caro?" she asked gently, and he opened his arms in response.

The pair embraced. He buried his face in her hair; it smelled of the green apple shampoo that she used. She smelled delicious, and she felt like Home.

He could have stayed like that forever, he thought, but duty, as always, tugged at him, and he broke away, kissing her on the crown of the head.

She watched the door long after he had departed. The hug had been a comfort to Clara too, and she knew that when all this was over, she must tell Luca that she loved him and wanted to be with him forever.

Nino was waiting by the stone steps to the theatre when Luca arrived.

They went into the, by now, empty foyer and met the Carabinieri officers who had first attended the scene.

They recounted what they had been told by witnesses, and then Luca and Nino walked through to the auditorium, where Eunice's body was being processed, ready for transportation to the morgue.

Looking up to the box, where she had fallen from, they

could easily see how the height and momentum had resulted in fatality.

"Let's see what evidence is in place in the box," Nino said.

He was eager to see if the killers had left fingerprints or fibre evidence that could bring them some way closer to the culprits.

On the way up to the box, Luca was introduced to the theatre manager. They enquired about CCTV and were pleased to hear that there was a state-of-the-art system in place that they could view once they had seen the location of the crime.

The box was comfortably appointed, with pale mint green walls and a red plush carpet. The edge of the viewing aperture was upholstered in red velvet, and there were small fixed tables along its length to allow theatregoers a place to rest a program or opera glasses.

The chairs were freestanding and could be moved to get the most advantageous view.

The chair that Eunice Bemrose had been sitting on was upturned and lay on its side.

The technical team was fingerprinting it, but as this was so frequently used by many people, there were hundreds of prints and partial prints jumbled together on the bent wood frame.

The velvet rim of the box was scuffed and the technical team was photographing the marks in the plush fabric.

Luca and Nino could imagine the large woman being lifted and pitched over the edge. There must have been two assailants.

Eunice Bemrose was too heavy for one person to successfully manhandle without causing her to fight back.

The element of surprise was a factor obviously, however.

As they calculated this, Gianni came in to inform them that interviews with Eunice's widower, Ivan, and the rest of the party had been conducted.

He reported that they had left Eunice alone when the interval began, after the first act. They had all made their way to get refreshments and had left her sitting close to the edge, looking down into the auditorium, watching the rest of the audience.

"CCTV," said Nino emphatically. "Once again, it's down to CCTV."

They followed the theatre manager to the security room and settled down to view the evening on the bank of four screens.

The camera operator explained that there were several bundles of cameras focused on all the public areas, from the steps outside the theatre to the stage.

With a quick click of the mouse, he accessed footage from earlier that evening.

The coloured images appeared on the screens from four separate angles, each provided by a separate camera. The picture quality was crisp and clear.

As they watched, they saw Domenico Scalla ushering his party up the steps. Eunice and Ivan Bemrose were easy to spot, as Eunice was such a large figure, and her ostrich feathers could be seen even through the crush of the foyer.

The main interest then, was what happened after the Bemroses' party had entered.

Nino and Luca concentrated as they watched the foyer empty, as people took their seats. The time counter on the video showed that Act one was in full flow when Nino spotted two identically dressed men in costume walking up the stairs in the foyer.

It was a back view; one was slightly taller than the other.

They were wearing cream, frock-coats and white wigs with ponytails tied in black ribbon. Luca asked the camera operator to switch to the cameras that monitored the curved corridors, that led to the doors to the boxes, over to the back section of the auditorium above the Royal box.

There was a delay when the camera showed an empty corridor, and for a moment, Luca thought that they were wrong in their hunch.

A minute later, the identically dress pair, seen from the front, walked briskly along the red carpet.

They wore black, impassive full-faced masks, hand-painted with a gold leaf design. It was impossible to see their eyes through the small openings in the masks, and their plastered lips were expressionless.

Nino realised he'd been holding his breath as they watched the assassin's progress.

They both let out a low whistles. They saw the figures stop at the door to Eunice's box and carefully, and slowly open the door to enter.

They continued to watch, keeping an eye on the minute counter at the bottom of the screen. Stealthily, the

91

door to the box slowly opened again, and both men came out.

They showed no outward reaction or interacted with one another in any way.

They briskly walked back, the way they had come and disappeared from view.

The camera operator switched view to the foyer and they observed the pair, leaving swiftly, down the steps as the ushers from the main foyer began to run towards the auditorium, indicating that the murder had happened.

Luca requested that the relevant footage be downloaded to a USB drive for them to add to the evidence files for Prosecutor Avedo.

With renewed purpose, Luca and Nino thanked the theatre staff and left La Fenice.

They went to a gondolier bar and stood at the counter to have an espresso as a pick-me-up. They needed to write up their reports immediately, while the information was fresh in their minds.

It was going to be a long night, yet again.

They felt that there was no time, between murders, to make any proper headway before they were pitched into a new death.

Gianni knocked at their office door as they sat reviewing the evidence that they had for each murder, cross-referencing and evaluating every tiny detail.

He brought his typed account of the interviews with the rest of the Bemrose party.

He had made an observation of his own, which he was eager to share with Luca and Nino. They cleared a chair of files and paperwork, and he sat down.

"I noticed that Eunice and the rest of the party had all begun their evening at the Palazzo Dolfin Manin, off the Grand Canal, near the Rialto," he began.

"It's a coincidence, perhaps, that we had occasion to go to interview Isabella Manin at the Palazzo after the murder of Massimo Lungi."

Luca looked at Nino; in their experience, there were very rarely coincidences that turned out to be just that.

Usually, this led to something.

"Was Eunice Bemrose a friend of the Manin family?" Nino asked.

"No, it was a city reception, before the Ball of the Doge. The Manins run the Palazzo for the city. It's not theirs anymore. They are essentially caretakers!"

This information heightened their interest.

Owned by the city? It was just possible that this fact could sow the seeds of a grudge against modern Venice.

"I think we need to go and interview her again. Is she married, or does she run the Palazzo alone?"

Gianni was able to tell them of the twins, Isabella and Rocco, who had direct lineage to Ludivico Manin, the last Doge of Venice. A prickle of energy ran up Luca's spine.

Two nobles, living in their ancestral home, but not owning it. Having to do the bidding of the city authorities.

This felt like grounds for a motive, especially with the view that he held, that the heart of this mystery was a comment on how the great city of Venice was being diminished in the wave of kitchness and mass tourism.

Day 6 of Carnevale

Luca was up early. For once, he was preparing breakfast for Clara.

She wandered out of her room, rubbing sleepy eyes, attracted by the fragrance of coffee, freshly brewed.

She was heartened to see Luca, looking his usual self, much more focused.

He had lost that troubled look in his dark brown eyes.

She mentioned that he seemed more positive this morning, and he grinned as he handed over her mug of steaming coffee.

"We might have a break! In fact, I think we do have a break. We have a meeting with Prosecutor Avedo, this morning."

He had a definite spring in his step. Clara felt her mood lift to match his.

They may not be out of the woods, but they were definitely making positive progress.

In the waiting room at the prosecutor's office, Luca was pacing. His pent-up nervous energy crackled around the room.

Nino wished he would stop. What if this wasn't the breakthrough that Luca thought?

Nino felt jumpy, really nervous. The revelation from Gianni the previous night, had affected them both equally, but in different ways.

Dario, Prosecutor Avedo's assistant, came through at that moment to take them in to see his boss.

Luca almost overtook him as they walked briskly along the corridor.

Nino rolled his eyes at Dario, who merely smiled an understanding smile, he'd seen it all before.

Bianca had been getting a lot of complaints from the city authorities and also her superiors in the Italian government.

Until now, they had managed to keep the chatter and speculation to a minimum, but the longer it took to resolve, coupled with the continuing daily murders, the harder it became to keep a lid on the gossip and comment.

Already, La Nuova had printed the possibility of a serial killer, which really didn't help matters.

The fact that the killer or killers had moved away from tourists had definitely helped to dampen the narrative.

Last night's murder of the rich American, Eunice Bemrose, however, had reignited the tourist threat once again.

She fervently hoped that Conti and Greco had something useful to tell her. She clicked open an email from Umberto Grazie in Pathology.

As the deaths were coming one a day, Umberto had begun grouping the results of the post mortems into batches.

This email covered the findings from Massimo Lungi and Dino Tolle.

Lungi had been killed by strangulation with a ligature,

pulled tightly around his throat from behind. There were no defensive wounds or anything to suggest that Lungi had resisted.

Equally, other than a sizeable quantity of red wine from his lunch, there were no traces of drugs in his system.

He hadn't been subdued chemically.

Dino Tolle was a different story. He had high levels of alcohol in his bloodstream, but he had been stabbed with a poisoned blade, in the same way that Betsy Noakes, the first victim, had been killed. The knife used was a rapier – something with a very long, thin blade, which seemed to be the same for both murder one and murder four.

She printed out copies of the report for Nino and Luca and buzzed through to Dario to send them in. When Dario opened the door to usher in both detectives, Luca burst passed him.

His excitement was palpable.

"Good morning, gentlemen. I hope you have some positive information to share," Bianca said wryly.

She indicated the two chairs in front of her desk, and Nino sat.

Luca began to pace. "Sit down, Conti! You're wearing out my carpet!"

Looking contrite, Luca sat. He opened his leather document file and drew out a typed report. He handed this to the prosecutor with beseeching eyes.

"Please read this, Prosecutor Avedo. I think we have a significant lead."

"I think I gathered that from your barely concealed excitement!" With that, Bianca began to read. Luca watched her intently.

She was interested to note that whilst Conti was like a coiled spring, Greco looked almost depressed and apathetic.

Maybe this breakthrough was only apparent to one of the team. She gave up musing and began concentrate.

The clock ticked. Luca drummed his fingers on his knee, and the sounds from outside on the canal, carried into the otherwise silent office.

Time seemed to standstill.

It was as if the room was holding its breath, waiting for Prosecutor Avedo's judgement and evaluation.

"*Molto interessante*," Bianca finally spoke. "So, we have a link to the Manin twins at the Palazzo Dolfin Manin. Do we have anything concrete, anything that will allow us to arrest them?"

"No, that's the problem," said Nino morosely.

"Why so miserable, Greco? You haven't shared your partners enthusiasm from the moment you arrived in my office. Why?"

Luca looked at Nino in surprise.

"I thought you were on board with this too, as much as me." Nino took a moment to gather his thoughts.

"It's too vague for me. We have a link, yes, but we have no direct evidence. We have CCTV of costumed figures around the time of each murder, but we don't have evidence of it being the Manin pair. Until we have something that clearly indicates that it's them, I cannot be content." He sighed. "It's day six of Carnevale, and I am troubled by the inevitable call that will come, of another death. This is a false dawn to my mind."

All three sat in silence for a moment, mulling over what Nino had said. He was right in many respects.

Luca rubbed his face. Bianca felt the positive energy seep out of the office, as if it was running like water under the door and away.

She knew she needed to pick up their spirits. If apathy and powerlessness set in, they may as well give up and call the Carabinieri from Rome.

"The obvious step, to my mind, is to interview the Manins. Eunice Bemrose was at the Palazzo. It's normal to interview everyone that the dead woman encountered on her last day on earth."

Begin there and see where it takes you.

"Could we put surveillance on the twins?" Luca asked.

"No, that could be problematic," Avedo cautioned. "We may have to build a case against the pair. We can't risk an allegation of entrapment."

Nino and Luca had found outside seats on the vaporetto.

They were the only ones sitting outside in the morning sunshine.

It was chilly today, and all of the other passengers were taking advantage of the heated central cabin.

This gave the two detectives time to speak about their strategy for interviewing the Manin twins.

They had decided not to make an appointment. It was better to take them by surprise to see what that revealed.

Nino was doubtful that they would get any closer to the perpetrators, but Luca was adamant that they were the killers. They decided that Luca would lead the interviews, and Nino would observe.

Ideally, they wanted to interview the twins individually. "Twins can have a telepathy. Sometimes they think as a pair," Nino said. He still looked nervous, and his concern was rubbing off on Luca.

So much was riding on this development. It really felt like 'make or break.' The spectre of another day of Carnevale was in the back of their minds.

Would there be another murder? Or would today be the day that they broke the case?

Isabella and Rocco had a full schedule, they had back-to-back tours, but first, they had to clear the last of the catering boxes from the Great Hall. The previous evening's reception had been a success from the point of view of the city dignitaries, but for the Manins, there was still a lot of work to be done.

Returning glassware that they hired and the rest of the wine that the merchant let them have sale or return.

Rocco was impatiently waiting for the boats to arrive so they could clear the boxes from the hall and put the ropes up, ready for the first party of visitors.

He was waiting by the door, distractedly looking up and down the plaza for a delivery man with a trolley.

"Rocco Manin?"

"Hmm?" He turned absentmindedly towards the questioner. Luca carried out the introductions and requested an interview.

"Not now! Now is a terrible time! We haven't a minute this morning!" A flash of temper showed in his eyes.

Isabella heard the sharp tone in her brother's voice, and went to the door to see what was upsetting him.

She offered to go first.

After all, she'd been interviewed before; it was routine. It had to be done, and it was better to get it out of the way.

She indicated that Nino and Luca follow her into the Grand Salon, leaving Rocco at the door, waiting for the couriers to take the stock away.

Rocco made a show of walking out into the street in exasperation, then he turned and covertly, watched his sister and the two Carabinieri go, with a small frown on his handsome face.

As soon as she had seated Luca and Nino in the Grand Salon, Isabella realised that they were a rather different type of detective compared to the two who had interviewed her two days before.

That had been a respectful, friendly chat. This was far more serious.

They began by asking her where she had been on the previous night between seven and ten p.m. Isabella explained that they had been cleaning up after the early evening reception.

She said that Lilia and her nieces helped to clean up, but that the four waiters, costumed and masked, had left as soon as the guest had. They hadn't so much as cleared away a single glass.

She recounted they had taken their cheques as payment and had gone in different directions, two by two.

She recalled how comical it had been to watch them. They were mirror images of each other, both dressed identically in cream frock coats and white wigs.

She said that she had been surprised that they hadn't taken their black and gold masks off as they went off duty.

She imagined that the masks would be itchy after a few hours of wearing them. Nino made a note looked directly at her.

She was an attractive woman, with fine features and an aristocratic air about her. Her brown eyes were watchful, and she was clearly very intelligent.

There was something slightly cruel about her wide, generous smile, though – something hidden.

He got the feeling that she felt herself to be very much better than he was. Luca wanted to know what time Lilia and her nieces had left the Palazzo.

"I don't know exactly. Let's ask her," Isabella replied, smiling. The smile didn't reach her eyes.

Lilia was found and came into the salon, wearing an apron and carrying a duster. "We've only thirty minutes before the first tour! Can't this wait?" she began.

Luca explained that they were investigating a murder, and that this investigation took priority over everything else.

Lilia shrugged. "Ask your questions, then, but be quick."

She told them that she and the girls had left to get the vaporetto at seven thirty p.m. Isabella frowned "Are you sure it wasn't later? I was sure it was after eight p.m. at least."

Lilia shook her head. "No, it was exactly seven thirty p.m. I needed to get the girls home before eight. I looked at my watch as we left to get to the Rialto pontoon to meet the boat." Again, Isabella frowned. "Va bene," she said lightly.

Luca allowed Lilia to get back to her tasks.

Rocco came into the salon. His boxes had been collected. He told them he was now ready to be interviewed.

Isabella asked for leave to go and prepare for their imminent tour party.

As she rose from the table, Nino saw the glance that passed between the siblings. He felt an inadvertent shiver go up his spine.

Something was going on here.

He wasn't sure that it was murder, but there was definitely something strange about Isabella and Rocco Manin and their relationship.

The earlier show of temper had outwardly gone from Rocco's manner.

He seemed affable and slightly self-effacing, apologising to the two detectives.

"I get so worried about messing up a tour! We are employees of the city, as you are. I'm sure you understand."

The fact that the Carabinieri were answerable to Rome and the government wasn't something that Luca chose to point out, and he nodded in agreement.

"Where were you last evening between seven p.m. and ten p.m.?" he said in a flat voice, he wanted to come across

102

as asking purely routine and boring questions to keep Rocco calm, and perhaps get more from him than he realised he was giving.

"I'm sure my sister told you, that we had just finished a large reception and we had a lot to clean up." Rocco smiled and stretched his arms above his head like a cat in the sunlight.

A picture of relaxed indifference.

Nino watched him and noticed a muscle pulsing in his smooth tanned cheek. Something is not as it seems here, he thought, perhaps Luca's theory has substance.

"Did you leave the Palazzo at all?" Nino snapped back to focus on the question Luca was asking.

"I don't think so, wait! I went to get some more bin bags from the convenience store by the Rialto, that took me a short while because they were closed and I had to go across the bridge."

Nino made a note of this. It could be checked on the cameras on the Rialto.

"And after that, what did you do when the work was done?" Luca sounded bored. Nino was impressed by his seeming disinterest.

"We went up to the flat, Isabella cooked some pasta, and we had an early night. We knew that we would be busy today, which we are about to be – very, very busy. I must go and help her prepare. Is there anything else?"

Luca passed his card across to Rocco. "If you can think of anything else, please get in touch." Rocco got to his feet and so did Luca and Nino they could see that their time was up.

As they left the Palazzo a crowd of tourists following a tour guide's flag were approaching, they looked back to see a smiling Rocco and Isabella the doorway.

"Welcome to our home, Palazzo Dolfin Manin," they heard Rocco say heartily.

They glanced at each other and walked away to find a bar to have a coffee and discuss their observations and impressions.

Sitting at a corner table with two Americanos in front of them, Luca and Nino began to go through what they had learned.

"I purposefully didn't ask either of them about Eunice Bemrose. I wanted to give us a reason to go back and probe some more."

Nino nodded. "I really think that there's something wrong with that pair."

"They scare me!" Luca said. "There's something, just under the surface, something unresolved. Rage, just hidden and tightly held in check."

"Until it's not!" said Nino wryly. They drank their coffees in silence.

They watched the scene from the street outside. The light was playing on the slightly opaque turquoise water of the canal and people were walking along, some in the elaborate costumes of Carnevale, and others photographing them or ignoring them as took their fancy.

The sunlight cast deep shadows and also bleached areas of their colour. "That's what we are doing," said Luca almost to himself.

"We are casting light into darkness, trying to

illuminate this evil." Nino shook his head. "I think we're trying to stop madness, but it's not easy. We may have this theory, but we have no actual evidence. Isabella spoke about the waiters; they were dressed exactly as the killers of Eunice Bemrose. We need to find them all, we need to establish that they weren't the perpetrators."

"There's so much to do." Luca finished his coffee and got up. "I wish that prosecutor Avedo would authorise a surveillance of the Manins."

Ella Bianchi waited by the dock on the island of Murano for her party of thirty tourists. They were a group excursion from 'Captain of the seas' a vast cruise ship that sailed thousands of eager tourists around Italy every year.

It was a very, very lucrative business and Ella was happy with the money that she was making.

Today, she was taking the group to the Glass Cathedral for a glassblowing demonstration and then a walking tour of the island.

She was taking them for lunch at the Trattoria Valmariana. The food was good, and the maitre'd paid her an extra cut to keep her bringing the tourists.

She was adding to her salary nicely by getting the places that she showed tourists to pay her a friendly little gratuity to keep on her good side.

She enjoyed the feeling of power that this gave her.

She was trusted by Royal Sea Liners, who ran the ships, and she could make the fortune of venues and restaurants just by choosing to bring parties to them.

She could break their fortune too if they displeased her.

She tapped her red nails on her clipboard and scowled as she thought of that stuck-up pair at the Palazzo Dolfin Manin.

They thought they were above her. They laughed, actually laughed, in her face when she gave her terms.

€200 per tour was a tiny amount to give her for her patronage.

Did they misunderstand the business that she was offering to them on a plate?

Well, they weren't the only ones with a Palazzo open to the public, she would go elsewhere. They would notice then, and see the results of their folly.

As the Vaporetto came in to view, she shaded her eyes against the bright early spring sunshine.

The water was full of sparkles and the painted houses and shops of Murano look beautiful in the golden light.

She smiled her welcoming smile and stepped forward to meet her group for the day. They would love her friendly knowledgeable style. Every holidaymaker did.

As a small girl, she had wanted to be an actress, and this was essentially the same thing. She played the part of an efficient, friendly tour guide, and it resulted in excellent Tripadvisor reviews.

She was proud of herself and the role that she had carved out.

Clara and the other tour guides knew Ella and they were well aware of her methods to get paid twice.

This behaviour was frowned upon, and many of the independent guides wished fervently that she would get found out and her guiding permit would be cancelled.

106

It was difficult enough to make a living in this profession without venues being made to pay bribes to guides.

It gave a very bad impression, a "*bruta figura*." Clara tried to avoid Ella as much as possible.

The girl was privately very insecure, and Clara didn't like the way that came across as competitive arrogance.

If they found themselves at the same historic site, or at the fish market, on a food tour, Ella would raise her voice and muscle her way to the best vantage point, even if Clara had been there first.

The rest of the guides resented the way the Ella creamed off the cruise ship customers.

There was gossip that she had an overly close relationship with the Italian manager for Royal Sea Liners.

It certainly was always Ella who got their principal business.

One or two might get the crumbs from their table, if Ella was already busy. It wasn't the way to work and was causing increasing bad feeling.

As Ella began her day on Murano, Clara was meeting her group to begin a day of tours of "The Palaces of Venice." She had six lined up and a lunch off the beaten track of a wonderful fish restaurant, run by a family who had lived in Venice for generations.

Her third Palazzo was Palazzo Dolfin Manin, and she felt very nervous about it.

Luca had made her aware of his distrust of the Manin siblings and she knew that at the moment they were the top of his list of suspects.

She wanted to get in, complete the tour, and get out with all her clients still alive.

If they were the "Carnevale killers," as the papers were calling them, she didn't want to draw any negative attention to her group.

The killers were touchy in their choice of victim, which seemed to be influenced by an annoyance with the tourist industry.

She resolved to stay close to her group and help the tour along as much as possible so that the Manin twins didn't have any reason to become angry.

Clara was pleased with her group of clients, they were engaged and interested in everything that she showed them.

They were knowledgeable too and shared information between each other.

By the second palace they were all firm friends. Despite this positive mood, Clara was still apprehensive about the Manin Palazzo.

As they walked towards the carved wooden door, Rocco and Isabella stepped out to greet them.

"Welcome to our home, the Palazzo Dolfin Manin," Rocco said as they entered the cool of the entrance hall.

The group exclaimed at the carvings and frescos, their enthusiasm was infectious, and they began asking considered questions. Isabella answered fully and took half of the party forward into the Grand Salon.

Clara hung back with the other half and Rocco. The sounds of appreciation and wonder carried between the rooms.

Clara was aware that Rocco was regarding her very closely. She felt a prickle of disquiet. "It is good to see that not all tour guides like Miss Bianchi," he said at last.

"Not my favourite person," said Clara lightly.

"She doesn't do the job properly. She has a contempt for the guests, and I think she has a contempt for Venice too."

Feeling as if she had said too much, she fell silent.

"So, you don't require a €200 gratuity then?" Rocco had moved closer to her, and she felt a little breathless. He was handsome, but there was an edge of cruelty to his eyes.

"Absolutely not! Who suggested I would?" Her indignation made her speak a little louder, and one or two of the guests looked up in her direction, puzzled, from their viewing of the information about Ludovico Manin, the last Doge of Venice.

"I'm teasing!" Rocco put a hand on her arm,

"Ella Bianchi made those terms to Isabella and I! Needless to say, we refused them. The stupid woman hadn't done her research. If she had, she would've known that we don't pocket the money from these tours. That entirely goes to the city. She should've asked them directly for the bribe!"

"I had heard rumours that she was doing that. Not just with you, but with all venues and restaurants. She would bribe the Vaporetti too if she could, I think!" Clara felt more at ease. She walked towards the Grand Salon as Rocco began addressing the group.

She would tell Luca all about this and her impressions of Rocco Manin.

The tour ended on an extremely positive note and Isabella took Clara aside when Rocco was thanking the group, to say that she would be welcome any time.

Her respectful behaviour and that of her party was appreciated and 'noted favourably.' Clara smiled and said that she had rarely seen a group so inspired by a Palazzo.

Inwardly, she was thinking what does that mean? 'Noted favourably'? She would definitely pass that on to Luca!

On Murano, Ella had shepherded her group into the courtyard at the Glass Cathedral. She gathered them around her and explained what they were about to see.

She ushered them into the vast brick-built space and let them look at the tables of handblown glass work, in all colours.

She looked pointedly at the young woman behind the desk and nodded as she was handed an envelope, stuffing it into her bag. She turned and pasted a large grin to her face and invited the party to sit on the seats ready for the demonstration.

The lights dimmed and the glassblower entered the space in front of the kiln. Music began to play and a voiceover in several languages explained the history of the building and of glass making on Murano.

She watched the faces of the tourists, their attention rapped and engrossed in the magic, the techniques that the glassblower was using.

There was theatre and wonder, as well as instruction, and the whole party gasped, and some shrieked at the finale when the large hand-blown glass bubble exploded.

110

She gave her charges half an hour to explore the upper part of the cathedral space and see the exquisite chandeliers and glass sculptures on display.

As they broke into groups, chatting excitedly, she took the director of the venue aside. "I need to make an adjustment to your payment plan," she told him.

"It has increased by 20%, and I will need the increase in payment when I next bring a group here in three days." The director began to protest.

She silenced him with a look and the raising of one manicured hand.

"I would think very carefully about refusing my extremely generous offer, Gio," she said quietly. "There are other demonstrations of glass blowing on Murano. You wouldn't want me to go elsewhere, would you? Me and my tour groups?" Gio and his daughter looked at each other, and he shook his head sadly.

They knew that they were trapped with these ever-increasing costs. It was extortionate and wrong.

What could they do though?

The volume of paying customers would certainly be missed sorely if Ella Bianchi did stop bringing them. They were "*Sopra un barile*" – 'over a barrel' – and would just have to pay up.

Ella had particular specific retailers that she allowed tourists to shop at.

If anyone attempted to stray into an establishment that she didn't sanction, Ella would whisper that the merchandise was substandard, or Chinese imports.

It didn't matter to her that she was lying.

For her the primary focus was the payments that she collected surreptitiously from shop to shop.

By the time they filed into the trattoria for lunch, her handbag was bulky with envelopes of money. Her favourite part of her day was when she was back home in her apartment in San Polo, counting it all up at the kitchen island breakfast bar.

Lunch was tasty and enjoyed by the whole party. As they sipped their complimentary limoncello digestivo, Ella went to the front desk, where the manager handed her a plump envelope.

She inclined her head in acknowledgement and encouraged the group to make haste, back through the streets to the Vaporetto stop.

She would travel back with them to make sure they all got off at Zaccaria, ready to board the Royal Sea Liner tender to take them back to the Captain of the Seas.

When she had seen them depart, she would go home and count her gratuity.

As they docked, she helped some of the older clients off the boat. One or two pressed €50 notes into her hand to thank her for the excellent tour.

One elderly lady gave her a glass trinket that she had bought for Ella as a thank you. "I'm sure they don't pay you much, and you're so excellent at your job, dear."

Ella smiled and crinkled her eyes. "Thank you so much. That's very kind of you. You shouldn't have!" She looked at the trinket, a glass cat in blue and green hanging from a turquoise ribbon with 'Murano' in white glass script across the front.

The sunlight caught the colours and set chips of reflected colour scattering across the pontoon.

"I love it," she said, in apparent rapture.

As she watched the party wave at her and board the tender, she smiled and waved back.

As the tender motored away, Ella turned on her heel and dropped the glass cat into the water of the lagoon.

"Stupid tat!" she spat; she didn't even wait to see it disappear from view as it sank.

Clara was having a much more rewarding day. It might not be so lucrative, but it was better for her soul. She enjoyed spending time with people who were as interested in Venice and its history as she was.

She was always amazed that guides like Ella Bianchi got away with their actions.

Clara had seen her and a couple of other bad guides at work and could see through their sloppy facts and disinterest.

Quite a few of the facts Ella had told people were incorrect. *One day she'll be found out*, Clara thought.

She dropped into a grocery store on the way home and picked up supplies for dinner for Luca that they could either share or, if he was working late again, wouldn't spoil when reheated.

She was tired but happy with the way the tour had gone.

She was eager to tell Luca of her encounter with the Manin twins. It might help him in the progress of his investigation.

As she walked from the grocers, towards home the sky

was a soft peach.

The peach was streaked with a dove grey band of cloud. The peach light fell on all the buildings and turned them rosy.

The sheer beauty of this place struck her yet again. Something that happened for Clara, several times a day.

She loved Venice as strongly as one loved a parent or a partner.

It never stopped feeling remarkable to her that she was lucky enough to live here. Her heart was full and she was content.

Ella had very different feelings in her heart as she picked her way home.

She was irritated by the people and their tendency to stop in their tracks in wonder to gaze upon a particularly remarkable bridge or church.

It's just more of the same – just old buildings! The costumed Carnevale revellers annoyed her particularly.

Thank God it's only once a year! It was impossible to avoid them and their preposterous costumes.

They blocked the paths and narrow passageways and just got in the way.

She restrained herself from giving a woman in lilac frills and wig a hefty shove into the canal that she was posing beside. So very inconsiderate!

Finally, after what seemed like a long time fighting her way through the streets, she turned into the small lane that her building was on.

Oh no! she thought, *there's even one of those 'Poppinjays' here, right by the door to my building!* They

114

were sort of draping themselves across the door.

The woman was wearing a dark green velvet dress with gold lace.

She had a large fan and was posing, as these idiots tend to do, gently fanning herself as she turned this way and that.

Her mask was gold, covered in gold leaf, not gold paint. Her elaborate wig was jet black. She was right in front of Ella's door.

Ella marched up to the woman. "Not here! Get away from my house!" she roared.

The figure turned and moved its head in a slow, mimed bow, fanning itself all the while. It didn't actually move or step away at all.

"MOVE!" Ella shouted.

She went to push the figure away with a sharp shove.

As she reached forward, she felt something go around her neck from behind. She reached up, to remove it, but it tightened and tightened.

She scrambled at it, breaking a nail trying to free herself. Panic took over, and she realised that she couldn't breathe.

It was only a matter of seconds before she blacked out. Death came quickly after.

Luca and Nino were still in the office.

Luca was looking out of the window, thinking. He noticed the lovely peach light and appreciated how it painted the buildings and the canals in the same shade. Venetian sunsets were breathtaking he always thought.

The desk phone rang, and Nino, who was filing away

the latest reports, groaned. "No prizes for guessing what that's going to be!"

Luca picked up the phone.

"Pronto!" He nodded at Nino as he listened to the caller.

"You are right, of course," he said when he put the phone down. "We have the murder of a tour guide, and props have been used once again."

Luca pulled his jacket on and called Clara to let her know that once again he was going to be very late coming home.

"Is it another murder?" Clara asked. "Yes, and this one is rather too close to home. A tour guide, a woman called Ella Bianchi."

He heard a clatter at the other end of the line as Clara dropped the phone.

"I don't believe it!" she said, finally, when she picked up the handset again.

"I was only speaking about her today. I spoke to Rocco Manin about her, or rather, he brought her up."

Luca sat down again, "Please tell me what happened, Clara. I need to take this down as a statement. I will put you on hands-free. Nino will need to hear this too."

Clara told them both about the "Palaces of Venice" tour and her encounter with Rocco and Isabella.

She told them of his comments about Ella Bianchi and her bribes that she demanded for continued patronage.

She also mentioned the €200, that she had demanded from the Manins.

She finished with the words that Isabella Manin had

116

said to her, that they had 'noted favourably' her respectful treatment of the Palazzo and the Manins themselves.

Luca wrote all this down and told Clara that he would bring it home for her to reread and then sign.

"Another link to the Manin twins," Nino said, when Luca had ended the call. "This is increasingly pointing in one direction."

The technical team had rigged up a white tent to protect the crime scene. They had put large spotlights in place to illuminate the dark lane.

Luca and Nino showed their passes to the officer on duty and ducked under the cordon, to take a look.

What confronted them was shocking. The victim Ella, was propped up in her doorway hooked up by her jacket onto the door of the Apartment building.

She was masked. It was the mask of Pulcinella, a cunning thief character from the stock characters from the Commedia Del Arte, traditionally Nepolitan in origin, it was also akin to pantomime or Punch and Judy.

Pulcinella when depicted as a member of the upper-class, was a cunning thief and schemer. When part of the servant class, he was a bumpkin.

In both cases, he was a social climber, striving to raise himself above his station in life, an opportunist who always sides with whoever is winning.

His motivations were always self-interest.

The mask was made of leather, grotesque and black against the woman's pale skin. Her neck showed livid bruising, which suggested strangulation.

The wide, mocking mouth of the mask had something

protruding from it. Luca asked the technician to remove it so that he could see what it was. It was an envelope; in the envelope was €200 in crisp notes.

Nina and Luca looked at one another. "This is one hell of a coincidence!" said Nino.

"Yes, it is, unless €200 was her rate for everybody when she asked for a bribe," Luca answered thoughtfully.

The technical officer drew their attention to her handbag, which was stuffed full of similar   envelopes to the one inserted into the gaping mouth of the mask.

"Let's bag them all up and count them when we get back to the office. If they all have different amounts, then, to my mind, it all points us towards the Manin Twins once again. The fact that Clara and Rocco Manin spoke about Ella Bianchi, this morning, is very suspect. Mentioning the bribe, in fact, the exact sum, then to find that amount in the mouth of the victim." Nino shook his head.

Umberto Grazie arrived at that moment. He had been called away from an early dinner to process the body. He looked at the mask. "Ah! Pulcinella, the thief! I think our killers are making a point through black humour."

With that, he shooed Luca and Nino away and began to examine the corpse.

Luca looked up and down the street he couldn't see any CCTV cameras and there weren't any businesses here that might have a system that they could view.

He said as much to Nino. "Let's go to the main Calle, see if there any cameras that might have caught the masked figures entering this side street."

They retraced their steps to the main canal side and

walked along, searching for cameras. They found two.

One was a dummy, the restaurant owner told them apologetically; he had it as a deterrent.

The other was in a small supermarket. It was trained on the tills, but it also showed a view of the street from beyond the entrance door and the plate-glass window.

With more hope than expectation, Luca and Nino asked to see the manager and were shown into a cramped office which doubled up as a storeroom.

Squeezed in between the outers of olive oil and paper towels, they watched as the manager rewound the dated system to earlier in the day.

They began to review the comings and goings of the street.

At six thirty p.m., they caught a glimpse of two costumed figures walking past.

One was a lady in a dark green dress, but the other drew their attention. He was dressed as a man in a cream frock coat and white wig. The mask was black and gold, whilst his companion's mask was gold, entirely, against the jet-black wig.

The fact that the male figure was dressed as the waiters had been the Palazzo and also the assassins of Eunice Bemrose had been at La Fenice, stopped them in their tracks.

"We really need to speak to those waiters," Nino said.

They requested a recording of this part of the surveillance tape and then left the supermarket, giving their thanks to the bemused manager.

They went back to their office and put together a list

of things that they had to achieve the following day.

Interview the four waiters was at the top of their list.

That meant early morning enquiries at the mayor's office.

Red tape in Venice was stifling, but they felt sure that they would cut through most of it when they explained their purpose.

Day 7 of Carnevale

"Find the Carnevale killers!" screamed La Nuova's headline.

The editorial carried details of the latest death. It didn't have many concrete facts to go on, so what it lacked in fact, it made up for in colourful speculation.

Nino was reading it and shaking his head. Luca got a call from Prosecutor Avedo.

"Have you seen the paper this morning?" she asked by way of greeting. Without waiting for him to reply, she continued, "We need to hold a press conference. Speculation is dangerous. We need the help of every Venetian! The credibility and image of our city is under threat. Arrange it! I will speak to your commander. I'll require one of you to be there too, to answer any questions from journalists, within reason."

He understood her reasoning, and her point was sound, but they really didn't have time for this. There was already so much to do. They were still investigating Eunice Bemrose's murder, and now they had Ella Bianchi to work on as well.

"By the end of today, we will probably have another body to deal with too," said Nino gloomily. "Why can't these psychopaths take a day off?"

The press conference was scheduled for twelve noon.

It would be used for both the television news, and the papers.

The tale of the Venetian pair of murderers was too good, not to find its way into the national media, as well as generate interest from the American channels.

Two of their country women had been victims so far, after all. The heat was increasing, when Nino and Luca left the office. There were photo journalists waiting for them.

They made a swift exit on a Polizia local boat. For once, they were pleased that the officer, driving the small launch set off at speed.

This was getting more serious by the second.

They hated the implication that they were dragging their heels and not working diligently on the string of crimes.

Each one, on its own, was shocking, but to have six in a row, now, was unthinkable. And yet, this is where they found themselves.

It was the most stress either man had ever experienced.

They did feel privately, that they were making slow progress, towards something conclusive however.

That fact helped them to hold their nerve and keep pushing forward.

Umberto Grazie was compiling more reports. This time Eunice Bemrose and Ella Bianchi. Eunice had been fairly straightforward.

There was dark bruising on her upper arms, indicating that she had been lifted and then tipped over the edge of the opera box to her death.

The weight of the woman, coupled with the height from which she had fallen, resulted in a broken neck. She had also suffered a heart attack from the shock.

Which outcome had ultimately killed her was debatable, but she wouldn't have suffered either fate if two people hadn't picked her up and pitched her over the edge.

Ella Bianchi was strangled.

There were deep ligature marks on her neck, where some fine gauge rope or wire had been used from behind to kill her.

The staging of the body had been carried out post-mortem. He was examining the leather mask to see if it contained any DNA evidence indicating who had put it on her and who had strung her up.

As yet inconclusive, there were some cream, silky fibres in the knot at the back of the mask, caught in the strings that had been tied to secure it in place.

He put all this in his report and sent it to Avedo, Greco and Conti. He decided to finish for the day all this murder was taking its toll!

Luca and Nino had been granted interviews with the four men who had worked as waiters for the reception at the Manin Palazzo.

With a palpable feeling of excitement, Luca and Nino took the police launch to meet the first two of the four waiters, who were resting actors and shared a fisherman's cottage on Burano.

The island of Burano was across the lagoon, not far from Murano, the island of glass. Burano was famous for its lace-making and fishing.

All the houses were painted in multicoloured, eye-popping colours, including shocking pink, cobalt blue, and almost acid apple green.

There was a practical purpose for this tradition: the lagoon was prone to mist and fog that could last for days.

The bright colours insured that the fisherman could find their way back home, as the intense shades could still be seen through the murk.

It gave the little island a jolly feeling, and in the summer, it was always busy with tourists. Nino felt that perhaps these two actors, who lived here all year round, could have grown tired of the tourist invasion and could possibly have motive for the murders.

All of them, not just these last two.

Actors are used to playing roles, wearing costumes, and disguising their true selves. It was a distinct possibility.

Nino was the lead questioner in this interview, with Luca observing.

They decided this strategy, because Luca still preferred the Manin twins as perpetrators and Nino retained reservations.

It was almost a relief to have somewhere new to go, both physically, and with their working hypothesis.
The sky was a deep gentian blue, and there was no mist or fog today to confuse a fisherman. The bright colours looked intense in the sunlight. The police launch docked by a run of houses that popped with colour: orange, acid yellow and aqua, next to a very deep burgundy.

The combination wasn't restful to the eye, but the

festive, paint-box, jumble of shades made Luca smile as he disembarked.

The actors lived in a purple house. Its distempered walls had faded to a pleasing lilac over the years.

The door was open, and a woven striped cloth hung in the doorway, letting in the cooling breeze from the Lagoon but repelling flies.

"*Permiso*?" called Nino, and a tall, bearded young man appeared from the shadows and invited them in.

Matteo Ajello and Bruno Gallo were waiting nervously for their arrival. Matteo was bearded, tall, slim and elegant.

His housemate, Bruno was shorter stocky and very broad across the shoulders. He had a mop of curly strawberry blonde hair.

Looking at them physically, Nino knew immediately that this pair weren't the ones that killed Eunice Bemrose, or the pair that were seen on the CCTV near Ella Bianchi's apartment they were too mismatched in height and shape to be right.

In preparation for their interviews, both men had their waiter costumes on display. They had been given them by the agency that had hired them for the job.

They had the card of the shop that they needed to return them, and Luca bagged up the outfits to have them tested before returning to them to the shop themselves.

It would be useful to speak to the costume shop, as every costume that the killers had used, had only been used once, with the exception of these cream frock coats. That was an anomaly that needed to be investigated.

Nino began his questioning in a friendly manner.

He could see that Matteo and Bruno were nervous, and he also knew that they didn't fit the visual evidence that they already had.

They might be able to shed some light on the other two waiters and also what it had been like on the evening of the reception, and how the Manin twins had behaved.

Something had happened that evening that had resulted in Eunice Bemrose's murder.

The key to what had happened lay in the reception at the Palazzo, and these two men were firsthand witnesses.

As he began his questioning, they both visibly relaxed.

Matteo explained that they had read the papers and they were scared that they might be suspects.

They were trying hard to get their careers started, and a shadow like this on their characters would be enough to kill their dreams of a long-acting career stone dead.

Luca made notes, as both men spoke.

They were observant and intelligent and noticed a great deal about the event.

Matteo had walked into the catering kitchen to collect more canapés. He had overheard Rocco and Isabella talking about Eunice Bemrose.

He said that Rocco had been angry, and he caught the words, "She should leave check out early. We don't need people like her in the city."

Isabella had said his name in a reproving way. They had stopped as soon as he had walked in.

He said that he was glad of his mask. He didn't like the way they both turned to look at him, so he collected the platters and left.

Bruno had recollections of Eunice Bemrose herself.

He remembered that she had been very loud and very rude.

Rude about the city and also rude about the Palazzo. She had spent time telling Rocco and Isabella what they needed to do to improve and modernise!

Isabella had looked furious and had left the room. Rocco left a few minutes later.

She hadn't stopped her criticisms during the entire evening. She spoke loudly, to everyone, and no one, who may be listening.

Bruno had felt very sorry for her little husband, who seemed embarrassed by his wife.

Nino asked them about the other two waiters. Matteo looked at Bruno and shrugged.

"One was an English student. He was called Jack Sutherland. He's on a gap year working his way around Italy. He didn't really know what to do, and complained about his mask a lot."

"It itched," Bruno interjected and smiled.

"The other guy was an actor like us, Tomaso, I didn't catch his surname. I have the information for the agency we work for; they will have his full details. He's a nice guy – quite quiet and shy for an actor. When you see him on stage, though, wow! He has talent."

Mateo looked almost reverent at the thought of the fellow actor's skill. "How did you find the Manin twins?" Luca asked.

Both men looked thoughtful for a few moments. Nino

was pleased that they were considering each question so thoroughly.

At last, Bruno spoke first. "There is something about them that unnerves me. We were there to help make the evening easier for them, but they seemed almost annoyed with us. We arrived dressed in the costumes that the agency provided, as requested on the job sheet, but this seemed to annoy them. The woman, Isabella, asked where our clothes were. I didn't understand what she meant. She got quite snappy with me and then said to her brother something like, 'What use is that? We need those costumes for later.' He told her that it would be all right, and not to worry, but it still struck me as odd."

As Bruno was speaking, Matteo was nodding in agreement.

"Why should it matter how we arrived? Surely being dressed and ready to begin was preferable to having to find somewhere for us to change and store our clothes?"

Luca noted this down. Once again, he felt a prickle of excitement. For him, he was sure with every bit of information they gleaned about Isabella and Rocco, that they were the murderers. Still, the seemingly impossible part of the puzzle was to find the evidence of their guilt.

"Taking us forward to the end of the evening," Nino began, "tell us how the reception finished and how you left the Palazzo?"

"We couldn't wait to get away," said Matteo. "There was a real atmosphere created by the large American lady. Everybody wanted to get away from her, and onto the Doge's ball. Usually, we helped tidy up and clean, but as we only had our costumes to wear, we didn't want to get them dirty. They have to be returned clean and tidy to get our deposits back."

"You had to pay a deposit yourselves?" Luca was surprised.

"Yes! There are a lot of hidden costs to trying to pay rent and eat," said Bruno, with a smile.

"We just need a juicy play to come along or a good TV run, something that will make our names!"

"Did you all leave together?" Nino wanted to know.

"Yes, Bruno and I went left to get to Zaccaria, to catch the boat home. Jack and Tomaso went right towards Rialto. I think they were going to have a drink before heading back to their apartments. We couldn't wait to take off those masks and the wigs. We took them off as soon as we got out of the Palazzo. The relief to have air in our faces and in our hair was delicious!"

Again, Luca felt a prickle of energy. Here was a contradiction of Isabella's sworn statement. He could see that her image of two, and two men, walking away in mirror image, was meant to misdirect.

Clearly, they were hiding things. Hiding something that concerned those particular costumes. It was the first glimmer of evidence, albeit circumstantial.

He made a note and circled it, he would build this into the main body of his next report to Avedo, see if that would at least allow for a search warrant of the Palazzo.

Nino had finished his list of questions. They thanked Matteo and Bruno and walked out of the cool sitting room back into the sun and technicolour of the day.

129

Burano shimmered, and Luca suggested that they go and get a coffee to fortify them before returning to the city for the press conference at noon.

Nino looked at his watch. "We have just over an hour. Let's have a gelato in the sunshine and decide which of us is going to sit next to the commander at the press conference."

"I'll do it, if you buy the gelato, Nino!" Luca smiled.

"Done!" Nino shook his hand.

That was the outcome that he had hoped for. He didn't like press conferences and would be happier waiting in the background.

With that problem resolved, the two detectives headed to one of the gelato shops. The most pressing decision on their minds now was what flavour to choose.

The chance to sit in the sunshine and eat an ice cream was something Nino and Luca had forgotten was possible since the nightmare of the Carnevale killings had begun.

They could feel themselves relax as the warm spring sunshine bathed the square.

It was tempting to switch off their radios and play truant for the day, but the spectre of the press conference wouldn't go away.

They finished their gelato and began to walk back to the launch.

"Wait a minute!" Nino said, and turned, sprinting back to the square. Luca waited, puzzled. Nino reappeared with a tub of peach and mango gelato.

Luca looked at him questioningly, "It's for Giacomo. He had to wait with the boat in the sun. It's the least we can do."

As they approached the police launch, they spied Giacomo, sitting in the bow with his police hat over his face, dozing.

Nino barked, "Giacomo Malgeri! What is the meaning of this?"

Poor Giacomo woke with a start and jumped to attention, causing Nino to laugh and hand him his ice cream.

Luckily, the surprised Giacomo took the fright in good part.

Luca knew that back at the Polizia locale, Giacomo was known as a prankster. It was fun to see the boot on the other foot for once.

As they motored across the lagoon, back towards Venice, the sparkles danced on the water. The holiday mood began to diminish.

There were dark indigo clouds over the city, and the tower of Saint Marks was picked out in the sunlight, a striking peach against an inky sky.

It felt like a metaphor, the pressure building and brooding over Venice for as long as the crimes remained unvanquished.

At twelve noon, all lights were on, all cameras trained on the podium. The long table was spread with the Lion of Venice flag.

The room was full of chatter and the smell of stale tobacco and body odour.

The journalists, cameramen, photographers, and hangers-on were all crammed into a room that comfortably was designed for half their number.

The door to the left of the podium opened, and flash bulbs exploded in a cacophony of light and shouted questions.

Luca, the Carabinieri commander for Venice, the mayor of Venice, Luigi Brugnaro, and Prosecutor Bianca Avedo, entered the room and climbed onto the stage.

They took their seats as the clamour became a crescendo.

The commander was in charge and firmly sat silent until the baying mob realised that nothing would be said until silence had resumed.

Luca felt sick in the glare of the cameras. All eyes trained on them expectantly.

The commander began with an introduction to each member on the podium. The mayor asked for calm and then referred back to the commander.

He invited questions, firmly requesting they be asked one at a time and indicated by raised hand, not shouted out.

They had begun.

It was normal to expect such pent-up energy and interest. After all, this was the seventh day of Carnevale, and every day since the beginning of the festival there had been a Murder.

Up until now, the Carabinieri and the authorities of the city had stayed tight-lipped. This was a reckoning and an outpouring of curiosity and fear.

Luca knew that once the general questions were out of the way, eyes would fall on him. "What were they doing?"

132

"Did they have any leads?"

"Was Venice safe for tourists?"

"Was it the far right?"

"Was it the spirits of old Venice?"

"Was it terrorism?"

The questions multiplied in volume and sensationalism.

He looked squarely down the lens of one camera, took a deep breath and told them all that he could. All that he knew.

When he finished speaking the clamour of additional questions began.

They were all taken down with one strong word by prosecutor Avedo: "Silencio!" The room hushed, and flashes popped.

"We have work to do, for as long as we are here with you, we are not working towards catching the killers."

More shouted questions began. Bianca raised her hand.

"Every single Venetian has a duty to look around them. Consider what they know. It is vital that we catch these monsters before another soul is lost. Somebody must know something. They always wear costumes. Someone must have noticed something strange – perhaps with a neighbour, in their building, in a coffee house, a bar. Think! We have dedicated a phone number and email address to this purpose. Let us know anything that you think might help. Venice needs you now, more than ever."

As she finished her impassioned speech, there was a moment of hush in the room.

The mayor took this opportunity to rise and leave the stage. The others followed to the sound of more shouted questions.

Luca felt sweat run down the back of his neck, his mouth was dry.

He felt as if he had faced the baying mob and he wasn't sure if he had won.

Nino joined him in the side room to the mayor's office.

"You were great Luca!" he said, patting his friend on the back. He looked shaken, though – they both did.

The press conference had reminded them, if it was needed, just how much was resting on their shoulders.

More than ever, they realised how serious the situation was and how far away they were from a concrete solution.

Prosecution of the killers seemed a million miles away, and they feared that in the hours that remained of today, there would be another murder.

It was just a matter of time.

Ducking out of the rear door of the mayor's office, straight onto Giacomo's waiting police launch was extremely welcome.

Outside, there were press and camera crews, desperate for more of a story than the press conference had given them.

They still had interviews to conduct, particularly with Jack Sutherland, the English student, and also with the mysterious Tomaso.

As they sped away down the Grand Canal, Luca phoned the number Matteo had given them for the agency, who engaged the waiting staff.

He was also planning to contact the fancy dress shop specialising in Carnevale costumes. At this stage, they had to chase down every avenue, to try and solve the crimes.

In the end, it was a trip back to Guidecca, the Spine Island, to meet with Tomaso Soriano, the actor Matteo had so admired.

He was waiting tables at the Hilton, in the old pasta factory, and his Maitre'd, had given him some time off to speak to Nino and Luca in private.

Since the televised press conference, the mood in Venice and the islands was one of cooperation and determination to shrug off the citywide 'Bruta Figura.'

Luca thought that this new feeling of cooperation from all quarters could ease things along, and he said as much to Nino.

Nino, still rather gloomy on the subject, was concerned that they would be overrun by cranks. "We have every call being evaluated by good officers and run past the Commander before it comes to us." Luca suggested. "We will only get the genuine leads. We haven't got time to sift through it all, ourselves."

Tomaso was as Matteo had described him: quiet, serious, shy, but with quick, dancing eyes that took in much and weighed up every observation.

He was a medium height and slim.

He was certainly the right build for the killers of Eunice Bemrose. Luca watched him as Nino began to ask questions.

The way Tomaso engaged with them, was too open, too genuine.

He would have to be one hell of an actor to be able to cover up being a ruthless killer, in the face of direct police questions.

Especially now, when the whole city was speaking about the "Carnevale killers" as the media had dubbed them.

Tomaso recalled the seeming anger of Isabella Manin, when he had arrived in his costume and she had shown her frustration and annoyance, sending him through, to where Matteo and Bruno were already putting out glasses and platters of canapés.

He had been fascinated by the dynamic between Rocco and Isabella Manin. They seemed extremely stressed, but hiding it well.

He told Nino that he had a strong impression that the twins had always possessed 'two faces,' as he put it.

They could never forget that they were Venetian nobility and had a certain way to behave, even though that was often at odds with their true feelings.

"I think Rocco Manin, particularly, would make an excellent poker player," he said with a smile.

"He can act as well as I can, as well as Matteo or Bruno. I wouldn't trust him though; I feel there is a whole mine of resentment and hate, just below the surface."

Luca made a note.

Nino glanced at him. Luca felt that Nino was beginning to see what he saw.

The more questions they asked, the clearer it became that Tomaso was not responsible either for the deaths.

His alibi checked out, as he lived in staff quarters at

the hotel on Guidecca and shared a dormitory room with three others.

All of them remembered Tomaso's return, as they had laughed a lot at his costume and tried his wig and mask on.

Nino asked the same questions again, phrased another way, but once again the answers were the same.

He tested Tomaso's truthfulness a couple more times, but could tell that there was no guilt here.

They thanked him and left to return to Zaccaria, to meet with the student, Jack Sutherland. As soon as Nino clapped eyes on Jack Sutherland, as the police launch docked, he knew with certainty that the waiters weren't the perpetrators at all. None of them.

They didn't fit with the images from La Fernice's CCTV.

Jack was built like a rugby player, broad and thick-necked. He could imagine that being dressed up in an itchy costume would have been an ordeal for this bear of a young man.

It was also very clear to see that Jack would have had very little aptitude at serving dainties to the guests at the Aperitivo at the Palazzo.

He would have been more at home shifting furniture or loading and unloading boats. Jack had been very reluctant to have two Carabinieri detectives visiting him at his hostel. He didn't want chatter and gossip between the rest of the backpacker fraternity.

He had suggested that they meet at Zaccaria and walk and talk.

It was difficult to conduct a formal interview this way, and Nino hadn't been happy about the plan. Now that he saw that Jack wasn't a criminal mastermind, he was glad that the three men were on a more informal footing.

Giacomo was briefed to motor the police boat back to their boatyard and knock off the day. This solicited a huge grin and an extravagant bow from the prankster, who gunned the engine as he left the pontoon in a wave of wash to rival that of any cruise ship.

The working day was not done for Luca and Nino.

They had an appointment at Marega Renzo, the long-established shop on Fondamenta de l'Osmarin.

It was a short walk through the streets into the heart of Castello.

This was a quiet part of town, off the beaten track, not a tourist hang out.

Luca had made an appointment with Signor Renzo, the great grandson of the founder.

As they walked to find the costumier, they tested their increasingly compelling theory, about the Manin twins and their guilt.

Luca was aware that he was getting carried away and was glad that Nino, usually the impetuous one in the partnership, was encouraging him to examine every angle.

Opening onto a small, pretty canal, the Marega Renzo had a broad paved Calle in front of it. The shop was double-fronted, and the windows were full of beautiful, craftsman-made masks, wigs and costumes.

"*Permesso*," Luca said as he went into the shop, so dark inside, after the bright sunshine of the street.

Everywhere they looked were beautiful handcrafted things, in proper fabrics, velvet, silk and lace no polyester here.

They could tell that this was the domain of genuine artisans.

There didn't seem to be prices on any of the items, which indicated just how exclusive the merchandise was.

They were taking in the scene when a heavy silk curtain rustled, and a small, bespectacled, neatly dressed man with thick, dark blonde hair appeared.

Luca showed his identification and introduced them both. "Signor Renzo?" The small man smiled.

The smile lit up his face. He had quick, birdlike movements. He gave a little bow.

"I am he," he said.

He led them to a door, painted with scenes of Rome, and simultaneously called for a colleague to cover the shop.

The room they walked into was a large workroom, full of bales of coloured fabrics, velvet, and silks. There were mannequins with partly completed costumes on them, and a wall covered in sketches and pattern pieces.

Four freestanding sewing machines were over to the left, and a huge, worn, cutting table was set on the right, illuminated by the soft light coming through a window shaded with muslin. At the back of the room was faded, worn green velvet sofa and two hard wooden chairs. A coffee table strewn with fashion magazine stood between them.

Renzo indicated that both detectives sit on the sofa and

he perched, primly, on one of the chairs and waited expectantly for their questions.

Luca began, "Signor Renzo, we have questions concerning some costumes that you hired to waiters employed by 'Venice staff solutions' for an Aperitivo at the Palazzo Dolfin Manin." Signor Renzo nodded quickly, once, and went to a shelf to collect a large ledger.

"Si" he said, opening the pages and moving his fingers down the neatly written lists. "Four costumes, in a range of sizes." At this, he giggled.

A high-pitched girlish sound. Nino glanced at Luca and made a discreet note. This man was certainly a character.

"The costumes are still outstanding I'm afraid," Renzo said, still consulting the ledger.

"I can't let you examine them, but I can show you some of the other sizes, identical in all other respects."

With that, he jumped to his feet, and went through another door, appearing some minutes later with a suit of clothing in a protective bag.

He opened the covering and displayed a cream brocade frock coat and breeches, wig, and shirt with stockings, just like the ones that Luca and Nino had collected from Matteo and Bruno on Burano earlier that day.

Luca nodded and told him that they would return the outstanding costumes to Marega Renzo when they forensic team had done a few tests.

Renzo raised an eyebrow and sniffed. "As you please," was all he said.

He took the suit of clothes, and smoothed the fabric carefully back into its protective cover, and took it back to the store.

When he reappeared, he looked agitated.

Luca asked if everything was all right. The little man sank dramatically onto his wooden chair and looked from Nino to Luca.

"No! I am missing two suits of these clothes! When I put that suit back, I noticed that there are only three sets on the rail, we should still have five in stock! It's one of our most popular hires during Carnevale, for gentlemen. It goes so well with the more extravagant costumes that the ladies favour."

He picked up the ledger and checked again. He shook his head and swore under his breath. "Would it be possible that one of your colleagues forgot to write up a hire?"

"No, that is impossible! I process every hire and write it into the ledger. My employees write out a form for every hire, and I transfer the information into the book. It is the only way that we can keep track of all the items we sell as well as hire. We use twenty artisans and makers, who frequently work from their own studios. This system has worked for two hundred years, it has never failed us."

Renzo seemed genuinely concerned and extremely upset.

Luca realised that if he didn't distract him, with other questions, the little man would become fixated on the anomaly, and they would make no further progress.

He decided to test the water by taking a risk.

"Signor Renzo, do you regularly hire costumes to

141

Rocco and Isabella Manin at the Palazzo Dolfin Manin?" Nino watched his face carefully, ready to pick up on any telltale signs or reactions.

"Not regularly. We hired out two Pierrot costumes for a reception they were having once, but I would imagine that they would just make use of their own wardrobe. The Manin family were known for their extravagant costumes over the years. Proper Venetian nobility, you understand – very, very fine family. Very fine! When Leonardo Manin sold so much of value, my grandfather attempted to buy the costume collection. That was the only thing that Leonardo refused to sell, however."

"If I cannot disguise myself, then all joy has gone from the city!" he was reported to have said.

Renzo looked into the middle distance and let out a sigh of reverence.

"Oh! To have secured such a collection! It would've inspired us in so many genuine designs from Carnevale from years ago." He removed his glasses and dabbed his eyes with a butter yellow handkerchief, quite overcome.

Renzo's revelation struck both Nino and Luca as extremely significant.

The little Artisan seemed oblivious to the massive difference he had just made to their investigations. It now became imperative that they convince Prosecutor Avedo to authorise the search of the Palazzo, or at least organise surveillance to see if they could secure a concrete link between the Manin twins and the costumed murderers.

If they could find the specific costumes already captured on CCTV stored in the Palazzo, they would be

142

closer to prosecution and arrest.

Nino took a fanciful moment to imagine a time when this would be over and life could go back to the normal, slightly lazy pattern that he favoured.

Luca really had the bit between his teeth now, and he could barely leave the costumier fast enough.

He made arrangements with Renzo for the return of the four suits of clothes used by the waiters and thanked him for his help and his time.

Signor Renzo saw them back through the shop, to the street door, but was clearly distracted by the whereabouts of the two missing costumes.

Luca and Nino walked back through the city to HQ.

They were silent as they did so, both processing what they had just learned and the implications of this knowledge.

By now, it was late afternoon, and they stopped at a pizza slice vendor to get a snack.

It wasn't what either of them wanted to eat, but it was fuel and would hold back their hunger for a while.

They needed to collate and put together a report for Avedo, putting a case for a search or surveillance.

Dominico Scalla had been very put out by the death of Eunice Bemrose.

He had been cultivating the Bemroses for over a week, in the certain belief that he would be richly rewarded with a large tip.

Now Eunice was dead, murdered; all that hope had gone. He was very annoyed.

He tried to keep as close to Ivan Bemrose as possible,

but the police had taken Ivan off the ship and put him up at the Danieli, to have better access to him and for consular assistance.

As the days progressed, Dominico could see the chances of a large payout disappearing as quickly as Lagoon mist on a sunny day.

Ivan associated the trip with his wife's death now.

Dominico couldn't understand his point of view. In Ivan's shoes, Dominico would have been delighted to have been freed from such a monstrous wife as Eunice.

He would have been rejoicing. Instead, Ivan was grieving.

And his daughter had flown out to collect him, and take him home to the states.

Dominico had tried to see him, to say goodbye, and see if there might be a tip for him after all, but when he approached them in the foyer of the Danieli, the daughter cut the meeting very short.

She was a younger, carbon copy of her mother and bulldozed her way past Dominico in an apricot velour leisure suit.

That just confirmed his wasted time and sacrifices. He went back to his apartment and brooded.

He texted Ella, but she was too busy to see him. She took him for granted too.

He was her bridge between Royal Sea Liners, his employers, and her ability to cream off so much extra from the venues.

Their relationship had begun as one of inequalities, and that was the way that he had liked it. She, starry eyed and admiring. Hanging on his every word.

He, the hero in his own mind, well-established with Royal Sea Liners and enjoying large and discreet tips from the wealthy customers that he flattered and indulged.

Manipulating them into impressive personal gratuities. "Gifts, for excellent service" was how he chose to think of it. Just payments to show gratitude, nothing more.

Their relationship had to be kept secret.

Sometimes, he felt the need to flirt and engage with the rich widows or rich trust-fund heiresses in order to get the money.

Ella too had to take care.

There couldn't be any provable link between them.

He exclusively gave her tours from the Royal Sea Liners' boats and if there was a link, then they would both be in trouble.

Gossip went on, but that was normal! As long as it could be put down to jealousy, there would be no problem.

Recently, Ella had become too high and mighty. She was too busy to see him.

How dare she? He had made her who she was.

He had spoken to her as she was going home after the tour of Murano. She had been very short with him.

She sounded annoyed that he had called her at all.

Since then, he had been calling and calling and it was always diverting to Voicemail. His fury was building.

She was ghosting him!

If that was the way she was going to play it, then he would leave her to it. He had plenty of other irons in the fire, many more pretty fish to fry.

He had been very taken by the beautiful Isabella from the reception on that fateful night. He would call her, see if she would meet him at the Florian for a Prosecco.

That sort of refined company was just what he needed right now – someone who would be able to offer some class to his tarnished world.

Pleased with this idea, he dialled her number while pouring himself another large glass of claret.

Isabella was in the bath. She ached after another day of holding herself in tension, playing the part of a cheerful, helpful advocate of Venice's city authorities.

Her true feelings weren't that at all.

She felt resentment and anger constantly. She knew that it wasn't good or healthy to feel this way. She knew that it was poisoning her soul, but she couldn't stop herself.

Everything was so different from her childhood. Everything she had been promised and had been taught had evaporated.

Rocco had a headache. He was tense to the point of snapping.

He had Nessun dorma on the sound system, and the music filled the room, beginning to soothe him.

Into the soaring notes, another noise sounded.

It was an unwelcome distraction, and he realised Isabella had left her phone behind when she went for a soak.

He picked up the device to kill the call. He turned it over and saw 'Dominico' on the screen.

What was that fool doing? Calling his sister? Rocco

felt a surge of annoyance. He connected the call and waited. Dominico didn't wait to hear Isabella's voice.

He immediately went into oily flattery. When he finally paused, Rocco said tersely, "Isabella isn't available now. I will tell her that you called."

That should have been enough to dissuade him, but Dominico had consumed half a bottle of claret by now and had never been very good at reading the subtext.

"You aren't her keeper, you know Rocco Manin. She's a grown woman. If she wants a bit of Scalla magic, then you can't stop her getting some!" He let out a lecherous laugh.

"I have a lot of money to spend on a girl like your sister. I'm in the market for a high-class lady. Hell! Who knows? I might even marry her!"

He noticed that the phone had gone ominously quiet.

"Hello? Manin? You still there?" There was just the sound of the final strains of Nessun dorma to be heard.

"*Vaffanculo!*" he shouted down the line into the silence.

He wasn't about to be disrespected by the likes of "Rocco-high-and-mighty Manin." He punched the call-end button on his phone and flung it across the room.

He began to feel very sorry for himself, as he usually did when drunk.

Nobody understands me and how fine a man I am! I am undervalued by these idiots. With that great surge of self-pity, he passed out into a drink- fuelled stupor.

It was after eleven p.m. when Dominico woke.

The smell of wine was overwhelming. He felt terrible.

He seemed to be in his bath, which he couldn't remember running or getting into.

The bathroom was in darkness, which was strange.

The water was cold. As he came round and his senses sharpened, he realised that his hands were tied in front of him.

He tried to slither upwards to see what was happening, but he couldn't get enough purchase on the slippery surface of the enamel.

He heard a noise.

There was someone else in the bathroom with him. He shouted, "*Chi e la*?" Fear creeping into his heart.

There was no reply. A minute later, a match lit, and first one, then many candles, began to burn.

He could now see a figure, cloaked and dressed as an elegant courtesan. Who was this woman?

She was busy lighting candles which now stood on every surface.

As the light grew in strength, he was horrified to realise that he wasn't lying in a bath of water.

It was red wine that filled the tub.

This was so strange, and he began to panic. The costumed figure turned, and he let out a cry of horror.

The woman was masked. The white, unadorned, blank face showed no emotion or feeling. He cried out again as she slowly came towards him.

She held a white-gloved finger to her plaster lips, as if she was asking him to be quiet. He recoiled and tried to push himself away from her steadily approaching arms.

It was to no avail.

148

She took his shoulders and forced him back down into the wine. She had immense strength.

She took one gloved hand from his shoulder and moved it to his head, forcing him below the surface.

He thrashed about wildly. He couldn't breathe. Wine was in his mouth, his eyes, his nose, his ears. He was drowning!

It took only moments for Dominico to die. Whether his past wrongdoings flashed before him in those moments, nobody can say.

The woman hauled his lifeless form out of the bath and wrapped him in a large dust sheet. She swaddled him like a grotesque baby.

When he was wrapped, she hoisted him onto her shoulder in a fireman's lift and left the bathroom.

The candles still burned.

It was Signora Malves who smelt the burning first. She went into the shared landing of the apartment building and saw smoke curling under the door of Signor Scalla's flat.

It was late, but she was a night owl and had yet to go to bed. She was quick-thinking, and called the Fire Brigade at once. She gathered up her Pomeranian, Chico, and left the building.

She knew that the two lower flats were empty at the moment, so she didn't need to wake anyone else.

It was cold out on the canal side, and she held Chico tightly as she waited for the sirens. She was glad that their apartments were not far from the Grand Canal, where the fire service had their base.

She looked back up to her building and saw that smoke

was billowing out of the bathroom window of Signor Scalla's Apartment.

She crossed herself, and said a prayer. She was willing the fire brigade to hurry, when she began to hear the loud sirens in the night.

She was relieved, and turned back to look at the main entrance to the building. It was then that she saw the figure, sitting propped up by the doorway.

It looked like a drunk man, slumped and costumed. She went up to him.

He was dressed in a white blousy shirt, doublet and red melon hose. His legs and feet were bare underneath.

She shook him by the shoulder to rouse him, but he just slipped further down.

She realised that he was cold. He was dead, and his hair was wet and smelled strongly of wine. As she got over her initial shock, she realised that she knew him.

It was Signor Scalla, from the burning flat!

This was very strange. She thought back to the press conference she had watched on the TV news earlier.

Venice needed her! With shaking hands, she dialled the Carabinieri. As she spoke with the receptionist, the fire brigade arrived, and she indicated the body.

She and Chico stood guard over Signor Scalla until the detectives arrived.

Luca had fallen asleep on the sofa.

Clara put a blanket over him, as she headed to bed.

It seemed that, for once in this long nightmare, there wouldn't be an evening call about yet another murder.

Clara could see that eating dinner at home on the

150

terrace, and talking about other things had done Luca good.

She was curled up in bed, reading before she fell asleep herself, when she heard the unwelcoming insistent ring of Luca's work mobile.

She jumped out of bed and dashed into the salon to try to get to it before Luca was rudely woken.

He was already sitting up, looking dishevelled and reaching for it when she arrived. "Pronto," he said, his voice cracking as the sleep finally left him.

She sank down onto the sofa beside him, as he spoke and listened.

When he had finished the call, he shook his head and ran his hand through his hair. "Another one," he said flatly.

The night air was cold and the smell of smoke acrid, when Nino and Luca arrived at the apartment building.

The familiar white tent was set up on the street and the door was propped open indicating, along with the presence of the fire service, that there was more to see inside.

They were greeted by Umberto Grazie, who seemed to have pulled trousers and a jumper over his striped pyjamas.

"We have a poor unfortunate, dressed up as an 'Innamorata.' Commedia dell'arte reference again." Luca looked at the body.

It was dressed as a male romantic lead, unmasked which made the red wine and death pallor all the more gruesome.

"Unmasked this time?" ventured Nino.

"Oh, the Innamorati are never masked, traditionally,"

Umberto said. "I must say, these killers are almost scholarly in their referencing."

"What's happening with the fire brigade?" Luca asked.

"It's made safe, not too much damage, I understand. Have a word with the commander. I think the source of the fire is our crime scene," Umberto replied, and then turned back to the corpse, dismissing Luca and Nino with a wave.

They entered the building, which smelled of smoke.

As they approached the flat of Dominico Scalla, they met Gianni, who was speaking to Signora Malves and holding Chico, her Pomeranian.

He introduced the pair to the Signora and handed the dog back into her arms. Together, they went into the apartment and found the fire commander.

He briefed them on the incident, and then led them to the bathroom.

Although it was blackened, and had some fire damage, it was clear to see that this was where the murder had taken place.

The bath was full of red wine, and every available surface was covered with varying sizes of cream alter candles.

Nino shivered, and thought privately that he might never drink claret again.

The smell was sour and acrid. A stench of burning mixed with heavy red wine and candlewax.

Agreeing with the fire commander, that his report would be with them by noon, they went to speak to Signora Malves.

She was an excellent and sensible witness and told them step-by-step what she had seen and done.

Gianni took them aside.

"I interviewed Dominico Scalla, the victim, when we had the murder of Eunice Bemrose. He was the tour director for Royal Sea Liners and was with them at the Palazzo reception and La Fenice."

Luca thought for a moment "Wasn't it Royal Sea Liners that was giving Ella Bianchi so much work? Could Dominico be linked to the previous murders? Thanks Gianni, we will investigate that link further."

Gianni went back into the building, and Luca and Nino headed to the office to process their initial findings for prosecutor Avedo.

It was three a.m. by now, but the adrenaline was pumping, and Luca was determined to convince Avedo to give them a search warrant or a surveillance team.

Everything was still pointing towards the Palazzo Dolfin Manin and the Manin Twins.

Day 8 of Carnevale

Luca cleared his desk and began to lay out a timeline of evidence and facts.

He knew that if he could persuade Bianca Avedo of the need to search or watch the Palazzo Dolfin Manin, he might be saving lives.

They had assumed that the murders would stop at the end of Carnevale, when Lent began, but Luca was less sure of that now.

The complexity of the murders was growing daily.

The sunlight of a new day fell across his desk, and he remembered the list of bribe values that they had taken from Ella Bianchi's handbag.

He added the list to his desk timeline.

There had been various values of money in each envelope; however, it hadn't been as a conclusive as they had hoped.

There were four envelopes that contained €200, so it wasn't just the Manin's that she had demanded that level of fee from.

Nino came in from meeting with the commander.

He told Luca that Gianni was being sent to Murano, to interview everyone who Ella Bianchi and her tour group visited.

"We will be able to see exactly what she was up to. If

she was demanding bribes from everywhere, that's bound to annoy people. That is motive, surely!"

Luca gave him a long look and said nothing.

"I know, I know. It's still got the hallmarks of the 'Carnevale killers,' who you are convinced are the Manin twins, and you're probably right, but we have to follow procedure."

Luca raised an eyebrow, and Nino laughed. "I know that such a speech is unusual for me! Come on, let's get a report together that we can take to Avedo." He rolled up his shirtsleeves and began to work with Luca on the evidence timeline.

Umberto Grazie was performing the post-mortem on Dominico Scalla.

He was very interested to find that the drowning was from a mixture of wine and water. This was far more practical and also more planned.

He wondered if the wine had been a last-minute flourish – a detail added to the staging of the death.

He wondered if Scalla had been aware that he was in a bath of wine.

Considering the terror that he may have experienced gave Grazie an uncomfortable feeling, and he shivered, despite the sunshine flooding into his office.

He began to type up his findings to send to Avedo.

He squashed the feeling that he would be doing the exact same thing tomorrow, for another poor unfortunate.

When would it end?

Bianca Avedo had scheduled a meeting with Luca and Nino for ten a.m.

She was receiving pressure from all sides, and she was having to strongly resist demands from the government to let Rome take over and charge into an arrest.

Someone – almost anyone – would do, to end the tension!

She had made the completely logical point, that taking this course of action wouldn't stop the murders.

However, the politicians couldn't see past the damage that a series of crimes of this magnitude were doing to Italy, and to Venice in particular.

She felt as if she was holding back chaos to allow Conti and Greco to do their jobs. She really needed some positive progress, though; she couldn't hold things back forever.

It was a subdued pair of detectives who presented themselves in Dario's waiting room. Both looked exhausted, and Dario felt sympathy for them.

They weren't working completely alone, but for Greco and Conti it must have felt like it.

He took them along to Prosecutor Avedo's office and watched them take the seats before her desk quietly and without the nervous energy of their last visit.

He gently closed the door and took a moment to say a little prayer to the Madonna, to help them find a breakthrough soon.

He could see that it was taking its toll on his boss too. She needed to break as much as Luca and Nino did.

Luca felt nervous.

He really, really wanted Bianca to see their argument,

and agree to focused, targeted investigation of the Manin twins.

He would prefer surveillance, but if all she would agree to was a search warrant, then so be it. They had to start to be proactive.

He handed their report over, and she put on her reading glasses. She looked over the top of them at Luca and Nino.

"I know just how hard you are working at the moment. It might not feel like it, but it is noted and appreciated."

Nino bowed his head and Luca rubbed his face.

They said nothing, just waited for her to begin reading. Time became glacial.

Nino watched the specks of dust dance in the sunlight from the window.

Luca counted the books on Prosecutor Avedo's bookcase, trying to distract his mind. It seemed like an age before Bianca took off her reading glasses and looked at them.

"I'm convinced by your very compelling argument. Well done, that is good police work. You have addressed every point. I am minded to authorize a surveillance of the Palazzo for 24 hours. We will place a boat moored on the canal Rio di San Salvador, by the Ponte Manin, outside the main door. That will also cover the two side doors. I will put three technical officers on it. They can share the shifts. Video and still photographs will that satisfy you, Conti?"

Luca raised his eyes heaven-ward in relief, and thanked Prosecutor Avedo, effusively. He turned to Nino and grinned.

"I'm sure that we will achieve the evidence that we

need from the surveillance."

"When will it begin?" Nino asked.

"It will be put in place as soon as possible," said Bianca. "But realistically, it will go in under cover of darkness tonight, and begin at first light tomorrow. There are many forms to fill in, and arrangements to be made, even with a situation that is so very urgent."

She raised her hands in a gesture of exasperated frustration. "What can you do? Wheels turn very, very slowly."

This was certainly frustrating, and Luca bit his tongue.

He wanted to point out the obvious: they were risking another life being taken, before the surveillance was in place to catch the killers.

He knew, though, that he should be content with achieving what he had.

The meeting ended on a hopeful note, and Bianca filled out the paperwork required to authorize the surveillance of the Palazzo Dolfin Manin.

She didn't want any more delay than was absolutely necessary and put the forms in her briefcase ready to deliver personally.

She was required to lodge the authorisation request with the mayor's office, the Carabinieri commander, and obtain a warrant from the courts too.

She was hopeful that all this could be done and approved today so that technical could move into position by one a.m., ready to watch and, hopefully capture the evidence they so badly needed.

As she came into the reception area of The Comune Di Venezia, she nearly bumped into Ernesto Rossi, one of the thirty-six members of the Venice City Council.

"What brings you to Ca' Loredan this morning? Aren't you out, leading our citizens in a hunt for murderers?" He was laughing and bathing Bianca with a fine spray of coffee-scented spittle as he did so.

Resisting the urge to wipe her face and gag, she smiled and made small talk until the secretary called her by name, and she was able to go forward to lodge her request for surveillance.

It seemed strange that only a few metres away along the Grand Canal was the Palazzo Dolfin Manin, the subject of the permit that she so urgently required.

Ernesto Rossi watched her departing figure and made an approving grunt. She was a beautiful woman, Avedo.

He didn't hold with women in positions of authority as a rule, but he had to accept that they were easy on the eye.

Patting his large stomach, he decided that he needed some elevenses before he began the work for the day.

He had some lobbying to do, and he needed fortification first. He jabbed at Vito's number on speed dial and pressed call.

He would take his long-suffering assistant with him.

Vito could take notes, while he had a little morsel at the Ristorante Sapori de Mare.

He would ask Rafael for a few grilled sardines for il secondo and maybe some lobster ravioli for il primo, just a light snack to get his brain working.

He wiped his forehead with his handkerchief and waited impatiently for Vittorio to attend him.

The restaurant was just along the Riva Del Carbon, near all the Palazzos that fronted the Grand Canal.

He knew it was a tourist magnet, but he like to show the 'touristi' what one of the ruling members of Venezia looked like.

Vito had a lot of work to do and couldn't spare time to attend an early lunch, away from his desk.

He had no choice but to drop everything though, once again, to accompany his pompous arse of a boss to the restaurant.

He knew that he would have to sit by and watch Ernesto, that overblown glutton, fill his sweaty face and proclaim loudly.

The man was an idiot, and liked to think he impressed tourists with his apparent power. Smiling inwardly, Vito made a small wager with himself on how many times Rossi would say, "As an elected representative of the city of Venice!"

His record to date had been twenty-three times, in a fifteen-minute conversation, last month. Setting himself little subversive challenges like this helped Vittorio cope with the man.

Vittorio graduated from the University in Rome, and he thought that a career in Italian politics could lead him places.

He had wanted to eliminate corruption in his beloved nation, and had early aspirations of representing Italy in Brussels in the European Union.

This job had seemed perfect. That was three years ago.

The daily contact with Ernesto Rossi had just about stamped any ambition out of him. He dreaded work and clawed his way through his day, until mercifully he was able to go home.

He refused to keep his mobile phone on when he was off duty. His mother was thankfully very religious and traditional and wouldn't accept such an electrical device in her house. He left the phone in his staff locker in the Ca' Loredan every night.

It still amused him the next morning when he saw how many missed calls had been made to it by Ernesto.

Ernesto knew very well the Vito couldn't take his phone home, but he didn't care to remember that fact.

Vito suspected that Ernesto liked to leave voicemail messages that sounded big and important to impress whoever he was with, not because he really needed anything.

He was all about how things looked, not how things really were. Vittorio knew that Rossi was a crook and on the take.

He was absolutely the human personification of what his young self had resolved to rid Italy of.

The irony was not lost on him.

Ernesto was waiting impatiently in reception for Vittorio.

He loudly berated his assistant for keeping such an important man, like him, waiting. Everyone heard and Vito could see some sympathetic glances sliding in his direction. He was so used to this humiliating treatment by

161

now that it barely registered.

Like a ship in full sail, Ernesto Rossi swept out of the door with Vito following, in his wake. It was a short step along the Riva Del Carbon to the Ristorante, but Rossi made a meal of the walk. Speaking loudly and gesturing expansively to create maximum interest and attention. Rafael, Rossi's favourite waiter, was standing at the door looking after the pavement tables. Only fleetingly did a look of displeasure passed over his face. Vito saw it and met Rafael's eyes; a wordless message travelled between them, one of brotherhood and solidarity.

Almost immediately, Rafael was all smiles. "Signor Rossi! What an absolute pleasure to see you again. Let me lead you to your usual table."

Ernesto was settled at a central table, where he could see everybody and everybody could see him.

He tucked a large white napkin into his collar of his already straining shirt, and reached a pudgy hand for the bread basket and oil.

Rafael brought the red wine, despite the fact that this was nearer to coffee time than lunch. He knew the rules and just what Signor Rossi demanded.

Vito was juggling files and moving the place setting aside so that he could take notes that Rossi would give him.

He knew from long experience that he wouldn't be allowed to eat or even drink a coffee. Like all things with an Ernesto Rossi, this was a power-play. Vito was very much a servant.

As it was early, the restaurant was quiet. There were customers taking coffee outside, but there weren't any

162

takers for the indoor tables.

Vito saw a look of irritation pass across his boss's moist face. "Where is everyone? Vito?" he snapped.

"It is a little early, Signor; they will come."

Ernesto harrumphed in reply, like a small child, who has been denied desert before his meal. They were silent for a while, Ernesto moodily eating bread drizzled with lots of olive oil. He also polished off half of the bottle of wine that Rafael had brought him.

Vittorio felt irritated too.

He knew what piles of work he needed to get through today, and none of it was progressing while he sat here watching this slob eat bread.

Some tourists came into the dining room and were seated for an early bird menu.

The arrival of ten young women from the backpacker hostel, who were taking a tour later, changed Rossi's mood considerably, and Vito began his note-taking.

Making a discrete note of his personal challenge tally in the margin. "As an elected representative of the city of Venice," Rossi began. Vito marked 1.

Ernesto wanted to talk through his arguments to reverse the law passed some years earlier, to allow the cruise ships back, directly into the lagoon.

Back to the Zaccaria area, in front of the waterside entrance to the Doge's Palace.

This was at odds with almost every other Venetian, who was sick of seeing huge white cruise ships looming over the beautiful ancient city.

There was something supremely off putting, in being

peered down upon in your salon, or on your terrace, by tourists standing out on deck, watching you, as if you were an exhibit in a zoo.

The legislation had also been passed because of the environmental damage that boats of this size were doing to the fabric of the city.

The huge volume of water created by the wash from a cruise ship was enough to rival the annual Aqua Alta high tide, which flooded the city.

Ernesto was only concerned about the riches that the cruise companies would pay him to get the law overturned.

He tried out his arguments on Vittorio. He needed to have something compelling enough to convince over half the Comune to vote to reinstate the cruise ships.

He was aware that he might need to pay for allegiance, but the more he paid for their votes, the less he kept for himself, which he wanted to avoid.

He was focusing on the economic angle and the riches that would come to Venice once again. He also advocated levying a large tourist tax per head on the boats whether, they disembarked or not.

If every ship entering the lagoon paid a fee per head on board, they would generate millions of euros annually.

"…as an elected representative of the city of Venice, it is my duty to allow this valuable income stream to be reinstated!"

Vito marked '2' in the margin.

Rafael stepped forward with a plate of fragrant ravioli and a tomato cream sauce, lobster and parsley stuffed and

164

steaming hot.

He put the plate in front of Ernesto with a flourish and replenished his glass from a second bottle of wine.

He placed a cappuccino in front of Vittorio and winked.

Rossi was so captivated with the pasta and so busy mopping up the sauce with more bread, that he didn't notice the kindness being offered to his assistant.

Vito nodded a silent thanks to Rafael and took a restorative sip of the coffee.

In the kitchen of the restaurant, the chef, Federico, was juggling prep for later while managing meals going out for the early bird diners.

He could do without having to make lobster ravioli for that odious Rossi, but what could you do? He moved about the cramped kitchen skilfully, there was a trolley stacked with champagne coupes in his way, however.

As he nearly tripped over them for a third time, he swore. He needed them to be collected!

He had been asked by the Palazzo to loan them, and that was fine, but he needed Rocco to get a move on and come and take them away.

Otherwise, he was going to smash them to smithereens as he tried to juggle lunch service. "Caio Fede!" that moment, Rocco smiling, and in no particular hurry, came into the kitchen. He had a lad with him, and Federico was pleased to see the trolley wheeled out of the back door, and away towards the Palazzo Dolfin Manin.

Rocco propped himself up in the space between the fridge and the main workstation. He was clearly settling in for a chat.

In one fluid movement, Federico produced an espresso for his guest and turned the sardines that he was grilling.

He liked seeing Rocco, who was good company and knew how hard it was to be Venetian in this city of other people's dreams.

They were chatting happily as Federico worked.

In a lull, they heard the loud pompous voice of Ernesto Rossi.

He had finished his primo, and was exercising his vocal cords while he waited for his secondo to arrive.

"Listen to that guy!" said Federico, melting butter and garlic and beginning the tomato sauce to accompany the sardines.

"He's so full of shit! He wants to allow the cruise ships back into the lagoon! The really big ones." They listened for a moment and heard clearly Ernesto's conclusion to his speech that he proposed to use later, in session, at the meeting.

"I, Ernesto Rossi, an elected representative of the city of Venice, urge you to overturn this discrimination. This half-baked law prevents many thousands of paying customers seeing the beauty that is Venice. We should be opening our arms to their dollars, not excluding their wealth. It is our duty to allow the whole world the chance to see this wonderful place. We must remove the restrictions."

Rocco wasn't smiling anymore.

"Is that guy for real, Fede?" he asked quietly. "Who is he? He can't truly be one of the Comune?" Federico

166

explained all about Ernesto Rossi, and how badly he treated his poor assistant, Vito.

He went to call a waiter to collect the sardine dish for Rossi, but when he turned back, the dish and Rocco were nowhere to be seen.

In the dining room, Rossi was holding court.

He had noticed the glances of some of the neighbouring diners. He could tell what they were thinking, *Who is this guy? He seems very important,* and his feelings of self-congratulation swelled.

His narcissistic personality was fed by their apparent admiration. Just then, a waiter he didn't know, brought his sardines to the table. The man bowed low to him and presented the dish with the flourish. "Your Excellency!" he said. Rossi chuckled in pleasure.

"No, no young man! I am merely a humble servant of the great city! I am Ernesto Rossi, one of the elected representatives of the city of Venice."

The waiter bowed again and left the table.

As soon as he had gone Rossi had forgotten him.

He addressed his attention to his plate once more and Vittorio averted his eyes, as he sucked at the fishbones with gusto.

He wrote 5, neatly in the margin and waited patiently for this hell to continue.

Back in the kitchen, Rocco reappeared and threw the white tea towel from his arm. He had used it as a prop to go with his charade as a waiter.

Federico shook his head in disbelief. What a joker his friend was!

"Why did you wait on him, Rocco?" he said, laughing.

"I wanted to see the Pompous ass!" said Rocco simply.

"There will be a special place reserved in hell for his kind." Federico shook his head and began grilling steak and stirring sauces.

When he turned back to Rocco, he was surprised to see that his friend had gone. Shrugging he concentrated on the task in hand, and continued the lunch service.

Rocco left the kitchen, his anger slowly simmering just below the surface.

He needed to speak to Isabella. This rot needed to be cut away. There was no hope for Venice while its future and fortunes lay in the hands of men like Rossi.

The crusade had to continue; there was no alternative.

He found his sister in the catering kitchen. She was unloading the glasses loaned by Federico. "Oh! There you are," she said, standing up and stretching her back.

"I thought you would come back with Ludo. He struggled with that loaded trolley over the pavements."

"I had something I needed to witness," he said, closing the door to the kitchen so nobody else could hear what he said next.

In the dining room, Ernesto had finished his meal and his showing off.

He was ready now to go and begin showing off to a new audience: the rest of the Comune.

Leaving Vittorio to settle the bill, he left without thanking Rafael.

Vito had to run to catch him up, which was awkward carrying the large files.

As he got into the office, Ernesto prepared to have a post-prandial nap, while Vittorio went to his desk and began to tackle the mountain of paperwork.

He knew better than to make telephone calls, as that would disturb the by-now snoring Rossi.

He set an alarm on his phone to make sure that he remembered to wake him in time for the meeting of the Comune.

Bianca Avedo had methodically gone from office to office, gathering the permissions and warrants and approvals that they needed, to establish 24 hours of covert surveillance outside the Palazzo.

The final port of call was to the commander of the Caribinieri. *"Ciao Andrea,"* she greeted him as she was shown into his office.

She laid out her request and the various permissions that she had already collected. Andrea Revecco read through them and nodded.

"This seems like a good idea, Bianca. We really need something solid that links the masked killers to the Manin Palazzo – either to the twins or someone in their employ." She nodded.

"Yes, can you allow us three of your technical team to manage the surveillance?"

"I'm stretched at the moment, as you know. I could manage two technical and one ordinary. I was thinking young Gianni would be good. He has been involved almost from the start, and he interviewed Isabella Manin already."

"As long as he stays hidden," Bianca cautioned. "I don't want to risk her seeing him and recognising him as police."

Andrea agreed and issued the orders. He requested the three officers to attend him immediately and radioed through to the boatyard for the surveillance boat to be prepared. Thanking him, Bianca suddenly felt exhausted.

She realised that she had been holding herself at tension for hours. She didn't want to be the one who let down Conti and Greco.

She really wanted to provide them with what they had proved that they needed.

She left the commanders office and made her way to the small office that Luca and Nino shared to give them the positive news.

She knew that they would want to arrange to sit in the control room watching the footage from the live feed on the boat.

Bianca knocked at the door and went in without waiting for an answer. She was impatient to tell them the good news.

Luca and Nino were both standing, looking at the whiteboard, that took up one end wall of the small room.

Both had a marker pen, and were taking it in turns to add evidence points.

Luca looked around distractedly, and then registered who was standing before him. *"Prosecutor Avedo*! Sorry! We didn't know you were coming. Let me find you a seat."

He began to lift off teetering piles of paperwork from one of the chairs and put it at the side of their desks,

Nino sat down at his desk and Luca offered to get her a coffee.

Bianca sat down gratefully and asked for water. She didn't need any more caffeine today. With both detectives sitting before her, attentive as ever, and eager to hear what she had to say, she began to lay out the provision that had been made for one a.m.

She told them the plan.

The surveillance boat, an anonymous small cruiser, would be moored into position, and a tarpaulin would be spread over the cabin, as if it was moored for storage.

Inside, however, they would be two technical officers, who would have cameras trained on the Palazzo and be recording video, as well as streaming it to the Carabinieri control room.

The third officer would be Gianni, who had proved himself to be diligent and effective during the case.

So far, he had provided an excellent, comprehensive report from his interviews on Murano for the Ella Bianchi murder, and he had the right temperament for a long, probably boring watch.

Luca and Nino nodded in agreement.

"Gianni's first rate! We found him to be insightful and thorough," said Nino.

"We want to be in the control room as much as we possibly can to watch the live feed," said Luca anxiously.

Bianca felt as if he was scared that he would be refused the opportunity. She reassured him and he rubbed his face and gave a bashful smile.

"We have to decide what we do if we see costumed figures leaving the Palazzo. Do we follow? Do we apprehend? This must be decided so we have a strategy to follow."

Luca cleared his throat. "If we follow, that could blow our cover. The purpose of this surveillance, to my mind, is to find a link between the Palazzo and a crime. For example, if we record evidence of a masked woman leaving the Palazzo and then being caught on camera a t the scene of the next murder, we have solid evidence for an arrest or a search."

"I know that that risk is another death, but if we are wrong in our theory, then there will be another killing anyway. We would have to look elsewhere, and just now I have no clue where else to look!" He rubbed his face again; he looked shattered.

Nino looked thoughtful. "We have to be careful about putting all our eggs in one basket. It's a risk that we need to be aware of. We need to be aware that these 24 hours might offer up nothing. We have to be ready to be disappointed and not let it phase us." Bianca nodded.

"There is so much riding on this but you're both right, we must keep all other avenues of investigation going." She got to her feet.

"Gentlemen, I have asked to be kept informed by the excellent Gianni, and he will contact you too, also, if anything significant occurs. Keep working the other theories and questions that you have. Don't forget to chase every single lead. I know you want to observe, but see if you can do both. I know it's a lot to ask."

After she left, Nino and Luca looked at one another.

"We have a few hours now, before the boat is deployed to work up some alternative possibilities that gives us more time to watch the cameras from one a.m."

With a shared look of determination, they got back to work.

Vittorio's alarm sounded and he broke off from the emails he was working through to go into Rossi's office to wake him.

"Signor Rossi, it is one hour before you speak in front of the Comune."

He gently shook his boss's shoulder and the man jumped awake and was immediately in a temper.

"How dare you! I wasn't sleeping. I was merely resting my eyes, planning the strategy." He sat up and plucked in irritation, at a piece of paper, that had stuck to his plump, sweaty cheek.

He had been snoring as he 'rested his eyes,' Vito noted, but he knew better than to point that fact out.

Leaving Rossi to gather his thoughts, Vito went to get his boss a glass of water, and pack the briefcase that they would take to the meeting.

He had written the speech for Ernesto, using the arguments that Ernesto made at the Ristorante. He had made the points more coherent, though, and certainly more persuasive.

Rossi had no finesse.

He didn't even try to develop the ideas, or conceal the blatant reason for proposing this change in the law.

Greed and the acquisition of money was Ernesto's sole motivator, and he couldn't see that he needed to camouflage his aims if he was to stand even half a chance of winning the Comune over.

Not for the first time, Vittorio wondered why he helped his boss in this way. He loathed the man and didn't agree with his policies.

Why, then, did he do the spade work for him? It was baffling, and yet he had a compulsion to do his best always.

As he stowed the rest of the paperwork safely in the leather case, Ernesto lumbered into his office.

He snatched up the water and drank it down in one go, banging the glass on Vito's desk and barking at him to hurry up and stopped dawdling.

As usual, no thanks passed his lips.

Together, they left their offices and made their way to the ornate meeting room. The room glowed with the warm tones of polished wood panelling.

On the ceiling, the plaster work and painting shimmered luminously, illuminated by the Murano glass chandeliers.

Ernesto Rossi took his place and settled his large girth into the leather upholstered carver chair.

Vito put the speech in front of him and the briefcase to one side. He took his own seat just behind his boss on a small hard chair.

He was within whispering distance of Rossi and was on hand to assist him if necessary.

They were just in time.

The other thirty-five members of the Comune de Venazia, filed in singly or in small groups. When they were all assembled, the mayor's clerk came in and requested that they be upstanding for the mayor.

Luigi Brugnaro walked in, smiling, and asked everyone to be seated.

As he took his place at the head of the table, Rossi watched his progress and enjoyed a brief fantasy of himself in the role.

He would be much harsher if he was mayor.

Luigi was far too reasonable and fair minded in his views.

What was the point of power, if it wasn't used with aggression to gain the upper hand? He snapped back to the present as Vittorio touched his arm.

He realised that all eyes were on him expectantly. It was his turn to speak.

He shuffled his papers pompously and rose to his feet, grunting as he did so.

"As an elected representative of this great Comune of the Noble city of Venice…"

Vito marked a 6 in the margin of his copy of the speech.

In his head, he was speaking his words that this oaf was speaking.

They were his arguments, that came out, as those of Ernesto Rossi.

As Rossi finished, there was a low mutter from the rest of the delegates. It wasn't a mutter of approval.

The mayor opened the floor, and a barrage hit Ernesto in a way that he wasn't expecting and certainly wasn't prepared for.

He looked in panic to his side to Vittorio, who calmly handed him a typed sheet. He grabbed it and looked at the words, which swam before his eyes.

I shouldn't have had that second bottle of wine at lunch!

Or maybe I shouldn't have slept when I arrived back to the office! It was all Vittorio's fault!

As he calmed down, he realised that Vito had provided him with intelligent, thorough answers to all the criticisms and questions being hurled at him.

All he had to do was say them.

Speech and oratory were among his greatest talents!

He took a deep breath and pitched in with renewed gusto.

Meanwhile, the boatyard was a hive of activity.

The Carabinieri technical team were working as fast as they could.

Taking into account the last-minute request for a surveillance craft, and the amount of technology that would be needed to get a clear enough footage to be admissible in court. The team worked with a sense of excitement too.

Almost all of the forensics division had been involved in at least one of the murder investigation, and all were eager to see the 'Carnevale Killers' brought to justice.

Every new death felt like an affront to their hard work and professionalism, as though the killers were mocking them.

There was an immense pride in the Carabinieri at every level, and they really didn't like it when criminals got the better of them.

Gianni was getting a briefing from the 'two Salvos.'

Salvo Tuti and Salvo Favaro worked together on listening devices and covert CCTV.

The two had joined the technical force on the same day after graduating from university. While Salvo T hailed from Sicily, Salvo F was a native of Venice.

They had a shared interest in all things electronic and were happily geeky in their shared passion.

Gianni had a lot to learn, and he couldn't help but feel like a third wheel, amidst the jokes and brotherly romance.

Still, he knew he had something to offer that they didn't.

He had met the prime suspects and had seen – No! 'potentially' – their handiwork, firsthand.

He wanted to catch them as much as Nino and Luca did, and he was delighted to be part of the team.

To the casual observer, the boat was a grubby, old, anonymous craft. It had a faded navy cabin and a scrape, to one bow.

Inside, however, it was a hub of technology. Three upholstered seats faced a bank of monitors and recording equipment.

There was an infrared function and a series of sensitive microphones designed to pick up and filter the smallest of noises.

The computers, which processed the information gathered by the boat, were extremely powerful and had been customised by the two Salvos to give them the best possible chance of capturing the evidence, if it was there.

Gianni didn't know how most of the equipment

worked, but as he wouldn't be called to take a watch alone, he would have a Salvo by his side to help him.

The mayor called the session to close.

He concluded that, whilst Ernesto had made a compelling argument to repeal the law that prevented cruise ships from entering the lagoon and the city's waterways, it was too big a decision to be made by the Comune alone.

The people of Venice must be consulted, and a vote should be taken, almost like a referendum. Ernesto scowled and bunched his fists in temper.

This wasn't what he wanted. He wanted a clear passing of the proposal, so he could receive his payment from the grateful cruise companies.

This was going to take time and time was money wasted.

He had to hide his fury and there was nothing to be done but wait for the cogs to turn and the city wheels to move.

It would be months before the matter was debated again.

Vito knew that his boss was fizzing with temper.

He could see the pudgy hands clenched in fists, restraining themselves from beating the table in frustration.

Rossi's already florid face went beetroot magenta and a vein pulsed at his temple.

Vittorio was already working out ways to calm him down when they were called to order and dismissed.

Everyone rose as the mayor left the chamber.

Vito let the other delegates leave first. He knew that Rossi wouldn't want to speak with anyone.

Pleasantries would absolutely be frowned upon. They walked back to their office in silence.

Ernesto blamed him for the decision. This was a pattern that Vito had come to recognize and expect from his boss.

Ernesto Rossi was a man-child, not mature enough to understand that you lost just as many times in life as you won.

Politics was a process, which very often didn't go the way that the individual wanted.

He had no self-awareness and couldn't see that today's decision wasn't personally meant, as a slight to him.

Rossi was sulking and showing all the signs entering into one of his long grumps. Sometimes his intense sulking episodes could last for weeks.

Vito went ahead and opened the office door, fussing around Ernesto in an attempt to bounce him out of his gloom.

Vittorio was very glad that soon he could go home. He knew that his mother was making his favourite liver and polenta dish, so Venetian it should have had a red and golden lion flag decorating it!

He could almost taste it.

On the desk in Rossi's office there was a large box, from one of the bakeries local to Cannaregio. It was tied with smart black and gold ribbon.

Next to the cake box, was a bottle of expensive dessert wine, a fortified drink which combined white Shiraz and amaretto liqueur. It was one of Ernesto's favourites.

"What's all this?" Ernesto was nudged into speaking by the gift.

Vittorio took the card from the tiny envelope and read aloud:

'To Ernesto Rossi, representative of the Comune of Venice, with thanks and acknowledgement.

of the work you have done for Venice.' It was signed, 'An admirer of the city'

Vito opened the box. Inside was a cake shaped and beautifully iced to resemble a cruise ship.

Rossi demanded napkins, cake-forks, and plates; he was going to congratulate himself with this, even though the meeting hadn't gone his way.

This acknowledgement, tribute even, must be enjoyed.

Vittorio went to collect the plates, and Ernesto dipped a fat finger into the white icing of the hull and sucked off the Italian meringue frosting.

He looked happier than he had done a few minutes ago.

When the slices were cut and a glass of wine poured for Ernesto, Vito took his leave.

He took his plate back to his own office to finish the day's work and get ready to go home. He ate his cake thoughtfully. Maybe now was the time to move on. Working for Rossi had been unpleasant and stressful, but he could now see the level of his boss's corruption.

He would pursue the revocation of the cruise ship ban, and that would mean that Vito was on the wrong side of his own beliefs and his own conscience.

He had to remember his moral code and his early idealism.

He couldn't continue to help the corruption that sat at the heart of his beloved country, rotting it from the inside out.

He resolved to begin looking for another job the next morning.

Pleased that he had made that decision, he closed down his computer and put his mobile phone on charge in his locker.

He went quietly out of the shared office door, avoiding saying good night to Rossi.

He didn't want to have his mind changed, and he had endured quite enough of Ernesto for one day.

He pulled his coat more tightly around him.

After the spring warmth of the day, the wind had picked up as darkness fell, and it was blowing the fog into the city from the lagoon.

There was a chill and a dampness in the air, and he hurried home with thoughts of his dinner that he was about to enjoy.

Ernesto was demolishing the cake. It was as light a feather and rich with sweet icing and jam.

He was angry after the disaster of the meeting.

Vittorio had given him the wrong angle! If only he had a better assistant!

The cake was making him feel better, though. He read the card again, and felt pleased that he had admirers,

Those who saw the efforts and sacrifices that he made for them. The wine was tempting him, glowing amber in the crystal glass.

He saw Vito leaving through the dimpled glass that separated their offices.

Once he heard his assistant's footsteps on the stone staircase fade away, he smiled appreciatively and sniffed the wine.

The scent of almond, mixed with the sweet vine fruits, filled his nostrils. He licked his lips and drank deeply.

The sweetness mixed with the bitter almonds was more intense than usual, but he supposed that this was because of the sweet cake, already coating his palate.

To be sure, he refilled his glass and drank again.

It was only a few moments before he began to struggle for breath, as the potassium cyanide worked on his cells.

He became unable to process oxygen.

He fell forward unconscious, his face resting on the remnants of the cake.

His face and lips became cherry red, which stood out in a lurid contrast with the blue icing of the waves piped carefully onto the hull.

The fog was thick in the dark streets, and the foghorn began its mournful call across the city. The turn in the weather had emptied Venice, and there were very few people about.

The Salvos and Gianni launched the surveillance boat and began a steady paced journey across the lagoon towards the Grand Canal.

As they joined the great waterway, they admired the lights twinkling from the restaurants and grand palaces that ran its length.

The fog made all this opulent, faded grandeur seem ethereal and more magical than usual. They made the turn down the small canal, Rio de San Salvador, under the Manin Bridge. Killing the engine, Salvo F skilfully maneuverer the boat to the side of the canal, which afforded the best view of the doors to the Palazzo Dolfin Manin.

Gianni and Salvo T pulled the old faded, thick blue tarpaulin over the cabin and fixed it in place. The boat was anchored and ready.

It was 12:50 p.m. All three officers sat at their monitors, the surveillance had begun.

The surveillance cameras, trained on the Palazzo picked up the swirling mist that tumbled down the canal and hid the little Manin Bridge.

Nobody, costumed or otherwise, was about. Gianni felt sure that this would be a very long night.

Salvo F was given the first sleep break and went below to the tiny cabin into the single bunk leaving Gianni and Salvo T to keep watch.

Day 9 of Carnevale

As Vito entered Ca' Loredan and began to climb up the imposing stone staircase, toward another day of frustration and humiliation, he was broken out of his introspection by the sound of a woman screaming.

The screams went on and on.

He quickened his pace up the stairs and was overtaken by others, who were responding to the call of alarm.

As he turned down the corridor to their offices, he realised that the scream was coming from his boss's office.

He was one of a group of concerned men and women who came to the scene that had caused Rita, the cleaner, to scream.

Ernesto Rossi was still seated at his desk as Vito had left him the previous evening, but he was now slumped, face-first, into a partially eaten cake.

His lips were now a distinct cherry red colour and his usually florid face was an alarming pink.

Vittorio was amazed.

He couldn't process what he was seeing.

One of the others present began to phone the Carabinieri. This was an unexplained death, certainly, and even though it may have been a heart attack, that couldn't be assumed.

Especially at the moment, when so many deaths were

happening. The whispers began as the bystanders stood looking at the corpse "Carnevale killers?" was the main question on everyone's lips.

Luca and Nino had been in the control room, looking at the live stream CCTV from the boat outside the Palazzo.

Nothing was happening.

Luca felt despairing. He knew that they had 24 hours, but he was already agonizing over how to extend that time to 48 hours.

The call took them away from that anxiety and pitched them straight into another death. With weary resignation, they made their way to the Ca' Loredan to see what they had to deal with.

Another day, yet another murder. This was extremely stressful.

Umberto Grazie observed as the technical team carefully lifted Ernesto Rossi off the remains of an iced cake and bagged the crumbs.

They also took a crystal wine goblet and bottle standing next to it. One of the team sniffed the glass and recoiled.

"Signor!" he said and gestured to Umberto to take a look.

He tentatively sniffed and nodded grimly. "Bitter almonds, potassium cyanide! Look at the classic cherry-red colour to his face and his darker red lips. That is Cyanide poisoning." He carefully lifted Rossi's lips away from his teeth with a gloved finger. "See?" the gums were a dark purple. "The red colour sets in when you have a lack of oxygen in your blood. Potassium cyanide prevents the blood from absorbing and using oxygen. You essentially suffocate."

The technician nodded. He knew this already, but he loved the way that Umberto used every investigative post-mortem as a chance for people to learn.

Luca and Nino arrived to a very subdued Ca' Loredan.

The staff milled about in the foyer not sure of how to behave or what to do and where to be. "The sooner we get this body away from here the better," Nino said, quietly.

"…too many gawkers here to be helpful."

They made their way to the office where the cleaner had found the body. They were glad to see that Umberto and the technical team had persuaded the bystanders to go back to their own desks and let the police work begin.

Waiting quietly, with a stunned look on his face was Vittorio.

He knew in his heart that he had wished his boss dead a thousand times, but he knew too that he hadn't been the perpetrator.

He just needed to convince the detectives of that fact.

He approached Luca tentatively. "*Signor Conti*? I was Ernesto Rossi's assistant. I was with him all yesterday. I even ate some of the cake."

Luca looked at him in surprise. "How do you know my name?"

"Everyone knows you. I saw you on the news; you were at the press conference," replied Vito, frowning.

"I forgot. I'm sorry." Luca smiled ruefully.

"Let's go into your office and talk about your day with Signor Rossi yesterday and what happened."

Nino followed Vito and Luca into the relative calm of Vito's Secretary's space – a small side room, with an opaque glass screen dividing it from Rossi's office.

It would be possible to see that his boss was at his desk, but the opacity prevented details being seen, to afford some privacy.

They sat down and Nino took notes.

Vittorio was obviously shocked, but he was studious and intelligent. In a quiet voice, he told the tale of the day they had.

The eighth day of Carnevale and Ernesto Rossi's last day on earth.

He recounted the early lunch at the ristorante, describing what Ernesto had to eat and drink and when. He spoke of his boss's return to the office and then the meeting of the Comune.

Of Rossi's is fury that the revocation of the cruise ship law was not granted. This caused Nino and Luca to share a look.

This was again a skirmish in the battle between Venice and mass tourism. It fitted the profile of the 'Carnevale killers.'

They were particularly interested in Vito's account of finding the gifted cake on the desk   when they returned from Comune.

The fact that it was shaped as a cruise ship was a major red flag.

Vittorio told them that he had eaten the slice of the cake and was not unwell in any way. This led Nino to write a note about the dessert wine.

He circled the note to resolve to see if he could get Umberto to fast track the tests on the wine particularly.

They were pleased that Vito in his meticulous way had taken a note of the bakery who had supplied the cake.

He had done this in order to log it as a gift on the list of Comune interests.

He wrote the details out for the detectives, and Nino tucked the note in his jacket pocket.

He described pouring a glass of wine for Ernesto and leaving him alone with his thoughts and his cake.

He explained how difficult it was to work for Rossi and how he knew that Rossi was blaming him for the bill not being passed.

He confirmed what time he had left, and that he hadn't gone back in to say goodbye to Rossi. He was able to give a time of his departure accurately as he had noted it on the large foyer clock. CCTV footage would also back up his account.

Luca and Nino left in his office and went to speak with Umberto, by now clearing up his work things, to follow the corpse back to the pathology department.

Umberto shared his strong suspicions that the dessert wine had been poisoned and his view that the administration of potassium cyanide had caused immediate death.

Luca asked for a fast track on the toxicology report.

Grazie looked affronted. "Of course, young Conti! Don't tell me my job!"

He softened his expression and tone immediately upon noticing the stress and exhaustion on the faces of the two young detectives.

"I will make it my top priority; have no fear." With that, he picked up his bag and left the office.

Luca and Nino stood for a while, looking at the desk where Rossi had died. They decided to go and review the building's CCTV footage.

They expected to find a costumed delivery person with a large cake box somewhere in the previous day's footage.

They worked through the period that Vittorio told them that the Comune had been in session. They knew from his statement, that there had been no cake or wine, before they had gone to the meeting.

Nowhere, on any of the fifteen cameras, was there any recording of a costumed figure – just the city council employees going about their daily work.

With only minutes left of the meeting, Luca noticed a delivery man carrying a large box and bottle bag.

He was wearing the livery of one of the many courier companies that delivered throughout the city.

He went to the main reception and spoke with the woman on duty.

She directed him to leave the box and bag with her and signed his manifest.

He left, and she summoned a porter who collected the cake and bottle bag and began the journey up the main staircase toward Rossi's office.

They instructed the CCTV operator to switch to the camera on the top landing, and caught up with the porter, again walking toward Ernesto Rossi's rooms.

When he came out again, he was carrying the bottle

bag, but the cake and contents of the bag had clearly been delivered.

"We need to speak to the receptionist and the courier company. The bakery needs a visit too," said Luca.

They thanked the camera operator and hurried down to the reception. They hoped that the same receptionist was on shift today.

Time was of the essence, and they needed to make progress.

In the surveillance boat, a feeling of torpor had descended upon the three detectives. They had watched tour parties come and go.

They had witnessed a delivery of bottled water and another of folding tables to the Palazzo. They had seen Lilia, the employee who worked with the twins, leave and shortly after. Isabella had left with a shopping basket and then come back later with it full of groceries.

Nothing out of the ordinary, and nothing of interest.

It was disheartening and disappointing for all concerned. Gianni wondered what Luca and Nino were feeling.

This footage wouldn't get them any closer to solving the murders.

He gratefully went below to the cabin, to have his second sleep break.

He fell asleep immediately, his dreams full of masked figures, just out of reach.

The receptionist they had seen on CCTV was, thankfully, working the morning shift and informed Luca that the delivery was from Bar Pasticceria Ballanin, on

Calle San Crisostomo.

It wasn't far from Rialto.

Nino retrieved the slip of paper from his jacket pocket and checked what Vito had written on it.

It was the same.

They decided to visit the bakery first.

The courier had been used for delivering only, and they needed to see who had ordered the cake.

Leaving Ca' Loredan, they turned up their collars up, against the icy fog.

All the warmth of the previous week was forgotten as the grey mist filled every street and canal.

It reminded them that this was still February.

To accompany their walk to the bakery the fog horn sounded, long and low, through the ghostly city.

The bar and bakery that produced the cake, was warm and inviting, with all its lights lit. It shone like a beacon across Calle San Cristostomo, welcoming and sugar-scented.

The shop was busy, with people taking coffee and eating pastries.

There was an inviting display of Fritelle, as well as huge pastel-coloured meringues. There were fresh breads of all sizes.

Luca asked to speak with the manager, and Nino suppressed a stomach rumble and pulled his eyes away from temptation.

The manager, a pretty, competent-looking woman in her mid-forties, came forward and invited them into her office through the back of the shop.

They were seated in a small room and gratefully accepted the espresso and Fritelle that a waitress brought them.

As the sugary pastry with chocolate filling entered his system, Nino felt much better. The espresso, strong and piping hot, refocused his mind wonderfully.

Caterina Agosti, joined them and sat quietly behind her desk waiting for their questions. Luca finished his doughnut and licked his fingers.

Caterina passed him a napkin, and he smiled his thanks to her. With clean hands, he began his questions.

Nino hurried his last morsel, ready to record her answers.

"Signora Agosti, we need to know about a cake commission that you delivered yesterday to the Comune de Venezia at Ca' Loredan. It was distinctive cake, in the shape of a cruise ship." He paused to see what her reaction was.

She briskly tapped at her computer keyboard. "Yes, it was a rush job. It was phoned through at lunchtime yesterday – twelve noon. We had to rush to get it done. Luckily, the client was happy to go with our house Genoese sponge. We used one from the sales stock and carved and iced it to deliver before five p.m. That was the stipulation of the client."

Nino made notes.

"Yes, the client? Who was that?" Luca asked, his handsome face in a frown.

"We didn't get a name, it appears," said Caterina, frowning just as deeply.

"Maria, on the counter, is new here. She's eager but sometimes forgets the details."

"How did you get payment?" asked Nino.

"A lady came in an hour later to pay and brought a bottle of dessert wine to accompany the cake. She paid in cash."

Luca and Nino asked simultaneously if bakery had CCTV. Caterina raised an eyebrow.

"Yes, we do. I'm sure the woman will be clear for you to see. You may even recognise her."

Nino said a silent prayer, that the lady in question wasn't in costume and masked. Caterina pulled up the relevant hour of footage on her computer.

Luca and Nino joined her behind the desk to view.

In these cramped conditions, they watched and held their breaths.

The image sharpened, and before their eyes was a clear view of Lilia, the employee of the Manin twins, handing over money and a bottle bag, identical to the one already seen in the hands of the porter at Ca'Loredan.

Suppressing an urge to high-five each other, Luca and Nino finished the routine questions and waited for Caterina to download the CCTV footage onto a USB stick.

Thanking her, they left.

Once in the fogbound street, and out of sight of the bakery, they hugged each other in triumph.

"We have a link!" Luca said delightedly. "A solid link to the Palazzo Dolfin Manin!"

Carrying this important piece of the puzzle back to headquarters, Luca and Nino forgot all about the fog and the disappointment of the surveillance boat.

They needed to look into Lilia and see if she had anything on the database that would connect her to wrongdoing or similar crimes elsewhere in Italy.

She had connections to Burano they knew already. Could she be one of the perpetrators? All lethargy and disappointment had left them.

With this fresh information, they felt energised and alert. This case was such a rollercoaster.

When Luca got back to the office, he sent an excited text to Clara. "We are getting somewhere at last! We have a link!"

She received the text as she was shepherding a group of cold, damp tourists back from the 'Food of Italy' tour.

They had spent a lot of the morning hiding in warm bakeries and groceries along their walking route, as the fog was bone-chilling.

One lady from Britain had wrongly thought that Italy would be roasting hot and had only brought summer clothes.

She now wore a fleece-lined hoodie in a lurid purple with 'I ♥ Italia' on the front, bought from one of the many tourist shops and stalls at the base of the Rialto bridge near the Fish market.

She looked a lot happier now that she was warm.

Clara texted back an encouraging line. She led her group to the Drogheria Malvestio, Antonio and Lucia's wonderful grocery that had been in Venice for generations.

Lucia was now helping Antonio full-time, and she having given up her old job at the small supermarket.

The shop was full of tempting produce, and the tourists eagerly filled their baskets happily with dried pasta, specialty olive oil, and aged Parmesan.

As they shopped, Clara chatted with Lucia. The subject on every Venetian's mind was the 'Carnevale killers.'

"I know it's terribly evil and wicked," said Lucia, "but the murder of Massimo Lungi did us a great favour." She crossed herself and looked a little uncomfortable.

Clara nodded. "It does seem that the majority of the victims weren't the best people. One of the victims was a colleague of mine. She was awful – she used to take bribes from venues. She wasn't a good person, and she gave us tour guides a really bad name!"

As Clara left the shop with happy clients, all clutching paper shopping bags stuffed with souvenir produce, she reflected on the fact that the killers really seemed to be ridding Venice of some of the rotten elements of corruption and greed. It was strange to feel conflicted about something as shocking as murder.

Isabella had just put the groceries away and was making a cup of coffee for herself and Rocco. That evening, they had to set up a reception that was going to take place tomorrow at lunchtime.

It was almost the final day of Carnevale, and there would be many parties and events to mark the last day of frivolity, before lent began.

The tables had been delivered, and they had the champagne coupes from Federico's restaurant ready to use in the catering kitchen.

The canapés had been ordered, and the Prosecco would be delivered later. She ticked the items of her list one by one.

Her concentration was broken by her phone ringing.

"Pronto!" It was Flavia Ranier. Isabella sighed inwardly – she couldn't bear the woman. Flavia Ranier worked in the mayor's office.

She never let anyone forget just how important she was, and how the mayor wouldn't be able to do his job without her.

If Flavia was to be believed, it was she who ran the city, not Luigi at all. "Isabella, we need to have a little chat. We have to make some economies here at Ca'Loredan, as you know. For years now, you and Rocco have received your accommodation under a very reasonable arrangement. This arrangement is no longer viable for us. We have decided that we must begin to charge you rent – proper rent – for your flat in the Palazzo. The city pays you handsomely to live there and do a little 'showing around'." Isabella went cold. Anger, like bile, welled up in her throat. "We do more than 'showing around,' Flavia, as well you know!"

As if she hadn't spoken, Flavia ploughed on. "We've taken a look at rents for similar properties in the same area, and we are levying a rent of €2000 per month on the apartment. The tiny amount that has been previously deducted from your salaries will be credited, naturally, so that will offset some of the new cost." Silence hung between them.

Flavia could hear short, rapid breathing on the other

end of the line.

"This is not negotiable, Isabella. Tell Rocco. You begin to pay from the 1st of March." Isabella was leaning against the worktop, her heart racing.

She heard the phone click, the call ended.

She slowly put her handset down on the counter. She was shaking.

Somehow, she made her legs work, and went through the living room where Rocco was ironing the circular tablecloths ready for the reception.

He took one look at her face, switched off the iron, and led her to the sofa. "What has happened Cara? Who has died?"

She told him through tears about the phone call.

He let out a howl of fury and anguish. His nervous energy fizzed in the small room.

He began to pace and then abruptly went over to the window overlooking the Grand Canal. He opened the door to the tiny Juliet balcony and breathed in the air and sounds of the city. Their city!

After a few moments of calming reflection, he turned his sister.

"I will speak to her. You know things were left unsaid when I broke up with her. This will be part of that. She's hurt, and she wants revenge. I can talk her around."

With a new resolve, he pulled on a jacket over his grey cashmere sweater.

"I won't be long, Cara. I know we have a lot to do for the event. Keep to your list and get Lilia to help."

Isabella sat quietly sobbing on the sofa. This was the

final straw.

If she couldn't live here, in the Palazzo Dolfin Manin, then she didn't want to live anywhere. She felt more miserable and lost than she had ever thought possible.

Rocco turned up his collar against the creeping fog.

The tendrils of the mist seemed to tug at his jacket and wrap around his throat like a noose. He shivered.

He put his head down and trudged away towards Ca'Loredan.

In the surveillance boat, Gianni and Salvo F nudged each other. Salvo said quietly, "Suspect leaving Palazzo," for the tape.

They zoomed in and caught the bleak expression on Rocco Manin's handsome face. He looked as if he had the cares of the whole world on his shoulders.

This was very different from the face that Gianni had seen before.

It was as if Rocco had left his public mask behind. They were seeing the real man. In an instant, he had turned away and was walking.

His body language was still very much one of dejection and fatigue. Did that signify? It was so difficult to gauge.

Flavia felt quietly satisfied with her phone call to Isabella. She knew that Isabella Manin didn't like her, and she took great pleasure in taking her down a peg!

Striking a blow of her own.

Rocco had broken her heart when he had ended their year-long relationship.

She had been daydreaming about the proposal, and all

the while, he had been working on how to end it.

It still hurt and humiliated her.

She was Flavia Ranier! she practically RAN Venice! They were a perfect match.

He was from noble old Venice, and she represented all that was new and popular in the Venice of today.

They could have been the ultimate power couple.

It tugged a little at her conscience that she had taken a vague suggestion from the deputy mayor, Simon, and run with it to put the frighteners on Isabella.

It was true the Comune were looking for revenue generators, but realistically, when the costs were worked out, they were under paying the Manins and the grace and favour Apartment prevented them from losing what was an extremely cheap deal.

Simon had been talking about the rents that some of the Airbnb apartments commanded in the city and had mentioned €2000.

They could get that easily for the Manin flat.

Luigi had pointed out that they would still need caretakers, event managers and evening workers – all of which they already had with the Manin twins.

They also had their complete loyalty, if not to the Comune, definitely to the Palazzo. Their family lineage was a great draw and great asset. No one upset the apple cart. They must be left alone.

Flavia couldn't resist though.

She knew that the Manins could afford it. She was sure they could!

Putting her spiteful little stunt to the back of her mind,

she opened her spreadsheet and began working on the details of the last night of Carnevale's Masked Ball.

The Minister for Tourism, Danielle Santanche, was attending, and they wanted to send a message to Rome that despite these murders, Venice was functioning better than ever – glittering even!

She was engrossed in the planning and last-minute details for the Ball when her assistant, Viola, came to announce a visitor.

Flavia was just asking who it was, when Rocco came through the door. He hadn't waited to be summoned; he was there in front of her.

His hair was damp from the fog. Her heart and stomach constricted. She still loved him!

Viola left her to it.

She swallowed, and put on her professional face.

"What an unexpected surprise." She indicated the chair in front of her desk, but he just stood, looking down at her.

She felt nervous in the intensity of his gaze.

She began to think about saying that she'd been playing a joke. She didn't like the way that he was looking at her.

"What the hell are you playing at, Flavia? What is this nonsense about? Eh? What a ridiculous notion!"

Anger flooded her mind. She rejected the idea of saying it had been a joke. He was speaking to her if she was a naughty child!

How dare he?

She practically RAN Venice!

He didn't respect her romantically or professionally. She would wipe the smug look from his face!

"Rocco, you know full well that you have had an amazingly good deal from the city Comune for years now. We are all having to tighten our belts and dig deeper. We simply can't let you and your sister continue living under the terms you've enjoyed. We have checked rents in the same area. We considered evicting you. We can easily get €500 a night for your apartment on Airbnb or similar booking sites. The location of the Palazzo is second to none. Plenty of tourists would pay handsomely to be overlooking the Grand Canal in the Palazzo, which belonged to the last of Doge of Venice!"

She knew that she was getting carried away. Everything she was saying was a lie. She just couldn't seem to stop, though.

"You could rent a place in Dosodorro, or maybe Guidecca?" Rocco had such a dark look in his eyes that she stopped.

He suddenly sat down in the seat opposite. Quietly, he spoke. "Is it signed off? Is it settled? Is there nothing we can do?" She could barely hear him.

He looked broken, and she longed to hold him.

Her earlier temper disappeared, and she just felt sadness for what they had shared. She was too proud though – she had said too much to immediately back track.

She would contact him in the next few days, after the ball. Let him think that she had reconsidered.

He would be so grateful.

He would probably take her for dinner.

201

She looked him in the eye and shook her head once. He got up and left her office.

He didn't even say goodbye.

She watched him leave the building from her window. She felt a little panicky. What had she done?

"Oh, Flavia, you've gone too far this time!" she muttered to herself.

Luca and Nino were drawing a blank with Lilia Ferrara.

She wasn't on the police database, and seemed to lead a blameless life. She had a sister on Burano, who had two daughters.

They helped Lilia out at the Palazzo, for big events sometimes.

Her mother was elderly and unwell and had recently moved in with her sister. Lilia travelled into the city daily, from Mestre, on the mainland.

She lived in a small flat that she owned outright.

She was a widow, whose husband had worked at the oil refinery.

Nino was sitting at his desk, rocking on the back legs of his chair. Luca was at the whiteboard.

"I think it's got to be the case that the cake payment and handing over of the wine was an errand that Lilia was asked to do," he said, throwing a balled-up piece of paper, with other less likely scenarios written on it, into the overflowing waste basket.

Luca made a note on the whiteboard.

"Yes, as we have established, Lilia Ferrara is no criminal mastermind – not a criminal at all, to be frank.

She is, however, a loyal and efficient assistant to the Manin twins. That is the link that connects the cake and wine back to the Manins. If only we could get a costumed figure angle too," Nino shrugged. "Perhaps we contact Avedo now, ask her for an extension to the boat surveillance?"

Luca picked up his phone to make the call. Once again, he felt sick. It seemed to him that he was constantly oscillating between nervous nausea and bafflement on an almost hourly basis since this whole nightmare had begun, nine days ago.

Only nine days! It felt so much longer.

He felt that, just behind him, he had a line of eight dead people, impatiently waiting for him to find them the justice that they deserved.

The pressure was growing, as he also had the media and all of Italy lining up too. It was only a matter of time before they were taken off the case.

Results were being demanded. He was painfully aware that he and Nino only had one theory, despite looking in other directions.

Everything came back to Isabella and Rocco Manin.

Without hard evidence, though, they would lose the right to charge them, and to successfully prosecute.

In the boat, Salvo T and Salvo F were eating some of the reheated pasta that they had put by, in the cruiser's fridge. It was cold in places and boiling hot in others.

Salvo F commented on the irony that, in a unit crammed with extremely efficient electrical kit, they were being let down by a dodgy microwave!

Gianni was sleeping, his dreams once again filled with

images of masked figures, just out of reach.

Rocco sat across from Isabella at the dining table. Their accounts were spread out in front of them.

"We could sell something," Isabella said, dabbing her eyes, red-rimmed from so many tears.

"What?" Rocco asked, shaking his head in exasperation.

"We only have the costumes. They're the only bit of the Manin legacy left that doesn't already belong to the bloody Comune."

"Signor Renzo might be interested," Isabella offered.

"Signor Renzo would definitely be interested," agreed Rocco. "But he's a shrewd little magpie, that one! His price would be low. He would smell our desperation."

Rocco shook his head and got up to get another coffee. He came back with the grappa bottle and poured two small glasses.

"Come on, we know what we have to do. We can't play this game anymore. We have nothing left now to lose. Let's drink to our heritage, to the great Manins. Fortify yourself, Isabella. We have a battle to fight!" He raised his glass to her and knocked back the fiery shot.

Isabella squared her shoulders, shook her hair back, and met his eye. She nodded and downed the grappa in one.

She banged her glass on the table.

"Let's go to it! I have moped enough. I will fight fire with fire."

The daylight faded early in February.

When coupled with the thick fog, the gloom crept in

even earlier.

Tourists wandered damply about, visiting the sights, but the feeling of disappointment seemed to lay like a wet blanket over everything.

Those still promenading in the elaborate costumes seemed as tired as their polyester, faux fur, and plastic rhinestones appeared.

Everything felt a little tainted and a little spoiled.

Usually, the day before the end of Carnevale was full of energy and exuberance. Flavia looked out of her office window at the gathering darkness.

She was disappointed that the weather wasn't playing ball.

Good weather provided excellent opportunities for photos, which were important for advertising on social media platforms.

Venice was supposed to be full of sunshine and reflections – sparkles on the lagoon, that sort of thing.

This thick fog and damp cold weren't helping at all.

She still had work to do, she pulled her attention back to her computer screen.

She got her head down for a few more hours of graft before she could go home to a warm cosy apartment in San Polo.

Gianni and Salvo T were playing cards, with half an eye on the screens.

It was getting tricky to see through the thickening fog, and they decided that as soon as it became properly dark, they would activate the night vision.

It was far too easy for people to skulk in the shadows

when the fog was this dense. The game was accompanied by the echoing foghorn, which had been sounding all day.

Salvo glanced at the monitor that was focused on the doors of the Palazzo while Gianni shuffled the deck for another round of Scopa.

As he watched, he saw the door begin to open – slowly, stealthily.

He called Gianni to come and take a look. Both detectives held their breath as they watched two costumed figures emerge.

They both wore dark cloaks covering their clothing, but it was clear they had matching red outfits underneath.

The man was wearing a scarlet frock coat, black breeches, and a black hat with a white cockade. The woman's cloak was embellished with the Venetian flag, featuring the lion on a red background. Her dress was scarlet too and hooped.

The figures turned, and both wore black masks with gold detail.

Gianni gasped this was the same costume set as had appeared on the CCTV from outside Massimo Lungi's offices.

He went straight to his radio and called Luca.

Salvo watched and zoomed in the cameras to clearly track the progress of the two figures as they walked briskly away in the direction of Ca' Loredan.

Luca's radio crackled to life, and he heard the excited tones of Gianni. His eyes widened in surprise at what the detectives in the boat had witnessed.

As soon as the radio was silent again, he pulled on his

jacket and called Nino to follow him. They needed to see this with their own eyes.

They made their way down the corridor at a jog, and took the stairs down into the basement control room two at a time.

The excellent quality of the recording showed the two masked, costumed figures clearly, even in the swirling mist and gloom of the winter afternoon.

"It's them! We were right! That's the costumes that we have on film for Massimo Lungi. Here they are again, leaving the Palazzo. This time, though, the male character is taller. Before, the woman was taller," Nino said, frowning. Luca thought for a moment.

"We've assumed that those dressed as women were women. In costume, Carnevale mixes that up. That's part of the point – the joke, even. Men are women, women are men; it's all illusion and trickery. If the Manin twins follow their ancestor, Leonardo, whom Signor Renzo said couldn't bear to live life without disguise, then his great-great nephew and niece are probably the same. They interchange, cross-dress, share the charade!"

"Weird!" said Nino, shaking his head.

All the same, he had to agree that Luca's reasoning was sound. "What do we do?" he asked.

"Remember," said Luca, "we told Avedo that we would not follow. We are gathering evidence. We must keep cover and see what happens. At this moment, no crime has been committed. We might still be wrong about this."

Nino shook his head. "I don't think you are wrong. I

think that in a few hours, we will be dealing with our ninth murder."

They sat and watched the footage again, then went and got the disc with the saved film from Lungi's associates. They needed to compare properly; they would have to present this evidence to Bianca Avedo.

This would be vital in convicting the Manin twins, assuming that these were the ones under the black and gold impassive, plaster masks.

Flavia pressed 'send' on her final email for the day and stretched her back. She had been sitting too long.

She took off her glasses and massaged her temples, moving her fingers up to give her scalp a rub. Fatigue was weighing on her.

She got up and shook her auburn curls.

It was time to call it a night. She felt uninspired about the dinner waiting for her at home. It was a ready meal, from the freezer, that she had taken out that morning.

She thought back, sadly, to the food that she and Rocco used to prepare together. In her memory, the reality had taken on a golden glow, burnished by loneliness. She put on her jacket and shut down her computer.

She had a long walk to get home, and the fog wasn't lifting. The sooner she got underway, the better.

She switched off the lights in her office, and walked past Viola's neat desk and out onto the landing.

She noticed that Luigi's office light was still on, and she thought for a moment that she should go in and see him.

Remembering her journey ahead, she decided to leave

it until tomorrow.

Tomorrow was another day – a fresh set of tasks and problems to solve, and a massive day for Venice, with plenty of dignitaries to wrangle. She needed to bring her 'A' game to work to impress the Minister of Tourism.

As she left the foyer of Ca'Loredan, she shuddered as the damp, cold air hit her.

She walked in direction of Rialto, to cross over from the San Marco district into San Polo. At this time of night, and with the fog invading the city, the streets were quiet, along her usually busy route.

She lived in a garden apartment, very close to the beautiful San Rocco.

When they had been together, they had laughed about the coincidence that the church closest to her home was named for Saint Rocco.

Again, she squashed those memories.

Seeing Rocco earlier, and their interaction had unsettled her.

She wasn't far from home, she just had to cross the Rio de San Polo Canal and she would be practically there.

She thought about getting a Prosecco at the Ceranvolta bar, just across from her building, but she knew that she was just trying to put off the inevitable – the need to actually be alone.

Her heels were the only sound on the pavements as she walked the near deserted streets.

In the distance, by the canal, she saw two figures standing beside the bridge that she needed to cross.

They were costumed Carnevale revellers. One was

posing. She didn't pay them much attention, until the woman figure began to sing.

She had a sweet, melancholy voice.

She was singing the Baccarolle, the traditional folk-inspired song that the old gondoliers used to sing.

As the notes grew in volume, the male figure joined in.

They had wonderful harmonies in the mingling of their voices.

They stood by the canal now, singing together, focused entirely on each other, n ot acknowledging anyone else.

This pair were seriously good! She stopped and listened as the song ended. The female figure turned towards her.

Flavia clapped her gloved hands together and said, "Brava." At the sound of her voice, the male figure turned as well.

They both began to walk slowly towards her.

The male figure outstretched his hand. She noticed the thick, black, suede gauntlet he wore, with an embroidered gondolier on the cuff.

She didn't want to take the offered hand. Something about this felt wrong – a bit creepy.

The female figure was also offering her hand, this time incased in black velvet. Despite her misgivings, she felt compelled to comply.

The pair began the song again; they really were good.

She took their hands, expecting them to help her along towards the bridge. Their grips were surprisingly strong.

She felt confused as their grips tightened. The figures were still singing as they stretched out their other arms to hold her arms as well as her hands.

They were hurting her!

Now they were actively propelling her closer to the edge of the canal.

She tried to back away, but she was no match for the combined strength of the figures. She cried out! "No! Please, no!" but the sound of their singing grew louder, drowning out her words.

She could see now what was going to happen. She was going to be thrown into the canal. She could swim. She would just swim away.

Her mind was racing.

With one fluid movement, as the Baccarolle reached its crescendo, they picked her up off her feet and threw her bodily, into the water of the Rio de San Polo.

She hit the icy water with some force. It was deeper than she thought.

A good fifteen feet where she had been thrown. She kicked her legs and surfaced.

She came up next to a gondola, and swam to the side of the boat to pull herself up.

Her hands gripped the polished wood of the craft and she was beginning to haul herself up, when a gondola pole crashed down on her fingers.

A massive flash of pain took her breath away, and she fell back into the water again.

She looked up and saw the male figure, standing on the next moored gondola, as if he was about to punt off.

211

He was positioned in the gondola stance, his tricorn hat, with its white plume cocade, ghostly against the fog.

He lifted the pole and brought it down onto her upturned chest.

He forced the pole down, pinning her beneath the dark turquoise of the water as its oily surface closed over her.

She had no air left in her lungs, with the shock of the pain from her fingers and her chest. The pole pressed and pressed with incredible force.

She knew that this is how her story would end.

So close to her home, and in the city that had given her so much. Her vision blurred, as her life slipped away.

The two Salvos and Gianni were at their monitors in the surveillance boat, alert and focused.

Each had a different view to watch as they waited for the costumed figures to return. It felt like hours had passed before Salvo said, "Sono La!" pointing to his screen.

Slowly, a gondola appeared from the Grand Canal.

Seated in the craft was the female costumed figure and propelling it from the foot plate was the male figure, his black cape billowing behind him in the mist.

They made a turn under the Manin Bridge and came along the canal where the surveillance boat was moored.

The three detectives held their breaths and watched as the male figure ducked down to allow the gondola to pass below the bridge.

As they did, he raised a gauntleted hand to pat the bridge's stone affectionately.

This was rather too close for comfort.

Salvo T pulled air through his teeth in a low, soundless

whistle.

They watched in horrified fascination as the two figures glided right past their position.

The cameras picked up every detail of the progress of these two masked figures.

The male figure skilfully brought the gondola to the canal side and jumped nimbly onto the stone pavement.

He tied up the boat and extended his arm to his companion who rose and took it elegantly, and climbed out.

When they were both ashore, the strangest thing happened.

They linked arms and began to sing.

Quietly at first, and then louder and louder, an almost operatic version of the gondolier's traditional song, the Baccarolle.

Together, and still singing, their voices harmonising beautifully, they made stately progress to the main street door of the Palazzo Dolfin Manin.

They went through the door openly, not making any attempt to hide themselves, singing all the while.

Gianni and the Salvos looked at each other. "*Mio Dio*!" Salvo F said, crossing himself. They all felt very shaken, but they didn't know what they had just witnessed.

In the control room, Luca and Nino were transfixed as they watched the same scene in real time. "What the hell was that?" said Nino, eventually.

Both men looked shaken and troubled.

Day 10 of Carnevale

Luigi woke early as he always did and opened the shutters of his bedroom window to see if the fog was still lingering.

He was delighted to be greeted by an apricot sky and clear sunlight reflecting on the roofs and balconies of the city.

He let out a great sigh of contentment.

The last day of Carnevale for another year, and a sunny day as well! Thanking the Madonna, he looked down at the canal below his window. He was on the third floor and had an excellent vantage point.

He liked to check on his gondola before he went to get ready for the day, ferrying tourists around the beautiful canals of the city.

He really enjoyed his job. It delighted him to see their amazement and wonder at this fabulous place.

Sometimes, they cried.

Often, they came back year after year. He had some regular clients whom he had really got to know.

He glanced down and then rubbed his eyes.

His beloved gondola, his sole means of income, wasn't anywhere to be seen! What was even more shocking was that there was a woman's body floating.

Her dark auburn hair floated like a halo around her head. It reminded him of Shakespeare's Ophelia. This was monstrous!

He pulled on his clothes and ran downstairs to ring 112.

He felt as if his earlier optimistic mood had just been hijacked.

The call from Luigi was routed to Luca.

He was just then having coffee and a pastry on the terrace with Clara. They were also enjoying the fact that the dreaded fog had lifted.

It had disappeared so completely that Luca was beginning to think that he had dreamt the sight of two masked, costumed people singing the Baccarolle into the thick, fogbound night. As Luigi explained his lost gondola and also the body of a drowned woman, Luca recalled the horror of seeing the costumed pair returning to the Palazzo in a gondola.

He told Luigi that he felt sure that he knew where his craft was and that he and his partner, Nino Greco would be with him at his apartment very shortly.

He radioed Gianni and received confirmation that the gondola was still moored just opposite them in the surveillance boat.

He arranged for a normal police unit to seize the gondola, and for a technical officer to dust it for fingerprints.

They had all seen the costumed pair wearing gloves, but they had to follow procedure.

Ruffling Clara's hair, he drank the dregs of his coffee and dashed out of the door.

There was no time to waste. They had costumed

figures leaving the Palazzo, a stolen gondola, a corpse, and footage of the costumed killers returning in a gondola some hours later.

He couldn't get the memory of the voices singing, out of his head.

It was strange that this was the one element of the events of last night that had really spooked him.

In the sunlit sitting room at Luigi's apartment in San Polo, Luca and Nino sipped the excellent coffee Luigi had offered them.

He was a bright, sunny soul and was certainly shaken by the discoveries that he had made only a few hours ago.

He was overjoyed when Luca confirmed that his gondola had been recovered.

It was part of the inquiry at present, but when the technical team had released it, he could have it back.

The fact that the Carabinieri surveillance had captured it being used by the killers on tape meant that it could be handed back to its rightful and very grateful owner.

Luigi had already agreed to provide statements and be a witness when the case came to court.

Luca began asking what Luigi had done the previous day and how he had left his gondola. He explained that the fog and dampness had reduced his workload considerably.

People didn't want to sit that close to the water, floating through fog, seeing very little. They found it all too eerie and spooky to pay the required euros to hire him.

He had cut his losses as it was getting dark at about three p.m. and had tied up at his usual mooring for the night.

He had come in, closed the shutters against the damp and fog, and made himself a hearty supper.

As he woke so early, he had been in bed by nine p.m.

"Did you sleep through the night, or did anything wake you?" Luca asked, finishing his coffee and replacing the cup in the saucer.

"I did wake, yes," replied Luigi. "I thought I was dreaming at first. I heard singing, beautiful, melancholy singing. It was one of our gondoliers' Baccarolles. It was all about lost love and betrayal. It was a woman's voice to begin with, and then a man's joined in. When I realized I wasn't dreaming, I went to the window and opened the shutters, to see who it was. There were two figures in capes, over long, old-fashioned clothing, singing to each other by the side of the canal. I couldn't see any detail. I assume they were Carnevale-costumed folk, doing an impromptu performance. It was about eleven p.m., so not late, by most people's standards. It felt like the middle of the night for me, though – I always rise at five a.m."

Nino made the notes.

"Did you see anybody else when you looked out?" he queried. "Nobody. I didn't do more than glance to see what was happening." Luigi looked apologetic.

"Did you hear anything else?" Nino asked.

"No, the music sent me off to sleep again. The next thing I knew, it was morning."

They thanked Luigi for his hospitality and left to go see Umberto and the technicians working on the body that had, by now, been carefully taken from the canal.

The telltale white incident tent had been put up on the

canal side, and the first examinations were taking place under its cover.

There were people milling about.

After the days of fog, the whole city seemed to be out, enjoying the sunshine. There was a general feeling of relief.

This new, obvious sign of trouble was unsettling all over again.

Tourists stood in groups, watching the technical team in their white disposable suits as they methodically worked away.

Locals stopped to chat to each other on their way to get bread or coffee.

The rapid Italian rose and fell as they discussed what they had learned on this morning's grapevine.

Speculation was rife, and "the Carnevale killers" were everyone's fear. Luca and Nino were getting a fair bit of attention, too.

Luca was by now a minor celebrity from the television press conference a few days before. Luca heard cameras clicking and quickly ducked into the tent, with Nino right behind him. Umberto turned at the sound of their entrance. "Bongiorno Conti! Greco! Here we are, yet again," he said.

They looked to the subject of his labours, the body of a woman dressed in a business suit with dark auburn curly hair.

"Do we have any ID?" Nino asked. "We do indeed, the poor woman was still wearing her official office lanyard. This was Flavia Ranier, Podesta administrator at

Ca'Loredan. She was Mayor Luigi's right hand woman."

Luca shook his head. "An attack on the Comune de Venezia again! Did she have any links to the Manin twins, I wonder? We need to find out."

Nino made a note.

"Any idea of cause of death at this stage?" Luca asked tentatively. He knew it looked like drowning, but it was difficult to say for sure.

Umberto gestured down at the body. "I would say drowning killed her, but I have noticed that her fingers have been broken, and she has significant bruising to her sternum and chest area. That happened while she was still alive. I would suspect that, as in the case of Gunter Walner, she has been pinned down, under the water, until she drowned."

"I have some of the team dusting for prints on the remaining two moored gondolas. Perhaps she tried to pull herself up onto one to get out after being pushed in. I definitely believe this to be murder. That, I would say, for certain."

Luca and Nino made notes on all these points and then prepared to leave to let Umberto and the technicians get on with their work.

They needed to pay a visit to Ca'Loredan again and see what Flavia had been working on. Leaving the tent, they had to move briskly to keep ahead of the interested onlookers and a couple of opportunistic journalists.

They put their heads down and walked with purpose.

For once, they didn't chat through possible scenarios as they walked, it was too risky to be overheard and reported on.

As the detectives crossed the threshold of Ca' Loredan, the pursuing journalists melted away. The two security guards, in their smart uniforms, had scared them off.

Luca commented to Nino that it was rather like being hunted; he very much looked forward to the day when he could re-establish his anonymity.

Nino was just glad that he hadn't been the one in front of the cameras. He still had his privacy, thankfully.

They went straight to the front desk to inquire if Flavia Ranier's assistant was in yet; also, they would need to meet with the mayor, and that would take some arranging, especially today of all days – the last day of Carnevale.

The meeting and questioning of Viola could happen immediately, and with their visitor passes clipped once again to their jackets, they made their way up the stone staircase – this time to the offices of Flavia Ranier.

Viola, her assistant, was sitting at her desk typing busily.

On the appearance of Luca and Nino, she looked up and gave her professional smile. "Do you have an appointment? I'm afraid that Signora Ranier is not yet in the office." Luca showed his badge, and Nino followed suit.

He was rather distracted by Viola.

She was a beauty, with long dark hair and smouldering dark eyes. He felt captivated as soon as she glanced at him.

Luca recognised the signs and took the lead. He knew that Nino would need some time to get over the spell that

220

he clearly felt Viola had cast upon him.

There was no easy way to break the news, and Luca spoke quietly but clearly to Signora Ranier's assistant.

As his words registered, all colour left her pretty face.

She looked bewildered, and Nino rushed to the water cooler to bring her a cup to revive her. She took it dumbly and then began to cry.

Predictably, she wasn't an ugly crier, and Luca watched in fascination, as his friend and experienced detective turned to useless jelly before his eyes.

He looked sternly at Nino and ploughed on, realizing that he was for this moment, interviewing alone.

He asked when Viola had last seen Flavia, and between stifled sobs, she told how she had looked in at seven p.m.; her boss was still working away at the computer.

She had needed to get home, she explained, to begin dinner. She lived with her parents, and both were in failing health.

She was all they had, and she liked to give them one good home-cooked meal every day. Nino nodded so much at this that Luca expected his head to dislodge.

It was established that Flavia had been working on the plans for this evening's Finale Ball. A glittering affair, that would take place in the grand Palazzo Pisani Moretta.

The venue for many grand events, as it had a stunning ballroom.

"Was there anything that happened during the working day that struck you as unusual?" Luca asked.

Nino just gazed at Viola, with puppy-dog eyes.

"Yes, Signora Ranier's ex-boyfriend came by. He didn't wait for me to announce him. There was shouting, raised voices certainly; he stormed out and banged the door. I think Flavia still cared about him."

"Do you know the name of this ex-boyfriend?" Luca asked gently.

"Yes, his name is Rocco Manin, he lives and works at the Palazzo Dolfin Manin, off the Grand Canal."

Luca stopped writing and stared at her.

Nino regained his power of speech. "Rocco Manin seemed angry with Flavia Ranier yesterday? Do you know what it was about?" Viola bobbed her head. "I overheard her phoning his sister, Isabella, earlier. She was telling her that the Manins would be required to pay rent on the apartment that they currently get as part of their terms of employment to run the Palazzo for the Comune de Venezia. I got the impression that the news wasn't received favourably."

"That would do it!" muttered Nino.

Luca asked Viola to go over everything that had happened, from the phone call to Rocco's unannounced visit to his sudden departure.

With this new and explosive evidence, they were eager to speak with the mayor. They wanted to know more about the decision to change the Manin's rent.

Luckily, the news of Flavia's murder had reached the mayor, and he was as eager as Luca and Nino to talk.

Leaving the distraught Viola, they moved across the landing to the grandest of offices in the whole building.

Luca had met Luigi Brugnaro before at the press

conference and knew him by sight from television and newspapers.

Luigi urged them to sit and take coffee, which they gratefully agreed.

As he poured the coffee from the percolator himself, Luca explained the circumstances that led to the finding of the body of Flavia Ranier.

The mayor shook his head. "I can't believe it!" he said, visibly shocked. "Do you suspect the 'Carnevale killers'?"

As it was the mayor that he was speaking with, Luca decided to be candid. "Yes. We believe that we have a good idea who the murders are. We need to apprehend them as soon as possible. We can't imagine that there won't be a 'Grand Finale' to this Carnevale season. We have had a death every day, increasing in severity and drama. It is logical to deduce that there will be one big final murder tonight, and we must do all we can to stop it before it happens." The mayor listened attentively and made some small notes of his own.

As Luca finished speaking, he thought for a moment, and then, with brow furrowed, told them about the plans for the forthcoming evening.

The evening festivities began with an Aperitivo drinks reception at the Palazzo Dolfin Manin, before a Ball and dinner in the Palazzo Pisani Moretta.

He paused, and then, with a grim voice, told them that the honoured guest was to be Daniela Santanche, the Italian government minister for tourism.

Luca and Nino looked at each other. They knew now what was likely to happen if they didn't move quickly to stop it.

This was clearly the finale they had been expecting, and it confirmed hunch that all this death was a macabre comment on the level of invasive mass tourism that was suffocating Venice and most of Italy.

The murders were meant to make a point.

To shock the country out of its complacency and greed for foreign dollars. It was deadly serious and the Manins had to be stopped.

Luca wanted to know about the rent proposal. Luigi shook his head.

"No! That hadn't been agreed. I especially told Flavia that the Manins were too important to the city to risk upsetting them by charging them rent. They may get the caretaker's flat for next to nothing, but they are live-in caretakers, tour guides, events managers, ambassadors, and far more valuable to us than money. I told Simon and Flavia that we mustn't bother them. They agreed after they saw the costings, I'm baffled as to why she misunderstood and went off on her own with something that we absolutely discounted!"

Bianca Avedo had been shaken by the footage from the foggy night, when the gondola, conveying the masked figures, had arrived exactly opposite the Carabinieri surveillance boat. The singing had chilled her.

Then, she learned of the death of Flavia Ranier, whom she knew on a personal level. It was all getting too much.

She was the one pacing her office in an agitated state when Luca and Nino met with her on the way back from Ca' Loredan.

They needed a search warrant for the Palazzo Dolfin Manin.

They wanted to arrest Isabella and Rocco Manin before the last act of their monstrous, murder-filled protest.

There were only a few hours left to save the life of Daniela Santanche!

Bianca agreed immediately, and sent an urgent email requesting the warrant and accompanying permissions.

She needed to talk about it though, and while Luca and Nino really wanted to get back to the control room to arrange the end of the surveillance, speak with Andrea, their commander, to organise plenty of backup, they understood, however, the prosecutor's need to vent and voice her feelings.

This whole case had come closer to each one of them than they could ever have thought possible.

It seemed now that it was about the very essence of being Venetian. Closer than anything else to their shared identity, as proud people of Venezia.

Still pacing, she wanted to hear Luca and Nino's theories for why Carnevale had been hijacked this year, in such a horrible way.

Nino glanced at Luca.

He was the man for the theories. He should answer this one.

Luca sat silent for a moment, then quietly, almost to himself, began to speak: "Carnevale is one of the times of year that Venice shows its playful, naughty side. The

Manins come from old Venice; their ancestor, Leonardo Manin, held an impressive and extensive collection of costumes for Carnevale. We were told that by Signor Renzo at the costume shop. Carnevale brings hundreds of tourists, too, which has begun to make every normal Venetian nervous. We feel swamped; I feel swamped!"

He stopped and looked at them both. They nodded in agreement.

"Carnevale also offers a perfect selection of disguises. It's the time of year when it's perfectly acceptable to go about in public, completely disguised as someone else or something else. They could be sure of anonymity from witnesses, but also from the hundreds of cameras that observe our city 24 hours a day."

"You sound as if you admire them," said Bianca, finally sitting down behind her desk. "In some ways, I do. I admire the intellect and the idea, but I don't approve of the killing. Their main point is sound, that Venice is drowning under the weight of mass tourism, but I absolutely and fundamentally disagree with using murder to get the point noticed."

"Even if most of the later victims deserved some punishment," interjected Nino.

They all nodded.

"But why?" said Avedo, in exasperation. "Because they had begun this, and then they saw that it was an opportunity to settle some scores?"

Luca shrugged. "Only they really know. In our investigations, we found a link to the Manins from murder three onwards. That's when the murders changed and became 'vanquishings'."

"We think that Rocco or Isabella singly, did murders one and two without the others knowledge. Then three was the first that both of them did together, it went on from there," Nino said.

"Yes," agreed Luca, "the whole dynamic changes from three onwards. We have video evidence that two of them killed Massimo Lungi."

"Please try and get them to explain," said Bianca.

"It's that part of the crimes that keeps chasing around my head – the why."

Luca knew that they needed to get going, to put everything in place for the arrests.

"We must prepare. I will be sure to ask that question, Prosecutor Avedo. Don't you worry about that."

They rose and shook Bianca's hand.

She spent a few minutes standing, looking at the closed door before she shook herself and got onto the phone to chase through the warrant.

Andrea Rivecco listened intently to Luca and Nino's update and the solid evidence, that they now had, linking the murders to the Manin twins.

They briefed him on the Carnevale finale events that very evening and the presence of the Italian minister for tourism.

The fact that the pre-dinner drinks reception was to take place at the Palazzo Dolfin Manin, had him reaching for the phone to begin coordinating with the Carabinieri prefects and commanders of all local divisions to gather the manpower needed to apprehend the killers.

Gianni was summoned, glad to be on dry land again after 48 hours of surveillance.

He had proved himself to be detective material. Andrea planned to put him with Greco and Conti, as soon as this episode was over to begin training to become an investigator.

He would tell Gianni once this matter was resolved.

Luca and Nino were delighted that Gianni would be with them for the arrests at the Palazzo, along with ten of the regular force who were armed and in uniform.

With a palpable feeling excitement, the officers set out from headquarters, to make their way to the Palazzo Dolfin Manin.

Luca had the warrant and felt in his heart, that today was the day that all the deaths would stop.

It was mid-morning by now, and the sun had grown in heat.

Nino was glad that he didn't have to wear a uniform as a detective. The regular force boys looked uncomfortable in their dark navy.

As they approached the main entrance to the Palazzo, some of the regular force went to the side to cover the other doors.

Giacomo and two of the Polizia locale were stationed in the police launch, on the Grand Canal just by the Manin Bridge, to watch the water doors of the Palazzo.

It was showtime!

Luca went to knock, with force on the old wooden door.

Before his hand could reach ornate brass knocker, however, the door was wrenched open from inside by a harassed-looking Lilia.

"What do you want? Madonna! As if this day isn't disastrous enough already!" Luca then asked to see Isabella and Rocco.

"You want to see the twins? Eh? Well, wouldn't we all. The biggest event that this Palazzo has ever hosted, and they are nowhere to be found! It is a disaster!" uttering in an agitated fashion, she beckoned them all into the entrance hall.

Everything was in uproar. Delivery men milled about, with paperwork to sign and stacks of boxes of wine, canapés and provisions to be put away.

Lilia and her two nieces were trying to do it all; the feeling of panic was tangible Nino walked forward into the Grand Salon.

The tables with neatly ironed cloths were perfectly arranged, and the glasses were on trays, polished and ready.

Everything was set up for the event.

The only thing that was missing was the caretakers, Isabella and Rocco.

Gianni took one look at the situation in the entrance hall and began systematically to organise the chaos.

He got the normal force officers to direct the deliveries into the catering kitchen and the canapés into the fridges.

He moved the ice into the freezers and signed off the paperwork as he went, allowing the delivery people to leave.

When that was clear, he went to speak with Lilia to calm her down.

She could see that they were as well-organised as they usually were at this time on an event day, and her growing confidence calmed the atmosphere and her nieces.

Luca and Nino had spent this time going from room to room checking that the twins really weren't there.

Nino went out onto the balcony from the Grand Salon and let Giacomo know that he could stand down.

Giacomo saluted, turned the boat sharply, and gunned it back down the canal.

The large wake splashed against the water doors of the Palazzo and Nino suppressed a smile.

Leaving the majority of the Carabinieri downstairs to keep an eye on the state rooms, Luca, Nino, Gianni and Leo, one of the armed regular force officers, made their way up the back staircase to the caretakers flat.

Leo went first, his gun trained and ready for any potential ambush.

The sunlight flooded the stairwell and sent reflected sparkles from the canal onto the top landing.

The door of the flat was swinging open, gently in the breeze. Leo tentatively entered.

Luca, Nino and Gianni followed behind. They all held their breaths, not knowing what they might find.

As Leo opened the door to the sitting room, he let out a low whistle.

On every chair, and on the dining table, were costumes laid out neatly. Each one was recognisable.

The first, by the door, was black velvet with gold

adornment. A cape and gondola headdress on a black wig.

The mask in a box, by the dress was gold leaf.

Luca recognised this as the costume, worn by the assassin who had murdered Betsy Noakes so many days before.

Nino looked at the second costume, a dark turquoise silk dress embroidered with gold sea creatures. The gold trident was also there.

This was the costume from the murder of German tourist, Gunter Walner.

So, it continued, every murder represented by the costumes used by the killers, and caught on camera.

The detectives were silent, as they took in the scene and what it represented.

Nino got out his phone and began to video each item and record how it was laid out in the room. Everything was there except for the two cream frock-coats and black masks, from the costume shop of Signor Renzo.

Luca met Nino's eyes, Luca raised an eyebrow.

Gianni, discovered the letter on the dining table, propped up behind the towering wig from the most recent murder of Flavia Ranier and that of Massimo Lungi.

On the cream envelope, in ornate script, was written 'Signors Greco and Conti.' He put on a glove and passed the letter to Luca, who put on gloves to receive it.

The tension in the room crackled.

Luca opened the envelope and took out the paper. Signors, we are sorry to disappoint you.

We are not here to welcome you at the Palazzo, this time. Our protest is almost over.

Our manifesto follows:

Tourism is killing our beloved city. Venice has always been popular.

It is unique in the world.

The 20th century has brought greater and greater damage to her, however. Our beautiful Venezia, our mother and haven to every Venetian.

Tourists are killing her.

She is being swamped by plastic rubbish and the weight of millions of people crawling all over her.

Weakening her bridges, disrespecting her cathedrals.

Huge polluting ships come into her fragile waterways and flood her.

Pumping the poison from their bilges into the rich waters of the lagoon, killing the fish and turning the canals fetid and toxic.

Artisans are not valued, and good, honest restaurants, can't compete with the fast-food chains. Our way of life is dying.

Venetians can't afford to live in their city.

They are being pushed out by Airbnb rentals and hotels. Nothing is how it was.

We have very little power now.

We decided to make a stand and remove some of the rotten elements of our city.

We know that our acts haven't been enough, and we know that we too, will be removed from what is our birthright.

Our aim has always been to highlight this diminishment. To stop the cancer that is eating away at our beautiful Venice.

We are proud of the work that we have done, and would do it again given the opportunity. Our Venice, our mother, must be vanquished.

Rocco Ludovico Manin 2nd
Isabella Ludovica Manin
The last of the Manin family, (1578 to present)

"They are in the wind! We have no idea where! I feel that they will play their last hand tonight, either here at the Aperitivo or at the ball and dinner."

Luca said, and rubbed his face.

"We have to radio this in. We have to stop them!"

The lights glittered and danced on the water of the canal in front of the Palazzo Dolfin Manin.

Inside, the string quartet was playing, and the costumed waiters, along with Lilia and her nieces, filled the glasses and put out platters of delicious-looking canapés.

All was order. The Grand Salon shone and smelled of beeswax and flowers.

An idle observer would have noticed nothing different from any of the previous evening receptions that had been held before in this noble palace.

Looking more closely, the waiters, costumed and masked, had radios below their coats, and some had holsters that held loaded pistols.

The fourteen waiters were Carabinieri, all focused on preventing the Manin twins from committing their final atrocity.

A few palaces away, in the Palazzo Pisani Morreta, Luca, Nino and Gianni were waiting, dressed in costume, earpieces in their ears, hidden by the powdered wigs they wore.

Their faces sweating, beneath impassive plaster masks.

Signor Renzo had taken delight in dressing them and had gone to town with Luca and Nino's costumes.

They resembled dandies, and Nino, in particular, was avoiding every mirror possible. He felt itchy and ridiculous, and it was laughable to be dressed this way.

It was necessary, however. They had hundreds of guests attending over the evening, and members of the press were stationed outside, taking photos of every arrival.

Glamorous motor launches buzzed up and down the Grand Canal, ferrying guests from Palazzo Dolfin Manin to Palazzo Pisani Morreta.

They were an hour away from the arrival time at the Aperitivo, and the excitement and tension were building.

Luigi Brugano, Mayor of Venice, and his deputy, Simon, arrived to greet the guests.

They had been fully briefed at a meeting at the Carabinieri HQ and knew that they just had to act as naturally as possible.

The officers, disguised as waiters, were watching and would react if the Manin Twins showed themselves.

It had been decided to minimise risk by conveying the Minister of Tourism directly to the ball, skipping the Palazzo Dolfin Manin and the potential for danger between

234

the two venues.

This didn't make the mayor feel any happier about the evening.

He was mourning the death of his assistant, Flavia and also the hard facts that the perpetrators of the daily murderous nightmare had been trusted members of Venice's nobility.

He had seen an email of their letter to Nino and Luca, and he knew that their manifesto contained quite a lot of uncomfortable truths.

He felt that he would have to speak to the Comune to put in place a working party to address the 'Carnevale killers' points.

Some good had to come out of all this darkness.

Guests in sumptuous costumes stepped delicately off motor launches and entered the Palazzo Dolfin Manin.

The tinkle of laughter and the hum of chatter drifted out of the open main door and travelled along the Cala. It was heard by the two costumed figures, dressed in cream frock coats and white powdered wigs, each with a ponytail tied with a black ribbon.

They wore black masks with gold leaf detail.

One turned to the other and bowed. The other bowed back; they turned away, automaton-like, and bowed in the direction of the lights of the Palazzo Dolfin Manin.

One took the heavy antique Gemini pistol from the frock-coat's pocket and weighed it in their hands.

They lifted it, and aimed it towards the throng of people and then lowered it and put the ancient safety catch back on again.

They sat down on the steps of the bridge.

Prosecco and chilled white wine were disappearing before the eyes of the officers. They had never imagined how stressful it would be to wait on demanding guests.

One group shuttled back and forth to the catering kitchen, where Leo and Bruno filled platter after platter with canapés.

Lilia bustled in, dressed as a serving wench, took five more bottles of Prosecco and five of wine from the boxes on the floor, and added them to the wine fridges to chill them.

She patted Leo on the back and said, "Brava!" These boys were doing an excellent job, despite their lack of experience.

She didn't have time to cast her mind to the whereabouts of Isabella or Rocco. She was shocked by what she now knew.

It was impossible not to have put the pieces together. It all made sense to her now. She crossed herself.

When she considered that she had unwittingly played in the death of Ernesto Rossi.

She remembered Rocco's smile as he handed her the bottle bag and the instructions for the bakery.

She was an accessory to murder! Mamma Mia! She had to help the Carabinieri as much as possible to show them that she really, truly, had no idea what the twins were up to.

She went back into the crush of guests, picking up a full tray of champagne coupes to deliver more Prosecco to the party.

Her nieces were tiring, and she wanted to give them a ten-minute break on the balcony before the Aperitivo ended and they had clearing up to do.

She knew that the three of them would be working alone on that task.

The police would all leave with the guests and travel on to help keep watch at the Palazzo Pisani Moretta.

It was going to be a long night, and she was grateful that those nice boys from the Polizia Locale were going to deliver her and her nieces to her sister's in Burano later.

People were beginning to drift towards the doors, eager to get along to the best seats at the dinner and ball.

The Carabinieri began to take things back to the catering kitchen and then joined each small group of guests at a discrete distance, quietly radioing their progress to those waiting at the Palazzo Pisani Moretta.

The movement between the venues was one of the potential danger points.

Nobody could have eyes on every rooftop, or down every canal, to intercept the threat posed by the Manins.

Soon, the Palazzo Dolfin Manin was empty, except for Lilia and the girls.

They took their masks off wearily and went to tackle the huge amount of cleaning up in the catering kitchen.

Lilia ran the taps into the large stainless-steel sink and then stopped. She thought she heard a noise in the entrance hall.

She left the girls, beginning to soak the glasses, and went through to the hall. The heavy oak door was swinging open.

It was too large and cumbersome to blow open, and she shivered as she closed and barred it with the iron lock.

If she had looked outside, she would have seen two figures, in cream frock-coats, standing staring at the Palazzo.

One of them put the large door key back in their coat pocket and they both turned on their heels and walked swiftly in the direction of the Palazzo Pisani Moretta.

They walked with purpose and determination.

Luca, Nino, and Gianni were coordinating the Carabinieri, who had been at the Aperitivo. Leo told them that there had been no sign of the twins.

They deployed the officers around the dining room, seating one member of the force at every table.

The security detail was checking tickets at the main entrance.

They knew what to look for and what to do if they saw Isabella and Rocco.

The kitchen staff had Bruno, fully armed, on duty with them, and he kept an eye on the rear door. They were as prepared as they could be.

The commander Andrea Revecco was assigned to sit at the top table where Daniela Santanche and the mayor would be sitting.

He had his service revolver on hand.

They would prefer to take the twins alive, but they wouldn't risk another life to do so. If they had to shoot to kill, then so be it.

They already had a handwritten confession and all the costumes. It was clear that they need not look for anyone else.

Luca couldn't settle. He kept scanning the room where the dinner would be served. Once satisfied, he went to the ballroom, and did the same.

Only to repeat the process again and again.

If he hadn't been wearing the stuffy full mask, he would have rubbed his face into a frenzy. The nervous energy was like nothing he had ever experienced before.

He felt guilty too.

He didn't feel that he had trusted his instinct sufficiently. He had known in his gut that the Manin siblings were where he had to look, and yet he hadn't acted decisively.

Because of that, more people had died at their hands. That would take some time to come to terms with.

Nino watched his friend, and despite the mask, he could see the turmoil that was consuming Luca's mind.

Nino didn't blame him.

Nino knew the twists and turns that they had gone through to get to this point. A 'hunch,' a 'theory,' wasn't evidence.

They had to be in the business of evidence gathering.

The need to construct a cast-iron conviction and successful prosecution meant that there were all sorts of rules to follow.

The fact that Luca had been correct in his theory just showed what an empathic detective he was.

They had to have the evidence first, before they could act.

Nino hoped that a sharp talking-to from Bianca Avedo

or the commander might stop Luca from beating himself up.

It wasn't his fault that the victims had been murdered. That was entirely the work of Isabella and Rocco Manin.

Guests, dressed in great finery with masks and wigs to match, entered the dining room and began to take their seats.

There was an orchestra playing, and the beautiful music began to soothe Luca's agitation. Once everyone else was seated, Luigi Brugano, the Carabinieri commander Andrea Revecco, and the minister for tourism came in and took their seats to polite applause.

As the three walked to the table, Luca, Nino and Gianni watched for movement around the hall – anything that could be a threat.

All was calm, and nothing happened. They let out a collective sigh of relief. So far, so good.

The waiting staff had all been checked and had been advised not to wear masks.

It would be too easy for the twins to change places with a waiter or waitress to get to the mayor or minister that way.

Gianni seated himself at the adjoining table to the minister. He was facing away from her, but his chair was back-to-back with hers, with just a short space between them.

He calculated that, if necessary, he could cover her position quickly enough.

Luca was to the right, and Nino to the front, along with their commander. With an officer at each of the other tables, they felt an uneasy calm settle over the proceedings.

Dinner was served.

As the waiting staff brought in the primo plate of lobster with mango or the risotto with fragrant truffle and wild mushroom, the entertainment began.

The lights dimmed dramatically, which bothered Luca immediately.

Dancers in beautiful costumes, embroidered with flowers and encrusted with sparkles, danced between the tables.

The orchestra played for them as they danced.

From the ceiling, two men, made up with grey body makeup to resemble stone statues, tumbled on cobalt blue silk lengths to the floor, where they joined the dance.

It was all bathed in a soft blue light, which turned turquoise the exact colour of the Venetian canals.

There was so much to see, and every sense was filled with the drama and spectacle of it all. Gianni focused on the corners of the room, while Nino's head moved left and right, looking for any break in the pattern before him.

Luca felt like crying.

He knew that this event had charged a hefty price for tickets, and it was a major moneymaker for the city.

The top ticket price was €5000, which was eye-watering.

It was also a potential crime scene, and he wished he could shout out for them all just to stop, go home, be safe, and stay alive.

He had no idea what the twins were planning, but this was the exact event that summed up their loathing of the crassness of tourism.

Only the elite from all over the world could participate, as the tickets for one night only ranged from €5000 down to €800 for a later arrival ticket (after the meal and entertainment were over) He shook his head.

This caused Nino to notice and radio him. His earpiece crackled.

"Are you okay?" he responded affirmatively. He explained that he was finding it difficult to focus with so much movement.

Nino gasped as a fire-breather on stilts, dressed as a flame, began his act next to him. This was sensory overload!

As the primo plates were cleared, and the second course arrived: delicious-looking thinly sliced fillets of beef served with lagoon oysters. There were also buttery celeriac fondants with carrot mousse and cavolo nero.

The performers moved around and new actors arrived.

The costumes took on the colour of the Venetian sunset, sumptuous in their silks and velvets. Singing began. Luca shuddered; it was a Baccarole, last heard across the fog and sung by two murderers.

This was the classical version, but it still felt too close for comfort.

Luca heard his commander, Andrea, in his earpiece: "So far so good?" he muttered his agreement.

This was exhausting: waiting in tension for something to happen, not knowing when or what it would be.

The constraining mask didn't help either.

It had said very firmly on the ticket that costumes and

masks were mandatory. Tuxedos and evening gowns were prohibited.

This meant that the twins could already be present anywhere.

At least with the dinner, the masks had to be raised to eat. Each Carabinieri officer knew what the Manins looked like.

Luca's head was spinning, as quickly as the dancer to the side of him, who was whirling on pointe shoes in a swirl of peach and lilac chiffon.

The guests 'ooo'd and ahhh'd.'

It was spectacular, he conceded, but it was too much of a distraction, to easily conduct a manhunt!

As dessert was brought forward – pear compote with dark chocolate mousse or a lemon tart made with lemons from one of the islands – the performers, who had been working between the tables moved away.

All eyes shifted to the orchestra, and the renowned opera singer who was going to perform. The lights dimmed again, and a spotlight found her as she began to sing, perfectly accompanied by the orchestra.

It was Puccini. She was singing excerpts from 'Gianni Schicchi,' the one-act opera inspired by The Divine Comedy.

The music carried everyone away.

At the back of the hall, the security staff had stepped forward from the foyer in to hear the music.

They had transferred their focus completely to the stage.

Behind them, two late comers, dressed in identical

frock coats of cream brocade, with white powdered wigs and small curly ponytails tied with black ribbon, came quietly up the steps. They had matching black and gold masks with delicate leaf pattern.

They went to the side staircase and quickly ascended.

One of the security guards turned, thinking they had heard something behind them. There was nobody in the foyer at all, and they knew they had just under an hour until the €800 ticket holders began to arrive.

They turned back to the orchestra once again, allowing themselves to be carried away by the music.

The soprano was beginning her final piece, 'O Mio Babbio Caro.' The music was sung so sweetly that many a mask was lifted, to dry the eyes.

As the last sublime note rang out, the whole hall erupted in applause.

So moved was the audience that they began to get up from their seats to applaud and give a standing ovation.

Daniela Santache, wiping tears from her eyes with one hand and holding her mask with the other, stood too.

She was close to the orchestra and had felt the full force of the emotion as it played out before her.

She was facing the stage now, applauding, her mask back in place.

From an elevated position at the back of the room, a gunshot rang out, breaking through the applause and causing screams and panic.

The second shot came from a slightly different place.

Gianni leapt from his standing position and hurled himself bodily across Daniela, winding her.

He cried out! He felt a hot, stinging pain in his shoulder. He had been shot.

Nino had been watching Daniela, when the second shot sounded. He had seen Gianni dive for her, knocking her to the ground.

He had also seen the dark red patch growing like a flower across the shoulder of Gianni's dove-grey silk coat.

He shouted an instruction into his mouthpiece, "Man down!"

He then turned, and ran for the stairs, his pistol already in hand.

Luca was ahead of him and shouted, "Side door!" loudly to all those giving chase.

He had seen the twins running down the stairs, ducking to the side fire door, and out into the night.

The radio crackled in their ears, and the calming voice of the commander spoke.

"Those closest to the orchestra, stay with me. The rest of you, follow Conti and Greco – they are giving chase. Leave by the side door. Shoot if you have clearance. Take care; they have nothing left to lose." With their orders given, the Carabinieri – man and woman alike – removed masks and ran in the direction of the murderers.

Gianni gritted his teeth; he was in a lot of pain.

One of the officers applied pressure to the wound, and a guest approached.

He removed his mask and introduced himself as a surgeon from the Ospedale Giovanni e Paolo. T he officer, holding a pressure pad made of a bunch of linen napkins, gratefully handed over the patient to expert hands.

Daniela was sitting, doubled over on a chair. She had some of Gianni's blood on her dress.

She looked very shaken and was struggling to breathe. Gianni had undoubtably saved her life, but he had knocked the breath out of her in the process.

She took the glass of water that the commander offered her.

The orchestra had left the stage with the soprano, and Luigi Brugano, the mayor, went to the microphone to apologise for the premature end of the evening.

He asked everyone to take care on their way home and use the available water taxis available. Danger was still at large, and it was difficult to manage the situation with so many guests and visitors crowding the streets.

Andrea Revecco walked out into the foyer to brief his security staff.

He needed them to prevent any of the late-arrival ticket holders from trying to gain entry further confusing the situation.

He prepared a statement to be given to the media, who had by now heard what had happened inside the Palazzo.

He knew that this situation had every chance of getting out of hand. He needed the media on side to manage the risk posed to the public.

Luca's lungs burned.

He had one of the twins still in sight, but they were running as if their feet had wings. He wished that he wasn't so trussed up in velvet and lace.

The costume was designed for gentle movement, not a sprint.

There was too much risk to stop and take off the coat, or the lace shirt ruffles. That would lose him the advantage he had, and he couldn't risk losing them.

He debated, again, shooting at the departing figure in the leg to stop them, but there were too many tourists and other people around to take the shot safely.

Nino's voice crackled into his ear, "I have one of them in sight. They're running for the Rialto Bridge. Take care. They're a lot of people about. I'm…"

His voice cut out, and there was a sound of a shot. Luca felt sick.

"Nino! Nino? Do you copy?"

Silence and crackling were all that Luca heard. That and the sound of his footsteps pounding the pavement.

"I'm OK!" Relief flooded his system. "My mic fell out! I still have sight of one of them."

"Thank the Madonna!" Luca gasped. "I have sight of the other!"

They ran, weaving in and out of the tiny side streets and up and down bridges, shouting, "Please stay back!" As they went, to the bemused people lining their route.

The white stone Rialto bridge was in sight now, more of a parade of shops than merely a bridge. It was always crowded.

There were several stepped walkways up to, and over, the structure. The central one led to the shops and was always packed with people. The side routes led to the left and the right, with views of the canal.

It was to the right that Luca went.

He began the climb up the stairs at a jog, almost all his

energy spent.

He came up alongside Nino, who was leaning on the stone balustrade, breathing heavily. Luca grasped Nino's arm and looked him in the eye. He mouthed, "Okay?"

He had no speech left.

Nino nodded and pointed upwards.

Following his friend's finger, he saw both Manin Twins, costumed and still masked, standing together on the parapet of the bridge, above the walkway.

They were holding hands and were quite still.

They looked down into the black waters of the night-dark canal. The walkway up to them and the other side was empty.

Thankfully, there had been enough commotion, for people to realise that they need to stay back.

On the other side of the bridge, however, there were flashes from cameras, as people videoed and photographed the unusual scene.

Luca recovered his power of speech first.

"Rocco, Isabella! Stay there! There's been enough death. There is nothing else to say. We understand how you feel. The mayor is listening! He will put measures in place to help reduce the damage you fear."

One of the masked figures turned their face in his direction. Rocco's muffled voice rang out.

"It's too late! Too much has been ruined. Venice is drowning. She is being killed by popularity. She is swamped by tourists, ruined by the masses who are determined to see her and, in so doing, kill her in the process. We are the last of the Manins. There will be no more of our noble line. We die as the city dies."

With that, the two figures looked at each other and raised their clasped hands to the sky and jumped in unison into the velvet blackness.

The sound of a splash was heard moments later, accompanied by the shouts of surprise and alarmed cries of the bystanders.

A Polizia locale launch sped under the bridge.

Giacomo and his team had been waiting, their engine idling, just by the pontoon for the Rialto Vaporetto stop.

Now they came through to the far right and trained their fixed search light on the water.

Luca and Nino leaned against the bridge side, utterly exhausted. They stared into the black water.

The ripples caught the lights from all the restaurants and illuminated palaces on either side of the Grand Canal.

They watched the search light pan left and right, but no figures appeared through the water. Giacomo looked up to them.

"We will need divers," he said into his radio.

Luca nodded, then realised that Giacomo couldn't see him clearly. He spoke into his mouthpiece to arrange a team to attend.

The crowd of tourists who had been held back earlier were now swarming over the bridge and leaning over to see what was happening.

The videos were being posted to Instagram and TikTok.

YouTube footage was being taken as they chatted excitedly, as if this was for entertainment.

Nino felt sick.

He touched Luca's arm.

"Let's get out of here! We need to report back to the commander and see how Gianni is doing." Luca nodded, dull eyes.

He felt a huge weight of sadness about the whole affair. What a sorry waste!

"Hey! Look! It's Detective Luca!" somebody shouted, and then the cameras and clamouring faces turned towards him.

"Andiamo!" said Nino, and he and Nino began to descend the Rialto Bridge at a jog. He wanted to get away from the interest and the gossip.

It took only a few minutes to lose the pursuers who didn't know the streets and canals as well as Luca and Nino.

Soon they were back at the doors to the Palazzo Pisani Moretta.

They met uniformed officers at the door and were ushered straight through to the dining room.

Andrea Revecco had put together a temporary incident room, and the officers who had stayed behind were working on their phones and radios to coordinate with HQ.

The scene looked surreal.

All the officers were still dressed in Carnevale costume.

All masks were gone, but some still wore their wigs.

As Luca and Nino came up to the desk that Andrea had set up using two of the round banqueting tables, he broke off his call and pulled out two chairs for them.

He knew what had happened from the radio information that had been relayed to him, but he wanted to hear first-hand what had happened.

It would also do Nina and Luca good to speak about it to help them come to terms with the shocking and traumatic experience.

He listened intently as they took it in turns to tell the tale.

Luca closed his eyes and winced as he recalled hearing the gunshot, and losing contact with Nino momentarily.

They asked about Gianni, who had been taken by ambulance boat to hospital, accompanied by the Doctor who had been a guest at the Ball.

They also wanted to know about Daniela Santache. She had been taken back to her hotel, the Danieli by the mayor.

She was shaken and bruised, but otherwise unhurt.

"Gianni Marino saved the minister's life, that much is certain," said Andrea.

"He is an excellent officer, and I think that he has more than shown himself competent as detective material."

Luca and Nino nodded enthusiastically.

"Would you two take him under your wing? I want to promote him to detective, and he will need to learn the ropes. Will you do it?"

Both Luca and Nino agreed enthusiastically. "We are going to need a bigger office though, boss!" said Nino with an exaggerated wink at his commander.

"The details can be ironed out, as soon as we work towards concluding the investigations," said Andrea, smiling.

The radio on the table in front of them crackled into life. "We have two bodies, Polizia locale are recovering them now. We will take them to Umberto at the mortuary. There are hundreds of people watching us. We need to get somewhere secured to be able to concentrate on doing our job!"

Luca confirmed to the commander that there would be lots of video flooding YouTube and the rest of the social channels.

It was unavoidable and ironic, when you considered the point that the Manin twins were trying to make.

Luca felt sorrow. He was surprised that he did.

He had thought that he would be infused with complete relief that it was all over, but he wasn't. He suddenly couldn't bear to wear that costume any longer, and he pulled off the jacket and the ruffles that were attached by velcro to his shirt.

Wrenching off the hot, itchy wig, he sat down and looked at the painted ceiling.

One of the other officers who had stayed with the commander brought him a cold glass of water, which he drank immediately.

"Thank you. I really needed that!" he said, as he handed back the glass. Nino looked shattered.

He was half in and half out of his frock coat, with no energy left to progress either way. The officer helped him remove it and then passed him a glass of water, too.

Both men were reliving what happened in the last hour as the adrenaline rush left them. There was a lot to process.

It was very late.

The commander made his decision.

They would need to continue tomorrow, but for now, everyone needed to sleep. Nothing would be gained by spinning the evening out.

He needed their brains to be sharp to apply themselves to the huge amount of work to be done. There would also be the inevitable press conference, and it was important that Greco and Conti looked alert for that.

He gave his orders, and for once Luca didn't try to change his mind. He was dead on his feet and couldn't wait to get home to a hot bath. He never wanted to wear breeches or ruffles and a frock coat again.

Clara was in a state of nervous agitation when she finally heard Luca's key in the lock. She was taken aback to see him in his costume.

She had seen him leave the house in his regular work clothes, and seeing him now dressed in silks and frills was almost too much.

"What have they done to you?" she said, and promptly burst into tears. He was across the room in a flash and gathered her up into his arms.

What began as a hug became a lingering kiss, which took them both by surprise. "Where is my friend Luca? What have you done with him?" she joked weakly. He smiled at her and pulled off the frock coat.

"I need a bath and I need to talk to you, which should come first?"

"The bath, I can't take you seriously dressed like that. I'll make you some pasta and we can talk then."

Luca didn't have any appetite for food. He had eaten at the ball, and then so much had happened. "How about just a beer?" he said, and Clara went to get one for each of them, while he went to run the bath.

Dressed in his jogging bottoms and a T-shirt, and towel-drying his hair, he joined her in the salon and sat next to her, where she was curled up with a blanket over her.

It was late, and he knew that he should probably wait until morning to talk to her, but he couldn't leave it any longer.

Their kiss, earlier, had given him hope, and he felt that he would never sleep if he didn't resolve things now, this very moment.

He pulled her legs across his and covered them both with the blanket.

They chinked their beer bottles together and drank deeply, taking a deep breath. Luca began. He spoke quietly; he didn't look at her but held her hand.

"I've known this for a while now, and I have to tell you what's been on my mind. Even through this nightmare, I have clung to this feeling as it has grown and grown. I love you, Clara, not as a friend, although you are my best friend."

Clara held her breath. To steady herself, she took a swig of beer. Could this be true?

"I know, with every certainty I possess, that I can't live without you. During this incredibly stressful time, you've kept me sane. It's an imposition, and it could ruin everything, but I have to know – might you be able to come to love me too? I want to be with you always."

He trailed off and looked embarrassed.

He swigged at his beer and rubbed his face. He still wouldn't look at her.

"Luca, Caro! can you doubt me?" She turned his face to hers.

He saw, in that moment, the outpouring of love in her eyes. He realised that she felt as he felt.

Such a massive surge of emotion was too much, and he burst into messy tears.

She was crying too, and then they were laughing and crying together.

It was as if the pressure of the last ten days had suddenly been released.

Joy overwhelmed them, and they kissed again, this time with the passion that they had been too scared to show previously, for fear of rejection.

It was extremely late – or rather, early, depending on how you looked at it. Luca knew that he had to get some sleep.

He got up from the sofa and took Clara in his arms once more.

She folded the blanket neatly on the arm of the sofa and took his hand. She led him to her bedroom where a soft peach light was already glowing. He didn't argue.

He went with her, his whole heart singing with the shared delight of the knowledge of shared love.

Nino felt groggy. He was experiencing an adrenaline slump the likes of which he had never experienced before.

He was drinking his second espresso of the day when

Luca breezed into the office. He looked fresh-faced and was grinning from ear to ear.

Nino took in his friend's mood and the feeling of joy that emanated from every pore. "You told her?" he said, smiling too.

"Yes, and Mamma Mia! she loves me too! I can't believe it."

Nino considered telling his friend about how obvious it had been to everyone else but decided to leave Luca to be delighted and amazed.

"That's such wonderful news. I'm very happy for you Clara is one in a million." Luca just beamed his agreement.

There was a sharp rap at the door to their office, and the commander came in.

"We need to have a meeting with Bianca now, and then we need to go over to the mortuary and see Grazie. Today will be packed with so much work, I'm afraid. We have a press conference this afternoon. The minister for tourism and the mayor will be part of it. We have to get our news out and give the media the facts. We know that there are many YouTube videos out there already, and we have to give the full facts to prevent speculation and conspiracy theories running riot."

He broke off and realised that during his speech, Luca had just been beaming at him – a smile so large it quite transformed his face.

"Conti, what has changed? You are smiling like the cat that has found the cream." Nino interjected, "Some upturn in Conti's personal life Signor!"

"Oh finally! The lovely Clara said yes? That is good.

It took long enough, eh?" Nino nodded and Luca looked amazed.

"How did you know?" he asked, looking baffled.

"How did you not?" asked Andrea.

"You are one of my best detectives, and yet you couldn't guess how the girl felt about you!" He punched Luca gently on the arm.

"Come on, we have work to do!" Andrea had reserved the conference room at HQ, and Luca, Nino, and Andrea joined Bianca Avedo, who was already waiting, with her files spread out in front of her.

Gianni came in, his arm in a sling. He looked pale and tired.

Andrea explained that Gianni was going to go on sick leave for at least a week, but they needed to debrief him before he left.

Luca pulled out a chair for Gianni and helped him sit down. They began with his statement.

"I was watching the corners of the dining room. There was so much going on at first. It became easier when the opera began, and I just kept my eyes trained on the dark edges of the room. As the applause started, I saw a chink of light flash from up in the balcony. It must've been the stage lights catching something metallic up there. It was new; that hadn't been there before. It alerted me, and then I heard the first shot. I jumped to cover the minister. I think I hurt her when I pushed her out of range. I'm so sorry for that." He looked contrite.

They let him continue. "I felt a sharp pain in my shoulder, and then I heard the second shot. Everything is a little fuzzy after that."

Nino took up the story. "We heard the shots, and I saw Gianni had been hit. There was a movement up on the balcony, and Luca and I gave chase."

Bianca cleared her throat. "Did you see the shots fired?"

"No, we heard them," Andrea said.

"I've spoken with Umberto, and he tells me that a single Gemini Musket – antique I believe – has been found in the large pocket of Rocco Manin's costume. There is also the large key to the Palazzo Dolfin Manin. We will need to get technical to look at the gun in detail, but we think that they had a Gemini pistol each. There were a pair of such pistols in the collection at the Palazzo. We will need to properly search the Palazzo anyway, but I guess we will find that these guns are missing from their display case."

Gianni told them that an antique musket ball had been dug out of his shoulder by the surgeon at the hospital the previous night. He looked pale as he spoke, and took a quick sip of water. Andrea could tell that Gianni was tiring, so he prepared to release him.

"Gianni, I want to congratulate you for your quick thinking and bravery. You have, throughout this whole case, shown initiative and dedication. As a result of this, I'm promoting you to the rank of detective. I would like you to join Conti and Greco and be part of their team as soon as you are well enough to return to work."

Gianni's face was a picture. His mouth literally fell open. He looked from Luca to Nino, and they smiled and nodded.

"We will be honoured to have you on the team," said Nino, gently patting him on the back, avoiding his injury.

"Thank you! That's all I've ever wanted," he said in a whisper.

Andrea helped him out of the meeting room, and Bianca, Luca, and Nino sat and waited. "Well done to both of you," said Bianca.

"The confession letter gives me the answers I was seeking. I wish we had them both to question, but I can see that it was never their intention to be arrested. They always planned to die, to further emphasise their point about the death of old Venice."

The three of them felt sad, when they considered everything that had led them to this point, there were no real winners.

Andrea came back into the conference room. He saw the serious faces. "This has been a lot for everybody. Let's use this opportunity to do our very best work, and really make sure that no life lost was wasted – not even the lives of the perpetrators."

Bianca, as prosecutor still needed to put together a report for the court, even though the guilty parties were dead.

She began a timeline, and with input from Luca, Nino, and Andrea, they filled in the known facts. Luca and Nino made notes of any unknown information as a starting point for their continuing investigation.

It was going to be easier now the deaths had ended with the death of the 'Carnevale killers.' themselves, but they now had the added complication of the press and other on lookers.

It was a different pressure to have, but no less challenging.

Andrea checked his watch, "We need to get to the mortuary for the post mortem on the twins. Bianca, are you satisfied that you have enough to begin your report?"

She agreed that she did, and the meeting was adjourned. Nino felt drained.

It was only just beginning and he already felt as if his brain would explode. Luca was smiling to himself, and looking full of beans.

Nino was pleased for his friend, of course, but he felt a little left out. Luca seemed to have it all.

They arrived at the hospital mortuary after a sunny, sparkling journey across the lagoon.

It was a beautiful day, and it seemed at odds with the drama and pain from the previous night. Carnevale was over, and apart from coriadoli confetti scattered on the pavements and catching the breeze, all evidence of the celebrations had left the city.

Venice felt like a hostess, cleaning up after a night of partying.

She was getting everything back to normal, ready for the Lenten fast. Nino stood in the bow of the boat and shook his head.

Did he dream it all? With the warm sun on his face and the occasional splash of water as they hit a wave, it felt entirely possible that it had all been a terrible, suffocating nightmare.

Umberto Grazie was his usual irascible self.

He had secretly enjoyed the fast pace of the daily, new body count. He felt that he had certainly formed a closer working relationship with the detectives, Luca and Nino in particular.

He realised that this case had stretched him, pulling him out of his rut. He had been freewheeling toward retirement, and this case had called upon every brain cell and synapse he possessed to keep up. He felt tired, but also strangely energised by it all.

With a flourish, he pulled back the sheet covering the bodies of Rocco and Isabella. They looked like wax effigies of themselves, as if they were sleeping.

Umberto began his report.

"They died from drowning. There was a sizeable amount of canal water in their lungs. There was a quantity of red wine and grappa in their stomachs too, but nothing toxicology would indicate that any additional substance was playing a part in their deaths. This was a suicide." He indicated a tray to the side of the bodies. "Within the pocket of Rocco, we found this antique duelling pistol, one of an identical pair, known as a 'Gemini pair.' Gemini, as in the twins, no doubt chosen from the Manin collection – possibly chosen for the fact that these guns were also twins." He paused. Luca was listening keenly and making notes. Nino looked dead on his feet. He sympathised; he felt that it had been far longer than eleven days since he had worked on Betsy Noakes, the first of the victims.

Refocusing, he pointed to a large ornate key.

It was as venetian as could be, carved and adorned

with decoration.

"This was also in the pocket of Rocco Manin," the Polizia locale boys thought it would be the key to either the Palazzo Dolfin Manin or the Palazzo Pisano Moretta. It's definitely old, grand, and looks as if it could have been from a palazzo.

Andrea looked at the key and Luca took a photo of it on his phone. They would show it to Lilia when they interviewed her.

Umberto led them to the clothing that the twins had worn. The soggy garments had the label 'Marega Renzo' stitched into the back of the frock coats.

"Signor Renzo's missing two suits of clothing," said Nino, holding a cream ruffled sleeve with his protective gloves.

"I wonder if he will want them back now," Luca said, making a note.

The meeting came to an end, Umberto replaced the sheets over the bodies of the Manin twins and removed his gloves.

"I will write up my report and send it along with the one I'm still preparing from the murder of Flavia Reiner. I must say, I'm going to miss this flurry of work – it nearly killed me too, but it was extremely stimulating." He raised a hand and made a shooing motion. "Go get this case concluded!" Andrea, Luca, and Nino left the mortuary. It was only eleven a.m. and already they felt as if they had done a full day's work. It was going to be a long slog.

The prospect of the press conference loomed up at them. I've just got to keep going thought Nino, gloomily.

The press conference was a much bigger affair than previously.

The mayor had insisted that they use the largest room in Ca'Loredan.

The case had attracted interest from every News group, there were cameras and journalists from all over the globe.

Andrea explained to Nino that he needed to be on the podium too, but that he, the Commander, and the mayor would handle most of the questions.

There was still a lot of work to do, and this conference was a chance to quell the gossip. The thought of standing under the glare of the spotlights, with cameras trained on him, made Nino feel distinctly unwell.

Nerves bubbled in his stomach, and he felt an overwhelming urge to run away – to be anywhere but here.

They lined up, in the corridor. The murmur of chatter from within the large conference room was loud enough to make Nino's stomach churn afresh.

The mayor, Andrea, Daniela followed by Luca and Nino, walked in to the sound of popping flash bulbs and shouted questions.

They took their places on the podium and looked out into the sea of faces and cameras. The mayor had prepared a statement.

He spoke eloquently about the murders and what they had learned about the reasons behind the deaths.

He acknowledged the pressure that mass tourism was placing on the city.

He announced that an inquiry would be launched into the crimes, and lessons would be learned from the Manin twins' frustration, which had morphed into a killing spree of such magnitude.

He managed to strike the right note of sympathy for the cause, and disapproval of the appalling methods that the Manins had chosen.

Daniela spoke. She had almost become the 10th victim of the twins.

She also represented tourism across of Italy and was well-versed in the difficulties that Rome, Milan, and other areas of the country were experiencing.

The sheer volume and type of visitors that were filling every corner of their wonderful country had to be carefully managed.

Going forward, she described this moment in time as a watershed, where they could look clearly, assess the problems and make efforts to change things for the better.

This speech solicited a wave of questions.

Nino zoned out; he was really struggling to deal with the clamour of the journalists.

He slid his eyes towards Luca. He was focused and calm. *How does he do it?* he thought.

Luca wasn't concentrating on the conference.

He knew that he and Nino needed to be there, but his mind kept drifting to Rocco and Isabella. He wanted to get back to the Palazzo Dolfin Manin.

He wanted to see what else had been left for them to find, to tie up the loose ends of the case. He really wanted to speak with Lilia, then he really wanted to get home to see Clara and explore how their friendship could evolve into the partnership they both desired.

The commander, Andrea, was speaking now, he explained about the injury to his officer, Gianni Marino. The questions surged once again.

A journalist asked Luca, by name, how he felt he could have done things differently, given that it had taken too long to stop the killers.

Luca cleared his throat. "We needed evidence to arrest the perpetrators. The use of costumes and masks made gathering that evidence very difficult. There was no forensic evidence or DNA left at any of the crime scenes because of the gloves, masks, and costumes used. When we found a link, we acted immediately."

"Do you think you were too slow to act, Nino Greco?" The pushy journalist turned to Nino.

He swallowed, leaned forward to his microphone, and, looking directly into the journalist's eyes, said flatly, "No."

The hall erupted with questions, shouted from all areas.

The mayor and commander got up and nodded to Luca and Nino. Daniela led the way as they left the room.

The noise and shouting continued.

Glad to be free of it, finally, Conti and Greco went directly along to the Palazzo Dolfin Manin.

Some of the technical team was already there, working in the caretaker's flat.

Lilia was mopping the floor of the Grand Salon,

looking as if the weight of the whole world was on her shoulders.

She smiled weakly when she saw Luca and Nino and propped her mop and bucket against the credenza.

She knew that she needed to give her statement.

Luca began by showing her the photograph of the key found in the pocket of Rocco's costume. "That is the main door key. It usually always in the lock. Last night, after the Aperitivo, I noticed that it was missing. The door was open to the night, and I bolted it from inside. I felt as if someone was watching." She shivered, pulled her cardigan tighter around her. "I think they were watching. Despite everything, they loved this place, this city, more than anything else." She began to cry quietly, and Nino handed her his handkerchief.

She took it gratefully. "They weren't bad people, you know," she said after wiping her eyes. "They have done bad things, but they were good people."

Luca nodded.

"Did you know what was happening? Did they share with you? Their plans?"

"No! never! I wouldn't stay silent. If I had known, I would've reported it."

She spoke with fire in her eyes. She was resolutely looking at them directly, unwavering now.

She felt that she was fighting for her own life in that moment.

Nino and Luca exchanged glances. It was as they had thought Lilia was an innocent bystander. She had been asked to do various tasks for the twins. One of them had

266

been to convey the poisoned wine to the bakery, but she herself hadn't been complicit.

They watched as she signed off her statement.

She raised her head. "What happens now?" Luca advised her to speak with the mayor's office. The Palazzo was still, after all, an important attraction to the city Comune, and they were sure that it would still function as before, even without the Manins.

Leaving Lilia to continue her chores, Luca and Nino made their way up to the caretaker's flat. Home, for so many years, to Isabella and Rocco.

They wanted to properly search the rooms to see if they could get more of a sense of why the twins had become killers.

Luca first looked in the kitchen.

He stood quietly and looked at everything.

It was a small, well-designed space. The bean-to-cup coffee machine was centre stage and was clearly the most used piece of equipment.

He began to open cupboards and drawers. The kitchen had everything that a keen cook would require, but some of the items looked brand-new and barely used.

He opened the fridge. There was some long-life milk, some pre-made pesto, some Parmesan, and some orange juice.

He got the impression that the twins used the flat mainly as a base to sleep, and were more usually in the rest of the Palazzo.

There was an empty Grappa bottle in the recycling bin.

Had they needed to fortify themselves before killing?

Certainly, they had quantities of the fiery drink in their stomachs when they died.

He looked in the tall larder cupboard, by the small kitchen table and two chairs. There were packets of pasta, the same brand that was sold at Antonio's grocery.

There were tins and packets, all of food that would take no time at all to prepare.

Nino was in the sitting room. It was a square room, quite small, but with windows along one side. He went to them and opened the door in the middle. He was immediately in Venice; the sounds and smells of the city came up to him.

He looked down from the little balcony, not much more than a Juliet-style space, and watched the movements and bustle of the Grand Canal.

Life was progressing as if nothing had happened.

This high up, you could see the city without engaging with it.

He looked across the rooftops of the other neighbouring palazzos and felt the hot sun on his skin.

He went back inside and let the sheer cream drapes fall back. They softened the view and slightly darkened the room.

There was a large L-shaped, comfortable, rust-red sofa, with cushions that looked as if they would have been more at home in the grand rooms below, in the main body of the Palazzo.

There was an ornate sideboard, and a bookcase filled with old books.

A lot of the titles were on subjects of Italian history,

Venetian nobility and art. The antique wooden dining table gleamed.

There was a high-end sound system but no television.

He went back to the bookcase. He began taking each book out and opening it to see if anything had been hidden, when Luca joined him.

The two technical officers, in their protective suits, came through from the bedrooms with their evidence bags.

They would process everything at HQ and send a report to Luca to add to the information for Prosecutor Avedo to use.

Luca came to a book with no title on the spine. It was bound in purple leather.

He drew it out and saw the Manin family crest on the front cover, embossed in gold. He opened it and called Nino to look too.

It was a diary.

Rocco Manin had kept a diary!

Neatly written, with beautiful, slightly dated-looking handwriting.

It began the previous year, and included the whole of this year's Carnevale period.

At first glance, it seemed that he had journaled about his feelings and his reasons for his actions. This was gold dust, and Luca bagged it.

He wanted to read it so badly – just to sit on the comfortable sofa and immerse himself in the day-by-day truth of the crimes from the point of view of one of the 'Carnevale killers.' He hadn't the time to do that, however, and had to continue the disciplined search.

The diary would have to wait. Isabella's bedroom was cramped.

She had many toys and objects from her girlhood around her.

She had a beautiful model of the Palazzo Dolfin Manin in the form of a doll's house. Nino opened the frontage and looked inside.

The Grand Salon, in miniature, was there with two dolls seated in chairs. The dolls were easily recognizable as Rocco and Isabella.

He shuddered and replaced the front.

The wardrobe was full of clothes, many of them grand gowns that looked to have been from previous Manins.

Nino got the impression that this girl had lived in the past.

She had preferred her youth and the glory days of childhood over now. There was a door to the bathroom, from Isabella's room.

It had clearly been another bedroom originally and felt more spacious than the other rooms. There was a full-sized bathtub and expensive bath oils and lotions.

The walls were turquoise and lightly gilded.

Another door from this haven led to Rocco's bedroom.

His room was almost austere. The single iron bedstead, stood in the centre. Above the bed was a heraldic depiction of the Manin family crest.

There was a single chair upholstered in red leather, and a dark wooden wardrobe and chest. Luca opened the wardrobe, and found a modest selection of men's clothes.

The chest was more interesting. It contained letters

270

and paperwork.

The handwriting was old, and the paper was marked with dark spots, showing its age. He glanced at a date: 1642.

It was a detailed archive of the Manin family.

Feeling as if he was snooping, he replaced the letter and took off his gloves. He felt as if the item they had sought – the diary – was all that they needed.

Glimpsing into Isabella and Rocco's lives felt intrusive. They really had very little, despite their noble lineage. Luca and Nino returned to the sitting room.

They each pulled out a chair at the dining table. For a moment or two, they were silent, just the ticking of a clock perched on the sideboard and the distant sounds from the Grand Canal cut through the intense quiet.

"Well!" Nino began, and then stopped.

"Makes me feel so sad," said Luca. "Not just now we know how they died, but how isolated they were. It must have altered their minds. They were, on the surface, wealthy, noble, to be envied, but where are their real friends? Their relationships? The life outside these four walls?"

"It's a gilded cage, a prison, really," said Nino. He pinched the bridge of his nose.

He had a thumping headache.

"We need to eat something," said Luca, recognizing the signs of a blood sugar dip. "Let's get something on the way back to HQ, and then let's start on this diary."

Munching on pizza slices from one of the takeaway vendors, they walked back to HQ. As a precaution, Nino

271

had put on a pair of dark glasses.

He didn't want to be recognised. He still replayed the horror of the press conference over and over in his head.

He now had a hundred answers to the journalist's question, but still, on celluloid, for all to see, was his actual response, "No."

He felt embarrassed, but there wasn't anything he could do about it now.

Eating definitely helped his headache, and he was eager to get started on reading and making notes on Rocco Manin's diary.

They wanted to read it as much as each other, so Luca and Nino moved their desk chairs next to one another to share the book.

They had notebooks to hand, and with a feeling of excitement and trepidation, they opened it t o the first day of Carnevale.

"I hate the life I lead," it began.

Nino looked at Luca, and they started to read.

The clock ticked, and the day darkened into evening. Luca stretched and cracked his back.

They closed the purple cover for the day, and Nino walked stiffly to the safe, locking the precious evidence away.

So much was swimming around in their heads already.

They had learned that Rocco had been the sole actor in the death of Betsy Noakes and Gunter Walner.

He had written eloquently about his views on the padlocking of bridges, and the damage it caused to the stonework.

He mentioned the side of an ancient bridge in Castello, which collapsed into the canal because of the weight of tourist-applied padlocks.

He had resolved to make a stand against the tourists who saw the forbidden signs and did it anyway.

He had been premeditated enough to dress in one of the Carnevale costumes of Leonardo Manin and carry a poisoned blade.

His victim was not predetermined; however, he almost made his point by the fact that he knew that if he visited enough bridges, he would catch someone at it, and he did.

He saw Betsy Noakes recording a video of the actual act of vandalism. His anger had surged. She was a dead woman from that moment onward.

His mood after the death, was one of self-righteous self-congratulation; he felt clearly   completely justified in his actions.

It was chilling to read.

It was written rationally, but so completely wrong that it shook both detectives.

Luca headed home.

Throughout his busy day he had not stopped thinking of Clara.

She was ever present in his mind and he hated being apart from her.

He let himself into the apartment, and the smell of rich, slow-cooked meat, wrapped around him. He let out an involuntary moan of hunger.

She popped her head out of the kitchen a big grin on her beautiful face.

He dumped his coat and laptop bag on a chair, and jointed her in the kitchen for a wonderful life affirming cuddle.

She ruffled his hair and handed him a glass of red.

Kissing her in thanks, he leaned against the kitchen units as she deftly basted the rolled joint of beef.

She had roasted vegetables too and made his favourite, indulgent English crispy roast potatoes.

As she made English gravy, they shared the news of their days.

Never had he felt so happy about these small, normal routine things; they were joyful, and he knew himself to be truly happy amidst so much trouble and stress.

It was as if the knowledge of their love and prospective future, had taken all the pressure away. He felt free and light-hearted despite the revelations in the diary.

Nino was in the next day, before Luca.

That in itself was unheard of. Nino had got his espresso, and then his second espresso, and was guilty contemplating his third, when Luca came in breezily.

He had brought pastries.

He was beyond cheery. Nino sighed; he was happy for his friend, but honestly, he was jealous. The fact that Nino had contemplated getting the diary out of the safe before Luca got in was a shadow of shame to his conscience. It felt worse that his lovely, genial friend had brought pastries.

He let Luca get the keys and retrieve the purple book from its place in the safe.

They were just settling down to open it again, to be

pulled back into the mind of Rocco Manin, when Nino's phone beeped.

There was a text. He glanced at the screen, and his mouth went dry.

What should he do? He nudged Luca's shoulder and showed him the illuminated display. "Viola" showed up first, and then a text:

"I feel so lost! Might you meet me for coffee? I feel as if I'm drowning! Please help."

Luca's eyes widened, and he looked at Nino. "Tonight?"

Nino typed sheepishly. "Yes please, after work," came the reply, immediately.

Luca looked at Nino again. "You got in touch with a witness?" Nino was fidgety. "Yes, she seemed troubled."

Luca smacked his palm to his head and rolled his eyes. "Seemed troubled? Mamma Mia! Nino! Caro!" He shook his head and play-punched Nino in the arm.

Luca was so happy at that moment, that his friend's rule-breaking didn't seem to matter. "Oh, go for it, brother! Andiamo!" he said, laughing.

"Let's get on with this diary."

They stopped their light-heartedness and sat down to read more revelations of the deaths that they had been puzzling over.

"It feels better to have Isabella with me now. It is our joint Crusade. She made me realise that we are avenging angels for the city. For our mother, Venice. Today, we have put a stop to the loss of proper Venetian businesses being eaten up by tourist shops, Isabella was marvellous.

She dressed as the nobleman. She intrigued that macho egotist Lungi. She made a mimed dumb play as I, dressed as the courtesan, glided around the room. He was so intent on her performance that it was almost nothing to slip the ligature around his fat neck. We are avenging angels and we shall avenge Venezia of every last cockroach who would damage her."

"Blimey!" said Nino. "I think he was quite quite mad. We obviously don't have Isabella's testimony here just Rocco's interpretation of her feelings but he really isn't rational."

"No, it's already a crusade by the third murder," said Luca, thoughtfully.

The diary continued, "…we are using Leonardo's costumes fully, they are being celebrated at Carnevale, as they were intended to be. I feel the approval of our ancestors. Each one is glad that Isabella and I are using them to make a positive difference. In every tableau, we take away some more of the tarnish from the face of our mother."

"Again, the use of Venice, as a mother," said Luca. "I'm no analyst, but I bet psychiatrist would have a lot to say about his state of mind."

"Something by chance today! This just confirms to me that our mother, Venice, is approving of her children's actions! I was taking a coffee at Bar Chiaranda when a girl and her friends began to tell the most terrible story.

"A proud artisan forced into poverty by mass production. Stealing his designs and making them in a factory in Asia. She kindly, unwittingly, told me who was

276

to blame. I have a very particular tableau for this one.

"I have been in the workshop by the boat dock. I have made mischief with wood and rope! We will offer up a sacrifice! La Peste! This is the best one yet."

"I can't believe how gleeful he sounds," said Nino.

"This is a lot to take in. I think we must get the first information across to Avedo. I think she needs to come and see this too. It will give her more context for her court report."

Bianca Avedo settled herself into the guest chair in Luca and Nino's cramped office. "What was so important that you make me come to you?" she asked, raising an eyebrow. "You could have come to me. Dario makes excellent coffee, you know."

"We don't like to have this particular piece of evidence too far from the safe," said Luca cryptically in response.

"I'm intrigued! Come on, I have stacks of work – literally stacks – on my desk. Everything has been held up whilst we were in the middle of 'the Carnevale killers! Ten days of terror', as La Nouva is calling it."

Nino rolled his eyes. "Journalists are my least favourite people," he said, as Luca carefully brought the book to the table.

He placed it in front of Avedo, who put on the protective gloves provided and her glasses. "Just read from where I've put the white slip of paper," Luca urged.

Bianca did as she was bidden, with a look of scepticism on her face.

That look turned to one of amazement as she realised

what she was reading.

"He wrote a diary? This is incredible. We can see the workings of his mind! What his reasoning was. This is remarkable, really remarkable!"

Luca had prepared a report for her, which quoted passages from the diary about the first five murders.

Nino was working on collating his report on the remaining four and the attempted murder of Daniela Santanche.

"Have you looked? Have you gone forward to the day of their deaths? Have you seen what he said about that?"

She looks squarely at the detectives.

"Yes, we have. It's very sad really," said Luca quietly.

"May I?" She turned the pages carefully to the ninth day of Carnevale.

It began, "So this is it. This is where we end it. We cannot endure the existence that we live daily anymore."

It was almost worth it to be the servants of all these idiots when we could still live in our family home, the place that sheltered Manins for generations.

We could do it, whilst that was possible. Now we find that we are being forced out, required to find more money than we have per month, to pay for the privilege of bowing and scraping and skivvying for the Comune.

In every piece of chewing gum I remove from a priceless carving, in every smear I rub from a mirror, something within me dies.

Isabella and I are tired of the effort it takes to simply keep breathing in our beloved city, so completely corrupted by the modern age.

We will take our revenge on those who are killing us, and killing our mother!

We will strike at the heart of the establishment in our final gesture. Then we will let our beautiful Venezia, city of canals, take us – reclaim and cleanse us in the waters, that we have seen flowing past our home for decades.

Our 'Grand Finale' will end all. To continue living is intolerable.

We must make our stand whilst making our choice.

I know that my words will be found, analysed, and chewed over.

Let me say to the readers: this outcome was begun when money weighed more than heritage, when status wasn't based on family line but on bank balance.

Corruption and greed are central.

It is the insidious rot that will kill Venice. Here, the writing stopped.

Bianca flicked through the remaining pages. Nothing more was written.

She took off her glasses, and ran her hand through her hair. "It's so very sad," she said almost in a whisper.

Luca and Nino nodded in agreement.

This whole case brought to the surface emotions that they hadn't expected to feel.

Sympathy for murderers!

Still somewhat subdued, Bianca gathered up Luca's report, with insurances from Nino that he would email his through when it was completed.

She patted Luca on the arm. "Thank you, both of you. This gives me a lot of evidence to use for my report to the court and the mayor. I want some good to come from all this sadness," she said. Nino went to his computer. He was already feeling nervous about his coffee date with Viola later.

Work was just a temporary distraction for him.

The light had gone out of the sky, and Luca had gone home to Clara an hour ago.

Nino surfaced from his keyboard and pressed 'Send' to dispatch the report to Prosecutor Avedo. He couldn't put it off anymore.

He had to be brave and go along to meet Viola. At the very thought of her, he felt terrified.

She was the most perfect girl he'd ever seen, and he was so scared that she might laugh at him or that he would be so tongue-tied that he would come across as foolish.

He had to remember that he had started this.

He had been the one to send her a message. He had broken protocol. And now, she was now asking for his help.

He had to calm down.

He gave himself a stern talking to.

He checked his reflection in the small mirror, that hung on the back of the office door, pulled on his jacket and switched off the lights.

He needed to hurry, he didn't want to be late. That would give a terrible impression.

The evening was chilly now, the sun had set. The first stars were already appearing in a clear sky. He walked along to the coffee house that Viola had chosen.

It was warm inside, and the windows were steaming

up from the lively company, already gathered within.

He pushed the door open and saw that she was there before him. She had a table for two over in a quiet corner, away from the bar and the crowd of people chatting and laughing.

For a moment, she didn't see him, as she was staring into the middle distance. She was completely in her own world.

He had a chance to observe her.

She looked so sad, so beautiful, but so very sad. She must have felt his eyes upon her.

She came back to herself and smiled at him.

Nino's heart melted immediately. She was incredible, and he knew that he would try everything he could to make her happy.

Nino and Viola were now sitting opposite each other, nursing Americanos. He let her talk.

She was really struggling with what had happened in the last few days.

Her world had been turned upside down. She was shocked at the murder of Flavia, her boss, who she liked and counted as a friend.

She was scared for her job.

Now she had nobody to assist, she was fearful that she would be sacked.

The Comune was full of competent staff, and she couldn't see any opportunities for another similar role.

Her job insecurity made her fear for the future of her parents, too. She was their only child, their carer, as well as the sole breadwinner.

All this uncertainty, and in such a short space of time, had really shaken her. She was grieving, too, and waves of sorrow kept overtaking her.

She knew that she shouldn't be at work. She had been told to take some time off, but having nothing to do but care for her parents and think, felt like a punishment.

She had opted to stay working, but she couldn't focus there, either. All of this poured out of her.

When she finished, she wiped her soulful dark eyes and gave Nino a weak smile. "I'm sorry! I'm such a mess!"

To him she was the embodiment of grace and beauty.

He felt as if he was if he was falling, he took her hand.

"Viola, to feel like this is normal. You have experienced tremendous shock in the last few days. In purely practical terms, tomorrow, go and speak to the mayor. He will understand how you are feeling. You were one of the two who worked with Flavia closely. Also, you must voice your fears about your employment to him. Once you know where you stand, you can make plans."

She wiped her nose delicately with a tissue, but kept her other hand in his. It felt good to sit like this.

Viola nodded. "Yes, I know, that makes sense. I'll speak to Luigi tomorrow." Emboldened, he cleared his throat.

"If the worst happens, and you have to leave Ca' Loredan, I can see if there are any staff roles at HQ. They always need efficient office support. All is not lost."

Luca and Clara were curled up on the sofa together, watching an old movie. The feeling of contentment and happiness radiated from them both.

Clara had made arrangements for her parents to visit for Sunday lunch, and they were planning to tell them then, that they were now a couple.

Clara knew how much her father liked Luca and how fond her mother had been of him when he used to walk her to school.

She was sure that they would be happy with the progression of their relationship. Luca had been thinking. "Clara, Cara, I think we have moved into your bedroom now, haven't we? Yours has the ensuite and the biggest cupboards."

Clara laughed. "How romantic you are Caro!" He ruffled her hair. "I have a point to make," he said, "have patience!"

She sat in mock attention, looking at him with big eyes.

He kissed her and continued. "Nino is all cramped at home now, his sister is living there again. It's not enough space for his parents, his Nona and his sister as well as him, only one bathroom. I know it's getting him down. I was wondering, could we offer him my room? It would help with the rent and give him the space that he needs?"

"That's a lovely idea, but wouldn't you two just talk about work all the time?" Clara asked. Luca looked thoughtful. "I think we would need to set some ground rules. It would be important for us to not make him feel left out too. We are a couple and he might feel awkward if we are too romantic around him."

The proposal made a lot of sense, and they agreed that Luca would talk to Nino about it the next day.

Happy with their decision, they went off to bed, utterly content with their world, Nino walked Viola home.

They had shared a light supper after the coffee shop, and Viola was feeling much happier and less lost than before.

She enjoyed Nino's company. He was clever and very funny.

She felt that he saw her as she really was, a vulnerable, slightly shy woman, who happened to have beauty, which often got in the way of finding a suitable, compatible partner.

Nino was surprised that Viola lived in Dorsoduro, not far at all from where Luca and Clara lived.

As they said goodbye at the street door to her building, she took him by surprise by kissing him softly on the lips. When he opened his eyes and looked at her, he knew that he had just fallen hopelessly in love.

He asked to see her again and she agreed to lunch the next day. Nino floated away on a cloud of happiness.

He didn't notice the long walk home at all. He couldn't take the smile off his face.

What a difference a few hours can make, he thought.

Bianca had her work cut out.

She had gathered all the reports from technical, pathology, and Luca and Nino.

She had the excerpts from Rocco Manin's diary and the case files from every murder.

She needed to distil all this evidence, and draw it to a conclusion that could be helpful and prompt positive change for Venice.

It could even become a blueprint for the rest of Italy.

This was so much bigger than anything else she had ever tackled in her professional career. She felt both daunted and inspired, in equal measure.

Asking Dario to cancel all other appointments, and hold any calls.

She took an A4 legal pad from her desk draw and sharpened three HB pencils. She was going to work at it long hand, before she began to type it up.

This was the method that she had used to gain her two degrees and professional exams to become a prosecutor.

She knew it worked for her, and she needed that surety now, as she tackled something that she wasn't confident she could encapsulate in one single document.

This was going to be a very long day Luca was in the office before Nino.

He couldn't wait to see what his friend thought of the plan to have him as a roommate.

Nino arrived unshaven and looking fed up. He brandished his razor and a can of shaving soap "My sister was hogging the bathroom and I ran out of time! I'll go along to the washroom and shave there. I know it's unprofessional. I'm sorry." Before Luca had a chance to say anything, Nino was gone.

To fill the time, Luca read the two reports that had come in from the normal force who had taken inventory at the Palazzo Dolfin Manin.

They confirmed that there were a pair of duelling pistols missing from one of the display cabinets in the library.

The information card was still there, and there was a darker area on the backing cloth in the ghostly shape of two antique, long-nosed pistols.

He looked at the photograph he had taken on his phone of the pistol found in the pocket of Rocco Manin. It matched for shape and size.

It could be presumed that Isabella's pistol was somewhere at the bottom of the Grand Canal.

Nino arrived back in the office, looking happier and clean-shaven. "I am sorry about that. My living arrangements are none of your concern."

Luca poured him a coffee.

"That is where you are wrong, brother. Clara and I have a question for you." As Nino sipped his coffee, Luca explained their idea, to add him to the tenancy of the flat and share the rent with him.

Even before he had finished speaking, Nino was nodding vigorously. "Yes! Absolutely yes," he said, shaking his hand.

He was so excited; he couldn't believe his luck.

Luca's bedroom was large and had its own small terrace overlooking the canals. It was big enough for a table and chair, where he could relax in peace in the evening sun after a long day. The bedroom came with a double bed, which was much better than the single bed in his boyhood room at his parents.

His sister could move from the sofa bed in the salon and have his room. It would all work brilliantly.

He told Luca about his meeting with Viola and how smitten he felt. He couldn't believe the positive turn in his

286

fortunes.

The best bit would be that he would only be a stone's throw away from Viola's apartment. He would also be a great deal closer to work.

Both detectives were very satisfied with the new arrangements and worked happily through their morning.

Bianca had finished a twelve-page draft of handwritten notes.

She opened a new document tab on her computer and began to type...

Epilogue

The official enquiry into the murders that had taken place over one Venice Carnevale went on for six months.

"The Gemini Enquiry" was far reaching. It was followed closely in the media and serialised daily in La Nouva.

The conclusions were drawn, and recommendations implemented. There was a stronger ban on cruise ships entering the lagoon.

A cap on permits and a larger tax for Airbnb and rentals was levied.

There was a fixed quota of souvenir vendors allowed to trade in every area in the city, to allow businesses that were useful to Venetian residents to thrive.

There was a tourist tax for day visitors to the city of €5, payable on entry.

The revenue generated was to be split between improving the lives of those who lived in Venice full-time and restoring the buildings and infrastructure.

The mayor had passed the findings of the enquiry to Rome to begin the process of putting laws in place.

Prosecutor Bianca Avedo had received an award for her work on the enquiry, which had sprung from her initial report.

Luca and Nino were sitting together on the large

terrace, which opened out from the salon of their apartment.

They were enjoying the last rays of the September sunshine.

Nino raised his beer bottle to Luca in salute, then popped a juicy black olive in his mouth. "This is the life, isn't it? What a difference half a year makes, eh?"

Luca agreed and offered his friend another Peroni.

He wandered back into the salon and joined Clara and Viola in the kitchen, where they were talking and drinking Prosecco.

As he checked the oven, he saw Viola hold Clara's hand and admire her single solitaire diamond on her ring finger.

Clara blushed, and Luca kissed her on the cheek.

"I was so relieved when she said yes," he said to Viola, giving Clara a squeeze.

"It might be you next," said Clara playfully. Viola laughed. "It's early days for us. We are taking our time to get to know each other. My parents like Nino though – that is a great start."

The meal was served out on the terrace, and all four savoured the tantalising aromas while helping themselves to salad and wine.

Luca proposed a toast.

He thanked Clara for agreeing to become his wife, and thanked Nino for being the best roommate and bringing Viola into their lives.

He grew serious.

"It is an unusual thing to say, but I want us to take a

moment to remember the last of the Manins." They were all silent as Luca raised his glass.

"Above all," he said, "I wish to propose a toast to this wonderful, unique city – to Venice, unlike anywhere else on earth."

"To Venice!" all four voices said.

As the glasses were raised, the chimes from several bell towers began to sound, and the cries of gulls drifted in the warm evening air.

The setting sun turned everything peach, and the fiery orb dipped low over the lagoon.